Theo

Theo

Ed Taylor

First published in Great Britain in 2014 by Old Street Publishing Ltd
Yowlestone House, Devon EX16 8LN
www.oldstreetpublishing.co.uk

ISBN 978-1-910400-03-6

10 9 8 7 6 5 4 3 2 1

A CIP catalogue record for this title is available from the British Library.

Typeset by JaM

Printed and bound in Great Britain.

Dedicated to Steve Street, *dikiy muzhchina*

the music, it was
the onliest thing.
                                    – Sidney Bechet

one.

what sticks to memory, often,
are those odd little fragments
that have no beginning
and no end.

– Tim O'Brien

Theo surfaces on his back and sits up, netted in white sheets cool and slightly ocean-damp, the dream before him, a scrim he sees through as behind it are the things in his room: the wall, the window, his stuff, all behind his father in a hotel room, with an eyepatch, and a model train track on the bed in a figure eight, and a knock on the door and a man in a blue uniform in a weird hat and Theo asking him, are you the conductor and now Theo awake in one place that's two.

He flops back down, the mattress bouncing a little, not sure of anything for a minute, then is asleep again, and his teeth are falling out. He is sitting at a table in a place like a bar, he's been to bars before with adults, there is music, and adults stare at him, and he wiggles his front tooth with his tongue. He reaches in and pulls and the tooth comes loose and others cascade onto his tongue, just fall out. They clack like plastic, but the teeth are small and sandy-looking, or sugary, grainy, and a little yellow. They look like candy. He looks up to tell someone, there is a man next to him. But words won't come out, just sounds, like an animal. He gets up from the table and tries to talk, but no words come out, just noises, and the people turn away from him: and then he wakes up again, remembering his dad's on tour.

Australia is so far away they have different days there. He wants to go: Australia has interesting animals. His dad said, we'll go mate, last time he came. Theo isn't sure when that was; before the tour, so it was months ago.

Everything else is waiting for his dad. Theo waits. He's getting better at it since he turned ten. Sometimes he forgets what he's waiting for.

He looks out the window and it's just blue. He hears nothing but birds; he knows robins, wrens, sparrows, thrushes, gulls, some wind. He's got a good ear, his dad says. Down past the terrace and the gazebo and the old pool and the rectangle that was a tennis court and the slanting back lawn is the beach. He thinks he can hear it, the ocean; he's on a ship. In a cabin. He has to go to the bathroom.

He untangles himself from bed and shuffles to the window, yawning so hard his eyes water. The sun's low and big, white bright, everything else gold early. Past the trees the white on the ocean is stairs. Waves. People surf on them, but not here. Is riding a wave like riding an animal. He doesn't think it would be like riding a horse, he's ridden a horse. If you watch the waves you can see how each one's different, and alive.

He takes off his pajama bottoms, stands at the window looking down and out, no wind, it's quiet, only the birds. The tiny ones he knows are called tits. Tits.

He thrusts himself out the opened window and lets loose. He watches his stream, a thin glass braid that frays and turns into little beads by the time it gets to the second floor, then it's like rain. He's at the very top of the house. On a mountain. If he jumped he'd get hurt. His head feels clean and empty.

No people sounds. The air's warm. Standing there he remembers the winter, when they didn't go downstairs for a while.

All the warm rooms were on the third floor, the living room with the fireplace and Gus's room and Colin's room. So they just stayed up there and burned things and opened cans, wrapped in blankets to go to one of the bathrooms. Then a morning he was bored Theo wrestled his arms into his overcoat and went out in the hall and down the freezing wide back stairs, carpet chewed, and there were crystals on the kitchen floor, white and shiny, blowing in, and down the hall toward the front door, the drifts curling and curving and Gus or Colin, probably Colin, had forgotten to close the front door and the white was inside, the white sky and the paired front doors' opening was rounded with snow at the bottom, snow blown in and everywhere, the whole first floor, snow on floors and walls, piled on paneling, everything, and tracks in a place the wind hadn't gotten – maybe a fox. Walking from room to room the windows were thick and you couldn't see through them, and snow everywhere, blown and dusted, lucky the rooms were so empty, and Theo started running and kicking through the white dunes, until he couldn't feel his feet in his sneakers and his bare hands. He knew he had gloves, somewhere. Maybe Gus could tell him.

In the sunny window now, Theo tugs on his pajama bottoms and laboriously ties the drawstring in a bow, concentrating. Then he turns from the window and toward the door, across the attic. The space is huge, and he's put his mattress against a wall so he won't feel lost. He walks past the nicked piano bench on which he arranged old photographs and letters and programs and postcards from the corrugated boxes and rusty trunks up there, left by previous residents of the house. It was an old house, like the last two.

The black and white photos are of people at the house a long time ago, around the pool when it worked, and at the gazebo; pictures of parties, of people in the rooms. He showed Gus and Colin the stuff he'd found after he moved into the attic, and they went crazy.

Gus, would you look at this. Holy fecking Jesus, that's Frank Sinatra. It's the bleeding Rat Pack, Dean Martin, and there's Peter Lawford. He married a Kennedy, for God's sake. Look at these other mokes – Colin flicked at the photograph with a painted nail. That was one of the days when he painted his nails and wore things that girls wore, like hairbands and make-up.

Those other fellows look like they might have some Sicilian blood.

It is the bleeding Gatsby mansion, after all.

I'm sure the agents say that about every house here.

No, I feel it, man, there be dragons. There's ghosts walking. There's blood, too, I'm telling you, matey.

That's enough. Gus snorted and frowned – you need a tighter leash.

Gus had frowned at Colin and cut his eyes toward Theo, made that face. The don't-forget-about-Theo face. Gus was Theo's grandfather. But sometimes Theo was glad Colin forgot. He wasn't a baby, he was ten years old.

Theo's favourite photograph, scalloped around the edges, showed a band playing in the gazebo, and people dancing, men and women together, on what looked like a nice day, but black and white. The band was all men and they wore white jackets, and one man had a baton, like an orchestra conductor, and all the men looked alike, the band and the dancers, their hair was short and dark and slicked back, and the women all had short hair but not slicked back, and everyone not in the

8

band was wearing white too, white suits and shoes, and there were a boy and a girl dancing too, at the lower corner of the photograph, both dressed like the grown-ups. A lady sat on the steps of the gazebo, watching everyone, and petting a white dog that had its tongue out. Even in the middle of everything, the dog was just a dog, with a dog expression on its face, kind of hopeful looking, Theo thought. Just enjoying the woman petting him, and maybe even though this was a big important party and maybe the lady would have to get up and help run the party or talk to strangers and make them feel welcome, or just get bored and leave, and maybe the dog would fret a little among so many strangers, it still wasn't worried. *Everything will be okay*, it seemed to believe.

Theo's round stomach pokes out as he navigates the wide plain of the attic. The dresser's looking at him, a long drawer open with a tongue of shirt hanging out. He walks the cool wood to the round rug island, which he dragged like a big pancake all the way up from the first floor. Now there are moths, tiny ones that dissolve when touched; they are made of dust. Theo felt bad the first time he touched one and it became just a smudge. He likes having them up there.

He has also moved his butterflies from his previous room, and stuck the branches in the spaces between the ceiling boards.

His dad had sent the butterflies in the spring. One day eleven boxes addressed to him from London arrived at the house. Colin was gone, Gus was asleep.

Each box was full of leafy branches with pupas on them like fruit, packed in Styrofoam and wet white padding. Theo knew his father had an office in London because things would come from there, and phone calls sometimes. There was a heavy envelope in one box, from Hotel La Mamounia, Marrakech.

> *hey pal alright – you & me both like to watch*
> *things grow & we both like SURPRISES/ see what*
> *pops out of these/like xmas crackers except MUCH*
> *better – be SURE & WRITE me/anything you send*
> *to office in ny or londontown will get to me ok ok*
> > *love & kisses on ya beautiful head*
> > *ps/take care of yourself love*

There were drawings and doodles around the edges, a flower and something that looked like an antelope or gazelle, and big zigzags. His dad had turned the paper sideways to write on it, in green ink.

Theo had a book about insects so he read and decided to stick the branches up in his room. Then when he changed rooms he moved the forest with him. It has been thirty-seven days. He counted. The pupas look like the skate purses washing up on the beach, leathery and dead. He knows egg, larva, pupa, adult. He knows imago is another name for adult and means ready to lay eggs, to reproduce. Sexual maturity it is called.

Theo has to be careful – sometimes walking around thinking about something he gets poked by a branch. He also knows the pupas should be in enclosed containers but the attic could be a big jar and he hopes that is good enough.

Theo walks around, closely looking at them now, skirting obstacles on the floor, his own and the stored things from previous owners. He pushes his hair out of his eyes to see better. Colin cut it last month so that it's not too much in the way; just trimming back the undergrowth, he called it, squinting from behind a cigarette, scissors shaking in his hand. Sometimes Theo gets nervous, but Colin hasn't yet cut him. So Theo sits quiet and motionless while it happens. His hair is over his shoulders and down his back, and he's had it pulled at school and had gum thumbed into it and glue poured into it.

It's beautiful, his mother says, always running her fingers through it. She likes it long. To Theo it's hot and in the way. And his face flushes when he thinks about school and the boys in his class. He thinks about the walk to class, in Manhattan, and his heart pounds still. He thinks about the wall where boys scribbled stuff at the hard playground, like a road with swing sets on it, the wall near the street and how words would get written and then the next day they'd be gone under new paint not quite the same colour. The writing spread elsewhere too, under the slides and swing seats, Sharpies and pens: *Mike sucks dicks Kings rule Peter pussy eater Theo is a pussy Stackpole is a fucking faggot,* students and teachers. *Adrian K fucks boys.* He didn't want to go, and his mother said it was okay, so he stopped. Then he didn't live with his mother anymore, or in the city. He lived with Colin and Gus, out here, but not in the same house. Different houses. They've been in this one a while now, longer than the others.

He tries not to think about school but can't stop. Sometimes it wakes him up. Dreams. When he lived with his mom in the city and stopped going they visited people, slept late. He slept in lots of different beds, drifting off to the sounds of music and voices. He wants safe hair, hair no one notices. But his mom notices, smiles.

Theo unlocks the attic door and walks out, closing the door behind him. His hand slides on the warm dark-wood rail as he walks down the top stairs, being quiet, because it's early and he wants to get outside before anyone notices him. It's a long way down, there are 113 stairs to the first floor – he likes to count them. Numbers feel good, it feels good to say them, and they fill the spaces in his head and keep other things out. So he counts, passing down out of the gabled peak of the sprawling house, moving down through the fourth-floor landing and the tricycles and mannequins that Colin dressed up in old-time clothes, ratty gold and crimson with tassels and braid, and the long halls called wings on each side, rows of rooms; probably no one up here, Theo thinks, but stays quiet anyway. He's a prisoner escaping. If he makes it out, he'll save the world.

Going down a monster's throat, must find a way out – light slashes in through the windows at the end of each hall; eyes letting in the light, inside a giant. Down the curving stair, watching for splinters under his right hand. Forty treads on the left staircase, wide enough that he has to stretch to take each in a single step and the risers high enough that he hops to keep to single steps.

He keeps going, past the 'art is anything you can get away with' painted on the third floor by somebody one weekend. They said he was a graffiti artist, but graffiti was supposed to be bad so how could you be an artist of it. Between the third and second floors each step is painted a different colour, another project by one of his mother's friends. As he makes the turn at the landing he passes a tiny city, or what looks like a city to Theo, little towers of clay built on the flat part in front of the big window over the front doors. Now Theo's inside an oak, spiraling down. When he's out and looks back he'll be seeing a huge tree. That's where he lives.

No sounds. Where are the dogs. Usually Paz curls outside his door, and the other two hear Theo descending in the morning, his thumps and sniffs and slaps at the railings, his sometimes muttering, and whistling sometimes. Not now, however: he is trying to avoid waking anything, including the sleeping giant. He slips down the last big set of stairs like walking in a movie, with faded red carpet that spills down starting at the second-floor balcony and then runs in a stream of wine down and into the middle of the black and white tiles under the big chandelier: like antlers except it has ladies' underwear, leis, fishing line, a shirt, a long beaded necklace, a scarf, a bicycle chain, a leathery banana peel, an orange paper kite, hanging. The bulbs don't light anymore.

He's down and onto the cool tiles.

Theo navigates among the tall things standing, Colin's chessmen made of driftwood and suitcases and plastic junk. He moves toward the front doors, through dust floating in the gold sun from the leaded glass beside the front doors. He's underwater, holds his breath. Gus usually puts a big piece of wood against the back of the doors to keep them shut at night, but he must have forgotten. Floor here is cooler and, grabbing a knob in each hand, Theo strains to open both doors at the same time. The heavy black slabs move, but slowly, and he has to keep pulling, backing up.

A silver car sits on the marble entrance steps. At the top of the steps the car's silver hood and grill and fender come to a point in the middle and stick out more at the top than the bottom: to Theo it's a shark.

That's what he heard last night. His mother is here.

Other cars sleep on the grass and along the gravel drive at angles. He notices the blue edge of something under the silver car's front bumper. Theo lowers himself to a knee and ducks sideways to look. Another cake box, with red ribbon. And a teddy bear. And a yellow plastic toy guitar neck sticking out from under the left front wheel. More offerings.

The last time, his mother fussed when he told her he'd eaten some of the cake that had been left – it could be poisoned, you just don't know with these people. Promise me you won't do that again.

Theo said yes, his face cupped in his mother's hands, her face inches from his, her eyes starry and dark. It was hard to say no to her when she was close like that, her eyes so big. But later when she'd vanished again he'd eaten a bite of cake, because he was hungry. And nothing happened.

Colin had then found that cake, where Theo had set it in the scullery, and Colin grabbed fistfuls and tamped cake into his mouth until there was no room, then he found the dogs curled on a sofa and tried to make the dogs eat some. Uninterested, they patiently stayed and allowed Colin to try, but shyly kept turning their heads. Colin stuck fingers in the back of Alex's jaw like pushing a button to open and managed to get a pink hunk onto Alex's tongue, but Alex shook his head and the wet cake slumped into a mound now dried and grey on one of the sofas. Theo couldn't remember which one.

At the silver car now Theo slides the box out from under, smelling the car smell of things he just knows as car, warming in the sun. He unties the ribbon, flips open the box, crouching. The cake is red, with icing piped in swirls and curves, and words Theo knows are French, and pictures. An icing guitar, and an icing skull.

He pushes the box out of the way and reaches under the car for the bear, on which a little greasy fluid has dripped. It has a ribbon, pink, and a little T-shirt that says 'rock n roll'. He stares at the toy guitar fretboard, a small arm reaching out from under the fat black tyre. When his mother leaves, he can collect the guitar and put it with the other things.

It has been a week since the last offering. Things appear in a variety of locations, occasionally on the back terrace, sometimes at the foot of a tree, but mostly on the front steps. Early one morning Theo had awoken and threaded his way down the long stairs and through the back hall toward the house's rear and across the ballroom, the leaning motorbike's bright lime-green against the far dark wall, Theo's head swirling and light-feeling and still mossy with sleep, and he saw a man in a tuxedo outside on the terrace laying a bunch of red roses in the middle of the tiles, alongside a black bottle with a cork. Theo walked to the French doors and stood, while the man carefully finished, then noticed Theo. He bowed, and turned, and walked toward the trees and the ocean. Theo walked out behind him, watching the man get smaller and disappear into the dense wiry low forest that stood up against the ocean and the storms and wind and salt just behind the dune line. The man had also left a book that said *Les Fleurs du Mal*. Theo yawned and his eyes watered. He stood for a while until he began to sway, and wandered back in and up the stairs and back to bed. When he came down later, Colin sat cross-legged on the terrace drinking out of the black bottle and wearing a wide Mexican hat made out of straw.

He's got the wrong celebrity map. He thinks he's visiting Poe's grave. But champagne cognac – he has excellent taste.

It's one of the side benefits of being a priest in this particular temple, eh.

What.

Nothing, my friend. Why don't we go fishing today.

Sure.

Theo had squinted up into the sun and down at Colin, the hat big as an umbrella. Then Colin had forgotten about fishing and gotten into a sword fight with somebody Theo'd never seen before who burst out of a room, and so Theo spent the day in the trees, reading and listening to the ocean.

Theo leaves the thick house doors open; the car looks like it wants in, and they are wide enough. He threads his way back through the chess field and then up the left staircase to the second floor, thumping on the carpet, a bleached colour with an old design but still sponge-thick. Theo keeps his hand on the banister all the way, feeling the cool red-brown, not thinking much. He reaches the top and turns left, where his mom usually ends up.

His mother often came with gifts for him: animals, candy, things she thought were pretty like rocks or pictures, hats, clothes, toys from places like Peru or Thailand, puppets, and sometimes weird stuff. An ashtray, a napkin from a restaurant, hotel shampoo, a piece of pizza, a record, a fistful of guitar picks, a drawing of her by somebody else – once with no clothes on – a feather, a flower. He figured that was when she was high. He knew what high was, knew what drunk was. It was a way people were, just like happy or sad. He also knew about bail, hearings, possession, depression, institutionalization.

His mother never brought anything for Gus or Colin: she didn't like them, although she'd never said this to Theo. He just knew.

Are you mad at Gus and Colin.

No darling. Why.

You act like it all the time.

No, my love. I like them. Gus is your grandfather and a man deserving of respect. A respectable and upright man, just as Colin is.

His mother's accent was different to his dad's. He knew she'd been born in Hungary but she said she grew up all over Europe and so, she said, she sounded like everywhere and nowhere. She called herself a pirate, said she and his father were part of the pirate nation. Theo didn't know what that meant, really.

People at school made fun of Theo's accent, which they said was faggy. Fag. Faggot. Which his dad said was a cigarette. Theo had lived in England, Jamaica and America so far. And other people's houses and hotels.

God help me, I'm starting to sound American, his mother said.

Is that bad.

His mother had laughed out a cloud of cigarette smoke. For your sake, I tolerate the place, my love. But there are better places to be.

Like where.

She exhaled again. That is a good question. If you could go anywhere in the world, where would you go.

He couldn't really think of a place: what were the choices. He didn't know. Every place seemed mostly the same so far.

I'd like to go to the bottom of the ocean.

She squinted at him, stubbing out the cigarette. That's an interesting choice. Could I come too.

17

He shrugged. Sure. Maybe Gus and Colin could come. And his dad maybe, in a big glass ball.

Why do you want to go there.

I wouldn't have to go to school.

He sort of knew what would happen if he said that, but he did anyway. She started crying. Oh baby. She pulled him into a hug, jangling with bracelets. She always wore a lot of things and he couldn't separate her from the sounds she made when she moved.

She had the smell. Sometimes he didn't know, she might seem okay, whether she was okay or not, until he smelled the smell. Then he would know. Colin and Gus had the smell a lot, and many of the people who came to the house. There were different smells but they all meant pretty much the same thing.

She cried a lot, and laughed a lot, and screamed, and punched and kicked, and danced, and staggered, and snored, and fell, and jumped – once from an upper hall landing and broke her ankle. He hadn't seen that, only heard the sounds and cried. He wondered what had made her jump, and whether he had anything to do with it, or with the way she acted. He didn't know, and he wasn't sure who to ask.

Now this morning Theo walks the long secondfloor hall, strewn with clothes and shoes, a bowling ball like Jupiter, swirly and pink, stopped against a door – he hasn't seen that before. At the distant end of the hall, in front of the big curved windows that remind Theo of churches from movies, pokes the silhouette of a big stuffed bird that he knows is an emu. His mother usually stays on this wing, but not always in the same room, and Theo doesn't like opening doors unless he knows who is in the room. So he walks, and listens. He hears something and turns: Alex has dragged himself up the stairs and, panting, follows Theo. Theo stops to scratch Alex's wiry head, bumpy with warts, but keeps listening. He hears ahead the sex noise. He knows what sex is, and he knows what it sounds like. He keeps walking down the hall, Alex tottering behind, to where the noise is. Noises. Two rooms. He stands outside, between the rooms, listening. He feels funny and kind of hollow. He also gets stiff, and knows about that. He doesn't want the noise to be his mother, but he doesn't want to find out. He listens longer, then scuffs back down the hall making more noise, hitting his hand along the wall as he walks, holding his hand on his pajamas. Alex pants behind him.

Someone may wake up, but Theo hopes not yet. Behind him down the hall a voice now sings, somewhere; muffled, hard to tell if it is a man or woman. Something in it makes Theo think: Mom. And he makes a face and runs, getting to the stairs and thumping down them, running down the stairs. The last time she smiled and flicked it with a finger, kissed him on the cheek and said it's okay, love, a beautiful, natural thing. That was awful.

Colin, somewhere below, is yodeling.

Gazebo, Theo thinks.

Theo keeps flapping down on the carpet, to the cool tiles of the entry hall, feet now slapping like fish, he likes the sound, and toward the swung-open tall slab doors and over the car hood, scrambling and out and down the stone steps and onto the gravel bit ouchouchouch like on hot pavement and onto the grass, moist because the sun hasn't reached this side yet, but everything is light, and he runs to the right, down the line of windows and the wild bushes crazy with flowers and stems sticking out and untrimmed and reaches the edge of the wing and goes right again and past more windows, running, and the trees are getting bigger, and he dodges a rusty bike he had forgotten about and runs into the rear lawn and toward the gazebo and there's a naked guy sitting in it, cross-legged. The man has long hair and a sharp face and something's wrong with his arms. They stop at the elbows. And he's naked. And his eyes are closed. Theo stops running.

New people always showed up: his mother brought them home or they followed her. Sometimes they were friends of Colin or, very occasionally, of his father. These he liked best; he liked them because they knew his father and being around them was a little like being around his father.

His mother attracted people, collected people, like pets. She called herself a broker, sometimes, said she should get a cut, she bridged worlds, that was her art, she said, a waving cigarette veiling her face as she talked to Theo sleepy in bed, him waking with her stroking his face, smiling lopsidedly at him, or crying. Sometimes, however, what she collected wasn't nice like that; when they wanted things and took stuff or got loud or pushed and she let them. Sometimes she screamed at them, hit them, got other people to hit them: he'd heard it. He'd seen her point guns.

It wasn't always clear what the rules were, what you had to do to make her mad. Theo believed it mostly depended on how long it had been since his dad's last stopover. Sometimes it happened after drinks and amber bottles with medicine labels and small ceramic boxes with flip tops and the skull with the top cut off and the white powder, yellow powder, brown powder, on book covers or tables or glass-covered pictures laid flat. Sometimes there was blood on the glass after. One time one of the dogs had gotten really sick after licking something from a low leather-topped stool. Theo was really worried. After that it wasn't hard to understand that it could do bad things to people.

He stayed away from all that as much as he could, but as much as he could wasn't much. Theo had to figure out a way around it kind of all the time.

Theo was hoping to have the gazebo to himself. Even though the house and the land are big, like the last house, sometimes it is hard to be alone. A lot of the time adults think he needs babysitting, or that they need to do what they call 'playing' with him, because there aren't other kids around. But it is the opposite of playing, and mostly he just wants not to be noticed. People fuss over him, rub his hair. Ladies hug him, make faces at him like they think he needs cheering up. Sometimes he finds someone looking at him oddly, their eyes half-closed, focusing, like they are thinking hard, seeing something else. Then they smile at him and act normal again.

The man in the gazebo opens his eyes, sees Theo and grins. He has glasses. Theo stares.

Come here.

Theo is unsure about whether to do it. The sun in his face makes him squint. Motion catches his eye – the heron flapping over its nest, in the big tree like a dead hand reaching out of the ground, grey-brown and smooth like driftwood near the dunes. Theo knows things about birds and thinks this one is lost – herons are freshwater birds that live on lakes. He hopes it's finding what it needs. Maybe it's not a heron.

It's okay.

Theo notices the man again, and slowly walks at him. It seems to Theo the bird would want a little more privacy for a nest, like a tree with leaves to hide the babies. But apparently the big ones like that build in the open so they can see. One parent's always there, for protection. Theo thinks about his parents, and then about teachers. Theo stops.

Why are you not wearing any clothes.

It feels better, man. Do you live here.

Yes.

Are you Frieda's kid.

Yes. This is my house.

Listen to the birds.

Are you high.

The man laughs, and then he frowns and stands. Theo steps back. He's seen this before and is glad there is plenty of room to run. He hears something: Alex and Paz and Baron sit behind him now, panting, looking at him, their dog eyebrows raised. He had forgotten about them and now feels better.

Standing, the man looks short, his penis like the nest with a dark purple baby bird Theo had found on the ground under one of the gnarled beach trees. His own penis is pale and wormy. What happens, Theo wonders, between now and then.

My mom asked if you could put some clothes on.

The man stares up and out and around. And down at Theo. Then he moves fast, his hair blowing, across the gazebo floor to the steps and jumps, landing and collapsing, then scrabbling up, grass sticking to him, and runs at Theo, his arms like flippers spinning at the air. Theo screams.

The dogs hop and jump, barking, Paz stumbling, Theo scooting sideways as the man gets closer, faster, saying something but Theo can't figure it out. Theo runs without thinking, the dogs frantic and the man suddenly there and grabbing and the dogs barking and the man laughing.

Theo away, watching, now the dogs calming, licking, the man on his knees, sticking his face against theirs, his arms like penguin wings rubbing the dogs.

Theo isn't sure what to do, so he looks at the brown ground, the grass like dirty hair, and then up toward a long-needled pine waving and shaking at him. There is a lot of wind early, making ocean noises. Theo feels himself moved a little by it as he decides to scuffle his way toward the cracked terrace that runs the width of the big house's back side, facing the trees in front of the dunes, the naked man now squatting on his haunches and the dogs trotting after Theo.

'Mansion'. Theo had found the word in the big dictionary with the tissue pages smelling like an old coat. 1. A large stately house. 2. A manor house. 3. *Archaic* a. A dwelling; an abode. b. A separate dwelling in a large house or structure. 4. a. See house. b. Any one of the twenty-eight divisions of the moon's monthly path. *Middle English*, a dwelling, from Old French, from Latin *mansio*, from *mansus*, past participle of *manere*, 'to dwell, remain'; see *men-* in Indo-European roots.

It is a big house. He isn't sure about stately, marked by lofty or imposing dignity. On the same page was *Their swords are ruste, their bodys duste, Their souls are with the Saints, we truste*, about something else. He passes the sundial at the side of the house.

> *Come, light! visit me!*
> *I count time; dost thou?*

Theo whispers the words to himself, walking.

Weeds poke up through the squares of the terrace, a hairy

chessboard. It would flinch and throw off all the pieces. You'd have to tame it to play. Pink and brown, faded and pale. He feels like stomping a puddle but everything is dry. The sun is a big flashlight in the sky, white in the white.

Then music. The music starts in the house and flies out the open windows on the third floor and drifts down around him. Colin is definitely awake.

Theo turns back toward the trees for an instant, shading his eyes with a hand. Colin sometimes didn't sleep for days. His mother, when she came, he wasn't sure about, because her door was always locked. Is she asleep or awake. Mostly awake, he guessed, because of all the noise and people when she came, which was always like a wave washing through. Things would be empty and quiet when Theo locked himself in, then in the morning people in the hall or on couches, sometimes looking dead, and different smells, and different things scattered around. Hello, my beautiful boy, she would yell at him from somewhere, above on the stairs or from an open door, or in from the outside, her standing outside naked one time staring up at something, her body broken into squares by the big iron and glass doors to the terrace. Theo remembers again he needs to find something to cover the broken panes with.

It is Wednesday, Theo guesses. He smells ocean. One of the dogs noses at him now, and Theo flicks his eyes down and smoothes Baron's head and leans into the big yellow and black shepherd, nudges him for an instant, then turns and moves toward the doors, hungry, too, flanked now on his other side by Alex, the thickest animal on the planet, Gus calls him. Theo feels sorry for the dog, who has seizures and pants when he walks.

The faded coppery dog's domed head makes him look like a human baby, although he is thirteen and totters. He needs something soft, his teeth going. Upstairs Colin yells now, and somewhere beyond the beach is the buzz and thump of speedboats, and the day is on its way. Theo slips through the French doors into the dark ballroom.

There is a Japanese magazine on the parquet floor, his father on the cover. His face very white, like a doll. Is that powder. *Aidoru.* Dog claws click and slide on the wood, the sounds loud. A piece of floor is missing since yesterday, Theo notes. He keeps moving.

Sand grains are scattered on the parquet. Theo feels them under his feet. There are crumbs everywhere: sand, salt, food, because people like to walk everywhere in the house eating. The dogs lick at the floor a lot, and at spills everywhere.

There's not much furniture but there are lots of pillows, and cloth. Blankets, tapestries, sheets, rugs, carpet in piles or folded or left limp and crumpled in the middle of a floor, as if the person wrapped in it vanished on the spot.

Theo skates across the ballroom, sliding his bare feet. A bird darts through the French doors he left open. It moves too fast for him to identify but he figures it is one of the little ones, sparrow or wren, always around outside, flocking to peck at grass or the terrace. All the people leave trails, or create them.

He skates over to a plant tipped sideways in a Chinese vase. It has deep green leaves with wine-coloured hearts and big veins and reaches toward the light. The shoots are arms extending, ending in brushes of little purple flowers. Theo sweeps the dirt back in with his hand and tips it up, pets it, and drags it over into a rectangle of sun. Then he skates the other way, toward the kitchen.

The dogs stare up as he yanks on the heavy pantry door and goes in to rummage for something to feed them. Dog food ran

25

out but no one has bought more, so Theo gives them peanut butter and things from cans, some of which they eat and some of which sits until someone else eats it: usually Colin or a guest.

That's what Theo's mother called them. Make our guests feel at home. Or friends. Theo wasn't sure about the difference, except the guests came less often.

There is a gunshot, loud and echoing, close. The dogs startle, whimper. Theo's ears dampen, and sound gets slightly muffled.

Theo sighs, leaves the pantry and shuffles back to the ballroom as the dogs orbit him, jumping. The sound whirls as crazily as the bird, moving now like an insect, flitting and erratic: scared too, Theo imagines.

Colin stands across the ballroom, wearing boots and a towel wrapped around his waist, his ropy arm up and pointing with a silver pistol at the bird. He points the gun at the floor and does something clicking with his other hand: chambering, he'd called it before.

Colin now has an eye closed and follows the bird with the gun, letting off another shot. Theo's ears hurt.

Colin, can you stop please.

Birds make me nervous. Too undisciplined. Or maybe it's just jealousy. One more for luck and then we're done.

Colin fires out through the opened glass door toward the ocean. Clears out the sinuses, that's for certain. Prevents constriction of the bowels, too, man. Nothing like a little cordite in the morning to remind you why you're alive.

He clomps across the ballroom, smiling with big square yellow teeth in the sunlight, as Theo turns and moves back toward the kitchen. He wonders what happens to bullets if they don't hit anything.

I am starving, Colin says. He walks past Theo with a pat

26

on the back and goes straight toward the refrigerator that still works. He yanks it open hard, the silver doors big as room doors, and bends to dig around. His towel falls, exposing his buttocks. Theo turns back to the pantry, and the cans: will the dogs eat canned peaches. Tinned is what Gus and Colin call them. Colin begins to sing something without words.

Theo scans the pantry shelves: there is food, and there are other things. A very old teddy bear with spots of furless fabric showing, but with both button eyes; a long piece of brown bamboo with a hunting knife roped to one end; caramels, bags and bags of caramels; some clothes, stacked T-shirts with things printed on the front from concerts; a small television, and silver-grey round flat metal containers in which are coils of film, a stack of them; a rake with teeth missing; a stuffed woodchuck and several antlers, like branches locked in a pile; oatmeal, a lot of it, because Gus likes oatmeal; a crate of canned smoked baby oysters; a stack of masks, all the same, of a bear face; an ottoman on its side; a box full of jars of honey, a box half-full of jars of jelly, and several five-pound bags of sugar, one that still hissed and shifted when picked up, and the others, hard blocks wrapped in paper; a tower of cans of Fray Bentos steak and kidney pie; a mummified grey mouse on a round piece of polished wood under a glass bell with a knob on top, which once held an Italian cheese Colin liked; a burlap sack filled with macadamia nuts, one corner of which has been gnawed open but Theo doesn't know by what, because he's seen people in here tearing at packages with their teeth; a row of boxes of Sugar Pops, like a shelf of books; scattered packages with Japanese writing, and different things inside, that look like candy but are the wrong colours, small round things and noodles and one he knows is rice crackers; cans

27

without labels; an old green and red cradle made out of tin with writing on the side that Theo can't read; Colin's ray gun collection, a pile of plastic and tin toy ray guns and a pile of other things like branches and things Colin has found that he thinks are shaped like ray guns – he keeps saying he needs to move it to a more suitable location; a sled; rows and stacks of coffee cans, some of which hold coffee and some of which hold nails, foreign coins, rubber bands, washers, salt, marbles – and one holds glass eyes.

Theo marveled over the eyes, because no one knows how the can got there, and when he is in the gloomy pantry he likes to hold the can and look down at them looking back at him, but in a kindly way. The eyes seem patient and wise, and all clear and white with the irises blue or grey mostly, like Theo's eyes. Sometimes he carries one around in a pocket, and he likes it there. He hasn't carried one in a while; he considers it a solemnity, like a ritual, although he isn't sure what a ritual really is besides something heavier than it looks.

Colin stops singing. Theo picks one of the few brown eyes up and carefully slips it into a front pocket of his pajamas, then on tiptoes pulls down one of the Fray Bentos cans, although Colin and Gus fuss at him when he 'wastes' them on the dogs. Seems it is time to shop. He is sick of smoked baby oysters.

Colin lies on his back on the kitchen floor, his towel crumpled under him. The soles of his cowboy boots have round holes – like eyes, but not wise ones. Colin is hairless and brown all over, his chest peaking in the middle like a bird's; ribby but with a little pad of fat on his stomach, where there is a long pucker like a mouth curving alongside his navel. He is sweating, even though it's cool now. He's patched with tattoos, lots of places, which Theo used to enjoy seeing revealed as Colin rolled up a sleeve or pant leg or took off something. His penis is tattooed with a series of dots and lines, which Colin said happened in New Zealand. Theo knows New Zealand; he likes knowing where things are. Colin also has a long set of wavy curves like lips tattooed in red and blue around his penis, starting on his abdomen. Theo felt funny saying the word, and funny thinking it. Colin said the lip things were the gates of paradise. Gus exploded when Theo first asked him about it.

Where did you see Colin's penis.

He was walking around with no pants.

He didn't do anything funny did he.

Besides walk around with no pants.

Yes, he didn't –

He was getting the brandy out of the green bathroom and I saw him. I asked him what that was. He said, that's the man monster, son. No, I said, what's around it. He said that's the gates of paradise.

Gus rubbed his face up and down with his thick hand: you tell me immediately if he does anything funny. Gus's words were a little slurred, blurry.

Besides the funny stuff he does, like, every day.

Like. Messes with you. Or tells you to mess with his.

His what.

Just tell me, son, okay. There's too many pervs in this circus.

Oh.

Theo remembered his mother's friend at the Chelsea Hotel. The one who wanted to help Theo go to the bathroom while his mom slept on the couch in the room with aluminum foil over the windows. Day outside and night in there. The bearded man at the party who rubbed against him. And being stuck on a soft loft sofa next to a weird man who put his hand on the back of Theo's neck and tried to hug Theo down onto his lap. But he was supposed to be famous and Theo's mom said the guy didn't mean anything, he was just affectionate. Was that true.

They never went back to his house, and Theo's mom sort of snarled every time someone else mentioned him, and she called him a name. The man was strong. He stopped because somebody needed a knife and Theo struggled up out of the big sofa and away.

Some grown-ups looked at Theo in a funny way different to the funny ways other grown-ups looked at him. But there were always so many around; he couldn't watch everybody. And they'd just be there, breathing, smiling. How do you tell which smiles are bad.

Okay, Theo said to Gus. I'll tell you.

You do that. Then Gus smiled and winked, slapped Theo's leg.

Was it a joke. Theo didn't get it.

That was the way things began, when they were all first together in the house. Now his birthday is just past – his tenth. And another school year begins in the fall, and he missed a lot of the last one: most of it. And he doesn't want to think about it. He steps over Colin, whose arms jut out from his shoulders; Colin's doing what he says are his exercises: what he calls it when he lies down somewhere and doesn't move.

A drawer hung already open, offering a spiky array of long silverware and kitchen things, and nails, stamps, brittle rubber bands, old bottle caps, and a blade of cracked mirror, like a hole in the drawer. Theo finds the heavy knife they open cans with and steps back over Colin to carry knife and can to the thick scarred table sitting in front of the skinny stained glass window that stretches from floor to ceiling. Colin said if money ever became an issue, that window was Tiffany and he'd have it on the auction block sooner than you could say reserve price. Through the window, outside is bright and tan and red and green and blue, and the bird in the ballroom can be heard as it still whirls, the calls coming from everywhere. Theo decides after feeding the dogs he'll help the bird escape.

Theo wraps both hands around the hunting knife's handle, raises it to eye level, and stabs down hard. He's gotten good, or stronger, and it takes fewer stabs to open cans now, especially as the Fray Bentos sit flat and low. Some of the skinny tall ones cause trouble.

Upwind.

Colin has spoken, eyes closed. Theo has learned not to ask questions, just to wait and Colin might make sense. The dogs snuffle over the mess Theo has placed in two ceramic bowls with painted daisies. The bowls seem old, like the attic things and other stuff they find in the house.

Your dad's coming soon.

I know. When.

When the tour finishes.

I know. When is that.

The answer, my friend, is blowing in the wind.

I dreamed my teeth fell out. And Dad and I were in a hotel room and somebody in a uniform came for him.

Eyes still closed, Colin starts talking. Last night I dreamed I was an archaeopteryx riding a train into a tunnel, and my mother was at the other end shining a big light and instead of coal the train was burning babies, there was a big car full of them behind the engine that the engineer was shovelling into the furnace by the pitchfork-full. And then my mother was a giant eel and I turned into a blue-eyed woman with red hair and a beard and ran away but the sun was blotted out from the sky by a giant foot wearing a glove like a hand and it was trying to stomp me or swat me. Then I woke up and had a smoke.

Don't make fun of me. Theo turns away.

Come on, my friend, I'm not making fun of you. I'm Hakim, the endless chronicler of Arabian nights. It's my job to entertain and amuse. Profound apologies offered if offense taken, man. None intended. In general other people's dreams are boring, but women like to hear about them. Write that down in your book. You'll need that one day. Along with a trainload of cash.

You want something to eat. Theo looks down at Colin.

Jesus no. Colin palms his forehead. Things aren't that dire yet.

Theo's bare feet on the scarred linoleum feel sand as he shuffles them standing there.

Theo.

Yes.

Did you know your name means god.

Yes Colin.

Have we talked about this before.

Yes Colin.

Have we talked about talking about this before.

Yes Colin.

Good man.

Theo carries the Fray Bentos can and the big spoon over to where Colin sprawls on the floor, and scrapes out the last bits of black from the can, and bends down beside Colin. Theo spoons the dark tarry sludge onto Colin's cheeks. Colin opens one eye.

Spoon's cold.

Aren't you supposed to be watching me and Gus.

That's what I get paid for.

Are you taking care of me now.

Every second. I'm on always on watch, patrolling with my thousand-yard stare. Colin winked.

Theo drops the empty can on Colin's stomach, which makes him howl and jerk, although his eyes are now open so he saw it coming. Colin smiles, the spoon slides onto the floor. Theo smiles.

Alex pads over to lick the can and spoon. Colin tips the can onto his stomach until a little gravy drips out for the dog to lick, which he does.

Theo watches for a few seconds, then leaves the kitchen, remembering weird noises from last night, and decides the idea of being alone might not work right now. He wonders if Gus is up.

Theo walks through the scullery, which he doesn't like, as a pipe burst during the winter and the wood walls and the floor warped and moulded once the temperature rose and the room got blotchy and smelly. One day, however, he plans to open the cabinets and see what is there.

Today he keeps moving toward the dark paneled back hall leading away from the kitchen to the front entry hall and to the rear stairs for the servants coming and going from their upper floor rooms, where they stayed to serve family and guests, bringing them drinks and food whenever they wanted. Theo often thought about servants and what it would be like to be waited on, or to be the person doing the waiting. What kind of work is waiting. He figured he'd be good at it. With grown-ups that's all that happened. Wait here. Wait there. I'll be down in a minute. I'll be up in a minute. I'll be out in a minute. In a minute. I'll be ready in a minute. Just a minute. Okay, I'll be right there. Hold on. Hold your horses. Keep your shirt on. What's your hurry. Can we do it later. Not now, how about later. We'll go later. We'll do it later. Sure, just let me finish this first. Let me sleep a little longer. It's too early for that. It's too late. It's not open. It's closed. Let's not do that now, let's wait. Just because. Be patient. You have to learn to be patient. Patience. Slow down, hoss. Slow down. Not so fast. Wait for me. Wait for me.

A spray-painted yellow arrow with a big fuzzy head that points toward the front doors runs the length of the hall. Someone sprayed a large bow perpendicular to the arrow, across the floor and up the wall onto the ceiling, but it just looks like a red D. Theo hears behind him Colin yelling or singing but the words are blurry.

Theo wonders why Gus hasn't come down yet after Colin shot at the bird. Maybe Gus didn't hear. Theo closes his eyes. He's blind and walks back down the hall, with a hand on the paneling. Try to go back through the kitchen to the ballroom and then outside. The furthest he's ever made it is from this hall to the middle of the ballroom. It's hard because it seems like something's always moved, or there's something new to stumble over that wasn't there before. Colin leaves things everywhere. It's lucky furniture's scarce, although Gus talks about buying more – more tables and chairs, things to sit on. Gus likes to sit, but that's because he's old, Theo thinks. Grandfathers are old.

Theo is sliding along the wall, his palm flat against the paneling, feeling the indentations and carving, and comes to an open place: the kitchen. He takes a step into something warm and wet, yelps and opens his eyes, lifting his foot, looking down. Alex has thrown up his Fray Bentos. He's old, too.

Theo hops into the kitchen and toward the sink. He pulls half-open a drawer next to the sink and puts his knee on the edge, the drawer digging in and hurting but he needs leverage to get onto the marble counter – he's done this before – so he pushes fast and wrestles himself up so he can get his foot cleaned off. It isn't until he sits with his feet in the steel sink that he notices – no Colin. And no dogs. He turns the water on and holds his foot under the tall curving bird neck of the faucet. Squawk. He rubs at his sole, his tongue between his lips, something he does when he's focusing. He never used to think about it and didn't realize he does it but people tell him it's cute, and now he notices and usually stops.

His dad's coming.

Theo closes the drawer with a foot and then hops down, leaving wet footprints, slapping across the ballroom, then running, toward the glass doors, which he wrenches open and flies out over the terrace toward the grass, and sees Gus already out and in his chair down at the end of the lawn, under his tree.

Imagine a game.

Theo says it to Gus. His grandfather is the bottom of a pool, something you could touch when you needed to know where you were.

Only one person can play, and they change it and rearrange everything and make everything different, the whole world of the game, and they play it till they die, and then they pass the game to another person, who does the same thing. But they don't really die, they just stop playing the game.

What kind of game.

It would be like your life, you would live it. You would play it every day, and everything would be part of it.

How do you win.

You don't win, you just play.

Doesn't sound like my kind of game. I like ones you can win. Or at least bet on.

Gus laughs, wheezily, sitting on a chair in the sun, his fat legs in shorts shiny and tight-looking, all the hair worn off. Theo leans against the left leg.

And the game's a secret. The only person who knows about it is the one who's playing it, because it changes every time someone plays it. You can change it any way you want. You just have to keep playing till you die, but it's not really dying, it's just dying in the game.

That sounds serious, not like a game. I like to stop after a few hands for a smoke. You wouldn't let me do that anymore.

You can do anything.

How is that a game.

Because it's not real.

It's not just a story.

No, because you change it, and only one person can play it at a time.

That's a story, ain't it.

Gus is from England, like Theo's dad. Gus mines in a pocket for a minute. Theo leans against it so it feels like a small animal burrowing. Gus's hand holds his Cross, worn as a pebble. Gus fought in a war, and his lighter had been there too. Gus jams a wrinkled, slightly bent cigarette between two fingers and flicks at the Cross, inhaling deeply and then coughing. He squints through the smoke and hands Theo the lighter, which Theo begins opening and closing, staring at it. It has writing on the side, barely there, hard to read, but Theo knows the letters are Gus's initials and Dirty Little Imp, which was a nickname from the British army, Gus had told Theo. Gus had been an infantryman, he said. Theo looked it up.

Gus exhales cloudily. So are we in a game now.

You're in the game.

I am, am I.

Yes. You're a key.

Like a door key, you mean.

Sort of. You're just a key.

Key to what.

I haven't figured that out yet.

So if other people are in the game, doesn't that mean they're playing too. So it's not just one person at a time. If you're telling me about it, it can't be a secret, can it.

Theo stops thinking about that, flicks the flame on and off, on and off, watching the orange. He wants to touch it. He likes the smell of the lighter: the warm brass and the liquid in it. Then he flips the top over and hands it to Gus.

Butane.

Has to be filled up just like a car, right in this little opening. Petrol where I come from. You come from there too, you know. You were born there. Gus laughs. Tell me more about the game.

Theo is walking away, seeing his dad's face. He turns: Does my dad know me.

What kind of a question is that. He loves you like a madman.

Where is he right now.

Gus hesitates. The boy turns back toward the trees and ocean.

I believe the tour's finishing up in Sydney, the words coming at the boy's back. But he's coming here to make a record.

Theo stops. Here.

He just told me last night. They'll let the engineers have a look and see which rooms are best. I was saving the news as a surprise. What do you think of that.

Why didn't he tell me.

You were asleep.

Does Colin know.

Yes.

Does my mother know.

I don't know. Haven't talked to her. She's here now, you know.

Yeah. I saw her car.

That's something to look forward to, right. Your dad might be here the whole summer. That's good news, right.

The times his dad had been around were oases in Theo's memory, bright clear sharp moments. They hadn't happened a lot since he was a baby. He knew there were different times, when his mom and dad lived together, but that was a long time ago. Theo didn't know why they didn't live together anymore. Whenever he had asked either of his parents they said different things. We're still together, we just live apart. Or your mother's mad at me right now, so I'm laying low. Or your father thinks I'm sick, but I'm not sick and I certainly will not be treated as if I am.

Theo wonders if maybe his dad would be bored at the house.

We need to get furniture. Where will my dad sleep.

Theo has walked back toward Gus, who is now looking at Theo carefully, like adults do, like Theo's a book but the print's too small.

Right. Everything'll be shipshape, a proper place. You can help us get the place ready.

I can show him the butterflies.

Right mate. Maybe they'll hatch by then, eh.

There's a man with no clothes on in the gazebo.

Gus's face closes up and his mouth tightens under his grey moustache, then he sighs. I'll go and have a talk with him in a minute, soon as I finish this fag. He shakes his head.

Theo turns and resumes walking, he's not sure where, his head down. He feels the ground rise and he's uphill, at the hump in the lawn where something used to be, a long time ago, a shed or building. Now it's just a slope up to a flat patch, like a stage made of lawn. Sometimes people sit here and play guitars.

One of his mother's guests rode a motorcycle up it once when Theo slept, really fast, but he ended up hitting that big tree – he left teeth in the bark. You could still see them, two big chips and his front teeth dug in and brown at the top now. Theo guessed that was blood. Colin said the man trying to fly was evolution at work. Theo didn't understand. Colin just said, it means the guy was not very bright. There was a long scar cut in the yard all the way back to the circle part of the driveway; the ground had been wet and the motorcycle chewed up the lawn, surprisingly sensitive, and nothing had grown back yet. Colin called it the border. One side is sanity and one side is madness. Which is which, Theo asked. Ah, that is always the question, isn't it, Colin said.

The border passes under Theo's bare feet.

The motorbike in the ballroom is Colin's. It snarls like an animal. He calls it his Italian spitfire. He tried to ride it up the stairs but he couldn't get further than halfway up to the second-floor landing. So far at least. He says he's going to try to ascend Everest: which means to ride to the fourth floor. It's one of his projects. He has a lot of them.

39

Before, Colin used to travel with Theo's father. Colin's a kind of minder but not like the others. He's more like Theo's dad Adrian than like the other minders. Theo knows his dad asked Colin to watch him and his grandfather, but Theo doesn't understand, because it seems like Colin is the one who needs watching and Gus is old so Theo's not sure why he needs minding. Colin is also supposed to get Theo to go to school, Theo knows, although he doesn't think he's supposed to know, because nobody's said anything about school.

Theo overheard Colin on the phone with Theo's father, talking by satellite. Theo's dad was in Thailand or South Africa, he couldn't remember, and Theo had talked and then hung around outside the door. Sure. The local district. Yeah. Forget the private, or – no. Those places give me the screaming meemies. Sure, I'll keep him from becoming any more feral but he does have his genes to contend with. Right. Heh heh. Bloody hell. Right.

Theo tries to stay out of Colin's way mostly, but it's hard because Colin's always finding him. My job, mate, he always says. Guarding the prince.

Theo tries not to get too excited about his dad coming but he can't help it. If his father makes a record, Theo knows he might be there for a while. He is not sure what his mother will think.

The air is getting warm and the ground's warm, and Theo stops and turns toward the trees. He hears birds, a lot of them, and there's an arrow low over the trees, almost too far too see, and it's pelicans. Up close they look like dinosaurs, something ancient, and Theo is silent when he sees them, feeling as if people should talk a different language around them. Everybody's forgotten that language, what people used to say. Pelicans and owls, he thinks. They know things. A real arrow skids past him on the thready, stiff grass, the arrow red with feathers and a round silver nose like a bullet.

Theo knows this is a target arrow. He whirls toward the house and looks up along the rows of windows: at an open one, Mingus, with his big head wearing a yellow rainhat but no shirt, his globular stomach in the sun, holding his bow and a hand, palm out. Theo smiles and holds out his own palm.

Mingus, under the yellow hat, smiles and yells something Theo can't hear. But he likes Mingus, who yells something else he does hear.

Give me back my arrow.

It's my arrow now, Theo yells, and runs toward it, picks it up. Running, Theo feels the sun. This day already hot. And grown-ups wake up early sometimes.

two.

And sometimes
we wash everything clean
as if by doing so we could
advance toward something.
We ought to simply describe
those sounds, those stains
on memory.
                                   – Alejandro Zambra

Theo hears surf and voices, the house waking, and runs with the arrow, past Gus smoking, legs crossed in shade at the lawn's far edge, just before the trees begin, toward the path and a snaking set of old wooden trestles between the humped dunes, sea oats and grass spiking on their backs. Theo then circles back onto the lawn.

Gus smokes a pipe too, a curving black one. Theo always expects sound to come out instead of smoke. Theo knows that Gus will walk back inside in a few minutes to watch television in his room. That's what he does a lot, and he drinks rum. Sometimes he argues or yells at people on the shows he watches. He likes *Wheel of Fortune* and *The New Price Is Right*, and the ladies on them, the ones who smile and point or turn letters over. When he thinks people are being mean to the ladies, he yells at the TV. Theo wonders if the man with half-arms is gone from the gazebo.

He turns, pretending someone's chasing him, and makes a wider circle so he can see the gazebo but not get too close in case the man's still there. The dogs are barking somewhere, one inside and one outside. The man is gone.

Theo warily approaches the peeling white gazebo, columns cracking and veins of vine on the lower parts. The grass is scratchy on his soles. He gets close enough to the gazebo to touch and does, and then begins walking with his hand on the railing's posts, sliding it from one to the next, and starts talking, a story, quietly. This one's about animals.

He tells himself stories circling, walking around the gazebo, but only when no one else is there. He's old enough to think maybe it's because he's lonely. Too many words and not enough space, which is weird because he lives in a huge house, houses, everywhere in different countries and surrounded by people all the time. But it's like he's in an aquarium looking out, seeing people outside doing stuff and looking at him, and what he knows in the water is so different.

Stories feel like they make things understandable, whether it's true or not. At least when he's doing it he's not thinking about anything else.

When Gus sees Theo walking in a circle and talking to himself, Gus hobbles out to ask him what he's doing, ask if he wants to play something or wants something to eat. Gus walks funny, with little steps and leaning over a little, bobbing like a toy. He says his legs hurt. Or his hip hurts.

Sometimes when Theo has been at the gazebo around sundown and no one else is around, there are voices. Men and women. And twice, music – old music. He didn't tell Gus, but he did tell Colin.

I've heard it too, mate. Out here on the bay there used to be rum runners coming ashore on the moonless nights, barrels floating in and bodies washing up at night, and during the day garden parties and lawn tennis and hot jazz in the gazebo, and those paper lanterns, and servants in white jackets. Like Faulkner said, the past is never dead, it's not even past. We're still in it, right now. But it's past me to light this bleeding cigarette.

Theo wasn't sure what Faulkner and the past stuff meant. Colin said this while trying to light a cigarette but sweating so much that he kept putting it out. He threw one down beside the mattress and plucked another one out of a pack on the floor. Colin's room had a huge broken wood bed that you had to stand on steps to get into, but Colin had the pieces apart, like Theo sometimes took apart sandwiches to eat them. Colin had laid the mattress on the floor and the box springs next to it and put some sheets and scarves on both of them, and so the bed was just a frame, which Colin used like a boxing ring sometimes: a couple of times Theo had seen Colin and other adults, mostly ladies, crouched inside the frame laughing and slapping at each other. Once Theo had walked past the door and seen Colin in jeans pretending to be a bull, Theo guessed, holding hands at ears with fingers like horns, and a woman with no clothes on holding a towel in front of him, saying, o-lay.

Colin was trying to light the cigarette from the one in his mouth but that didn't work, so he produced a box of wooden matches from the pocket of his canvas shorts after wriggling on the mattress for an instant. Colin was sick that day. He was sick a lot.

Theo. Theo baby.

His mom, calling. Theo stops the story, stops talking, but keeps his hand on the gazebo railing, circles around the near side, shady early, and then travels out of the shadow into the sun, facing the wall of windows and the dark cliff face of the house. She is waving. He's been around the moon, and now here is earth in front of him, far away.

Hi mom. He waves.

She blows him a kiss, smiling, wrapped in some kind of

white fur coat or robe that rises behind her head in a fan. Hello my beautiful boy. Her voice is hoarse. Can you bring me my cigarettes. I think they're in the car, darling.

Okay.

Theo knows that smoking is bad for you, that it can make you very sick. His dad smokes too. Lots of people do it, everybody around him it seems. Maybe it's not so bad. Everyone seems fine, except sometimes they cough a lot in the morning. His dad says cigarettes help him sing, that they make his voice lower. His dad doesn't like his singing voice, his dad says it sounds whiney and strained; sometimes he says he sounds like a girl. He usually sings harmony, but sometimes he's the main singer. Theo's heard some of his father's early records and his voice does seem a little lower now. When he talks there's a roundness to his voice like an old guitar, and an echo like he has a cold except all the time.

Theo likes his father's voice. He thinks of old wooden boats when he hears his father, solid and a little dark.

Theo decides to run to the car and the house front. He'd forgotten about the man with no clothes – that man is now far away at the edge of the front lawn, squatting on one of the pillars that used to have a gargoyle, yelling at a car driving past on the beach road at one end of the long driveway. There used to be a wall there, then there was a hedge, Theo knew from photographs, and then just bushes and the front edge of the lawn and sand and the road, and two stone pillars on either side of the driveway entrances.

The driveway is shaped like a horseshoe, curving at the house. The straight parts of the driveway are fifty yards long, Theo knows, because Colin once asked Theo to hold a watch and time him while he raced down it against Mingus.

Hold this, mate. Colin handed Theo a watch, big and silver. Colin never wore a watch.

Mingus wore his yellow rain slicker and a yellow rainhat, and carried a suitcase. Theo didn't know what he wore under the slicker, but he was barefoot. Colin, in cowboy boots, had a towel tied at his neck like a cape, no shirt, and carried a pitchfork.

All right you chocolate sonofabitch. Your people are born with those extra muscles, but my people have better shoe technology. So may the best civilization win.

You cracker cocksucker, I will run so fast I'll run into your future and fuck the woman you don't even know you're gonna marry yet.

Language, you goddamn savage.

Colin waved at Theo, and Mingus said, sorry, man. Mingus lumbered over and wrapped Theo up in a weird plastic bear hug, sticky and crinkly.

It's okay, Theo said, his voice muffled.

Theo could curse better than any of the kids at school, and that was one of the only things that slowed them down. So he didn't mind hearing bad words and ways to say them.

So let's go, Quentin.

Theo, start us.

How do I do that.

Say on your mark, get set, go. And then time us.

Mingus and Colin stood next to each other, jostling and poking, sticking legs out and having them slapped, oh no you don't.

On your mark, get –

They took off, flailing over the grass inside the horseshoe, toward the road, Mingus dropping the suitcase and Colin the pitchfork, Mingus taking one step for every two of Colin's, them yelling at each other words Theo couldn't make out, just the hoarse occasional bad words. Colin's cape fluttered, Mingus's slicker glided to the ground – he had on a hospital gown, like a dress on backward, with ties on the back. It had flowers on it. Theo followed, running too.

Colin did one of his football tackles, sliding feet first into Mingus' legs from behind and sending the big man into a slow motion stumble onto his hands and knees, like a statue falling forward. Then he started crawling, and Colin wobbled onto his feet and ran forward to try to sit on Mingus while he crawled, Colin hopping on one leg: Theo heard Mingus's voice drifting up, something spider monkey, and Colin yelling, hyah mule. Colin stopped hopping and flung himself forward to wrap his arms around Mingus, and they collapsed. Get the hell off me motherfucker, your skin is touching my skin. Ah paradise, Theo heard. He looked at the watch. He forgot to notice what time it was when they began.

Colin had rolled over onto his back and had his arms crossed over his face. Mingus was sleeping, on his stomach, head pillowed on his arms, face covered by the round flower of the rainhat.

What's my time, Colin yelled up into the air, not moving.

Theo arrived beside them: I forgot to see what time it was when you started. Sorry.

Rematch, Mingus yelled, the sound muffled by the hat, not moving.

Now Theo stops running for his mother's cigarettes; if he doesn't run, the yelling man won't see him. He rounds the corner of the house's east wing and stays close to the wall, keeping an eye on the man, who's still yelling, but there are no cars. He's yelling about God. It's hard to follow, what he's saying, but it seems like a conversation.

Moving among the stiff shrubs lining the house front Theo sidles toward the car, getting scraped by branches. Pieces of stone fallen from the house hurt to walk on, so Theo has to look down but also watch the man. Theo finally steps away from the shrubs and back onto grass. Then he remembers: opening the car door will make the man turn around. Theo worries. Maybe he can open very quietly. He'll look in the window first and see where the cigarettes are, and then. Maybe the car window is down – the ones on this side aren't, he can see now, but maybe the other side.

The man is not yelling. He's not looking Theo's way either.

Theo prowls to the house steps and the car, asleep in the sun. Theo must decide whether to go around the back of it, closer to the man, or maybe crawl over the hood. He crawls.

The metal's warm but not hot yet. It buckles once, making a sound sort of like thunder, and Theo freezes: the man turns around. Theo knows that the mission is vital; he has to complete the quest. He has orders and the game depends on his ability to steal back the magic.

Theo also figures he's close enough to get help of some kind should the man flip and turn weird again. So Theo keeps moving and slides down the metal, his pajamas riding up and legs sticking and hurting before the skin's released.

The windows on this side are down, as is Theo's head, which he slowly raises to look into the car. There's a person sprawled out on the back seat, snoring. The person has on a skirt that is like a checkerboard, red and black, and scratchy looking, and crumples up around her legs, but there is nothing to see unless Theo tries really hard.

She wears old sneakers that come up over her ankles, but no socks, and Theo can see blue veins in her legs. Her hair's spiky and dark and short, and in between is a black T-shirt with a picture of something on it, maybe a face. Her arms are very white and flung over her head; she sort of looks like she's been hurt, but she's just asleep, Theo assures himself. Her arms are bruised, however. He notices, under her head, something crumpled, like rolled-up clothes. And she has on sunglasses.

Where are cigarettes. Where should he look. How without waking the lady up. The man's behind him.

Theo's heart pounds. He whirls around.

The man's smiling and saying, shhh. Don't wake her up. The man is whispering.

What do you want. Theo doesn't whisper.

Just seeing what's going on. What's going on.

The man's still whispering. Theo wishes he wouldn't: I have to get cigarettes for my mom.

Do you know who that is, the man whispers.

I just need to get the cigarettes.

The man glistens: she played last night.

Played what. Theo is confused.

Her band played. That's funny. We play games, and we play music, and we play the fool, and we play the field, and we play a role. Are those really all the same word. It's like I love you and I love the Giants. Really.

I have to get the cigarettes.

Theo steps to the side and strains to look in. The back seat floor is a sea of litter. In the front seat, more stuff: food wrappers, some toys. Empty bottles. Magazines. A scarf. A sock. A bamboo flute.

Back off. Where is this.

The lady's awake. Sunglasses still on. She's not moving, hands still flung over her head.

This is my house.

Who are you. And where is your house.

Theo doesn't say anything. She stares, Theo thinks, but it's hard to tell behind the shades. Maybe she's closing her eyes again. She lifts one half of her mouth to smile and yawns.

My name is Theo. This is my house. Well, it's my dad's house. And this is Long Island.

Theo knows the house is rented and costs $11,150 per month, because he asked Colin. Colin said they pay through the nose because the agents know it's for Theo's father. Theo asked what pay through the nose means. Colin said it means we're being skinned, fleeced, we're being sucked dry by bleeding parasites. Do we have enough money: Theo thought sometimes about money, never sure how much there was. Colin laughed so hard he started coughing, and then he leaned on Theo for a minute, and then patted him. There is enough money, my young prince. Can I have an allowance, Theo asked. My man, you can, Colin said, and held out his hand, palm up. Theo knew this meant that he was supposed to slap Colin's hand with his palm, so he did. School kids did that, and now the grown-ups were doing it. But then Colin forgot about the allowance. That was last week.

Theo needs to remind him again: today.

The lady says, my name is Gina. Then she asks, who is your friend.

He's not my friend.

I'm the Seal. Nice to meet you. I like your work.

Yeah. Somebody mentioned you in the car last night. You're an artist, right.

Are you a friend of my mother.

Who's your mother.

Frieda.

So you're Adrian's son.

Yes.

The lady says nothing. The back of Theo's neck is tickling because of the sun. He remembers the cigarettes. Can you help me find cigarettes. My mom asked me to get them.

Mmmsure, she says, stretching, and leaning forward to sit up a little, pulling her skirt down and the shirt, shivering once. She strains to sit up more, and puts her ropey arms on the front seat back, then hangs her head over. You check the glove compartment yet.

No.

Try there.

Theo presses the knob on the car door and opens it, as Gina rests her head on her hands on the seat back, watching. Because the car's pointing up, he has to hold the door off his legs. He reaches into the glove compartment using his left hand, then he decides it's okay to sit on the front seat, and slips in as the door bangs shut and uses his right hand to fiddle with the glove compartment button. He's better with his right. He pushes, the compartment door flops open, paper falls out.

I just met your mom last night.

There's a grey gun under a strap in the glove compartment. Theo doesn't touch it and tries to move stuff around it to see. Nothing left but wrappers and gold paper bands like rings that Theo knows are from cigars. He wonders whose car this really is. The seat is sofa-long and wide, like the one in the back, and black and still cool: it's a big car, like the limousines Theo's ridden in, but not as many seats. Theo notices a syringe on the floor on the driver's side. Theo wonders when his dad will get here.

Hmm. I need to get out of here. The lady is sitting up now, looking around. Why'n't you check the floor right there, in front of you.

Theo looks around, pushes the glove compartment door up and snicks it shut. Down in the footwell on the passenger side he sees red: there's a pack of cigarettes under other junk. He tugs it out and spins out the door and back onto his feet and away from the car, letting the heavy door thunk shut. The Seal man is gone.

Gina is pushing her way up and out through the rear, ducking her head and stepping down. She stands for an instant on the steps, staring down at the banked car.

Theo says, where did you meet her.

Who.

My mom.

Mudd Club. Do you know it.

No. Do they play music there.

Yes. I was playing there.

What do you play.

Keyboards and sometimes other things if I have to. Do you play anything.

No.

Does your dad ever try to get you to play.

No. He says music either grabs you by the throat or it doesn't. And if it leaves you alone you're lucky.

Yeah. Could be. Do you think I could get some water.

Yeah. Come on.

Oh holy jesus. I didn't realize that guy had no clothes.

The Seal is struggling back onto one of the pillars at the entrance to the driveway. The beach road is getting busy.

Do you think he'll get in trouble.

Yeah, that's just not a real good idea. I'll go try to talk him down. Can you bring me some water, please. I'd really appreciate it.

She starts walking, the skirt swishing, shoes crunching. Her hair has different colours in it. Then she starts to jog, shaking her arms out. Hey, she yells at Seal, what's up.

Theo doesn't like it when people get in trouble, it makes him upset even if he isn't the one in trouble, especially if it's not the person's fault. Theo isn't sure it is the man's fault. Maybe he can't help it. Maybe he's angry about his arms.

Theo squeezes past the car into the main hall and then feels the cigarettes in his hand. He thinks for a minute and decides the water and the man first, then he'll bring the cigarettes to his mother. He jams the pack into his pajamas – he remembers the brown glass eye snug in there – and from the entrance hall runs down the left passage to the kitchen.

In the kitchen he picks up a glass and holds it toward a window to see if it's clean, and it sort of is. The faucet taps are stiff and old, so sometimes he has to strain, get a leg up to turn the water on. This happens when grown-ups who don't live there use the sink: Colin and Gus have learned how to turn off the taps so that Theo can turn them back on. Sometimes they forget to turn the water off and it runs all night. Theo always stops and makes sure it's off if he's passing through. He wonders if the lady would like ice, but then just pushes the glass into the stream.

Watching the water Theo wonders how the Seal got here. And where his clothes are. The glass is full.

Theo realizes he'll have to walk carrying the water or he'll spill it. So he walks, but fast, and water slops over the glass rim onto his pajamas and the floor. He's leaving a wet trail but he doesn't stop, just stares at the water's surface trying to connect how he moves with keeping the water inside the glass and it's not really working. Unless he slows he's just going to spill. Then he thinks he'll cover it with his other hand and run. And he does, but it's hard to run without using your arms. How does the Seal do it.

Theo reaches the hall, squeezes past the car and down the steps and into the full sun and sees a police car at the foot of the drive; no lights or siren but a police officer talks to the Seal, sitting on the pillar, and to Gina, who's got her hands on her hips. Theo stops. The gravel hurts his feet. He stands, watches, as the police officer turns and gets into the car, and the Seal shifts and crouches, and jumps from the pillar into the grass and then lies down on his back. He'll get itchy, Theo thinks. Gina strides back toward the house pushing hair out of her eyes.

Theo sees her see him and wave. He doesn't wave back, still holding the glass and covering it with his hand. She suddenly turns sideways and puts both hands over her head and turns a fast cartwheel, so fast her skirt doesn't even go down, and comes up smiling and running to where Theo still stands. He doesn't understand adults.

Thanks.

She takes the glass and drinks it all down. She is pretty. She closes her eyes while she drinks. Theo suddenly is thirsty.

Is he in trouble.

She shakes her head no: The cop just asked how he was, and asked him if he would do a favour and take it back up to the house. Does he do this a lot.

Theo remembers the cigarettes. I don't know. I've never seen him before.

Really. She squints down at him. She's taller than him but not by a lot.

It's a big house, Theo says. The grown-ups have lots of friends.

She's holding the glass with her little finger out, tilting it back and forth, looking at him, turns it upside down. Are there kids around here, she says.

No. I have to go see my mom now.

Okay, sure.

Theo runs back to the house, rocks hurting again.

At the front doors he squeezes in past the car and shoots up the right staircase two risers at a time, hopping because of the distance between them. He is trying not to think.

Theo runs all the way to the floor his mother stayed on last time she came, where her window was earlier. Aside from some clanging and banging from the second floor, there's little sound now except birds and wind up and in from doors and windows, which are open mostly everywhere. Birds get in, and bats, a flying squirrel last month. Sometimes there are nests.

Out of breath, Theo pants on the fourth landing. Someone squeals.

Is this him.

Ahead down the hall in shadow, another woman stands with her arm around Theo's mom, both, he can see, smiling. The other woman's taller than his mother, her hair shines even in the dark and she's got a big chest in a leather vest. She has tight bands of metal around her arms, jewellery, Theo supposes. And she's got a rug wrapped around her bottom half, which she's holding up with the hand not around his mother's waist.

His mother's in the high-collared white thing like fur. It covers her from head to foot.

Yes, this is my angel of mercy, his mother says.

Quick love, bring the cigarettes, says the other woman.

Hello baby, his mother says, walking out from under the arm toward him, stumbling a little. It feels early, is it early, she asks. Lots of times grown-ups ask questions that're not questions.

He reaches into his pocket for the pack, pulls it out and holds it out at the end of his arm.

You didn't open it did you, she asks, kneeling to hug him, his arm still extended.

Theo knows better: no, mom.

Thank you, my darling.

She holds his face in her hands and looks at him like the doctor, looking at the parts of his face and into his eyes. Good morning my sweet. Her eyes look very tired.

Good morning mom. Are you okay.

He leans into her, feels the softness of what she's wearing, feels the friend take the pack from his hand now curled around his mother's back. He feels his mother's ribs, her spine even through the thick thing she's in.

Yes, baby, I am fine now that I see you. I'll be downstairs in a minute. I'm going to get dressed. This is Marthe. She and some people came out with me last night from the city. You'll meet them later.

Sure mom. I don't know if we have any food.

Don't worry, angel, we'll figure it all out. Everything. I can't wait to spend the day with you.

You know dad is coming here to make an album.

She's still holding him and Theo feels her muscles tense, and she has to shift to keep her balance: No, I didn't hear that yet.

61

I don't know if that's a responsible thing to do, subject you to that kind of atmosphere. It is not necessarily a healthy one.

Why.

I'll talk to him about that. Or talk to his people. I'm not sure if I'm currently allowed to talk to him.

Why.

Oh baby. Let me get dressed and let's have a good day. Let's have some fun. Marthe, hold your goddamn horses.

The other woman has disappeared with the cigarette pack into an open door.

His mother rises and hurries away in a white swirl of fur into the room, shutting the door and locking it.

Okay mom, he says to her back.

Theo bumps back down the steps, wondering what a good day will be this time. Usually his mother likes to talk a lot early in the day, then she gets tired in the afternoon and just sits or lies down. Sometimes it's the other way around. Sometimes she can't sit still at all and she chases him, teases him, says, let's go on a boar hunt, or bowling, I've never been fishing, or let's play football. She meant soccer when she said football, Theo knew. Maybe they would actually do something. At the edge of the back lawn, near the trees, is the rectangle of brick-coloured clay with a sagging frayed net cutting across it as if to catch something. Maybe they could play tennis. If it's just the two of them it's different than if there are other people. Maybe Marthe likes tennis.

Colin had said yesterday that it was time for a milk run, so that could mean today, maybe. Colin and his mother don't like each other, but they have to get along because Theo's dad wants them to. Colin's supposed to look out for Theo's mother too, and she definitely doesn't like that. Theo's heard Colin and his mom discussing this: they snarled, and Frieda said how dare you, you fucking valet. Since his mother is here maybe Colin will do the milk run today.

Colin makes the trip once a month to Theo's father's office in the city. He picks up envelopes filled with hundred-dollar bills. Colin says this makes much of the household's more delicate transactions possible.

What does that mean, Theo asked.

I like the feel of money. But American money is so boring, designed by a cabal of Masons. But you take a pound, now, it's flash-coloured and you have to fold it up just to get it to fit in your kip. You want some square footage to your currency, hard-earned and stuffed into your pocket at the end of a shift, you want to feel that weight dragging your trousers down so you have to hitch your belt or start spending just to ease the burden. Say, do you know what precipitation that evaporates before it hits the ground is called.

No, Theo said.

Virga. It's Latin, means twig, but I'm not clear on why. Sometimes cash evaporates like rain in the Sahara, gone before it even hits the ground. Sometimes it's cold and hard, and sometimes you can float a battleship on it, and you can surf on it, get the thrill of your life, and it can dig the Grand Canyon, rip a divot out of the hardest stone. One day I'm going to ride nonstop across country on a bloody big Harley to the Grand Canyon, get off, stand at the edge and take a piss, then zip up and get back on and ride back. What do you say, you want to ride with me.

Okay, Theo said. If it's okay with my dad.

Colin was frying meat in an iron skillet the size of a car tyre on the big stove in the kitchen while he said this, smoking a cigarette, wearing a Yankees hat. He had a hunting knife in a sheath jammed into the back of his jeans.

Why do you have that knife.

Let me tell you the first rule of using a knife: never, ever, under any circumstances, use your knife.

Why do you have the knife then.

I'm not saying I haven't violated my own rule, but you can tell them as are not totally comfortable in wielding one. You use the knife to distract your opponent and then either run, or your friend lays him out from behind with a chair, or you kick him in the you-know-where. Then he's your man. The real key is always have a friend handy.

Here he turned to look at Theo, squinting through the cigarette and shaking the spatula at him, flinging hot grease but not noticing. Piece of priceless advice, offered free of charge. Ow – he lifted a foot and stopped shaking the spatula. How do you like your meat – black or grey.

Theo said, how many fights have you been in.

Not as many as some, Colin said. And always *casus belli*. I never took a poke unless someone did first or I could see they planned to.

Did you ever fight my dad.

Colin laughed, turning off the gas on the big stove, the kitchen blurry with smoke from the skillet. Your dad and I have had our strong disagreements and possibly wrestled a little. Certainly he's a hard-headed sod and stubborn as any human that ever drew the breath of life. Part of my portfolio is whispering to the king that he's mortal. At least I feel that's part of my job. Others may disagree. I can tell you, I've been on his team a couple of times when others have come at us. He can hold his own, your dad.

Why don't you like my mom.

What makes you think that.

I'm not stupid.

Very true, my friend.

Colin padded barefoot across the tiles to the heavy table at which Theo leaned on his elbows over an empty plate. Colin stuck a long fork into the pan and pulled out a slab and poked it onto Theo's plate.

Here now, get some life into you, put some flesh on your bones. We don't want anyone to think you're getting mistreated. It's more your mom not liking me.

Why.

Theo leaned his head on his hand and picked up the meat with his other hand but then dropped it: still too hot.

Christ. Silverware. Like a bleeding animal.

Colin yanked open a heavy old drawer and scooped a fistful of forks and spoons and can openers and a couple of knives and spilled them on the table. Choose your weapon.

Theo sat for an instant staring at the dull gleams, then grabbed a fork and jumped up from his chair and yelled, running at Colin. Colin jumped out of the way, holding cigarette and frying pan away on each side: zounds, a barbarian sneak attack. You will pay for your perfidy.

Theo came at him again, poking, growling.

Dropping the pan clattering on the stove and grabbing a long wooden spoon from a countertop, Colin whacked Theo on the top of his head, then started feinting with the spoon, and dancing around the kitchen, forward and backward, knocking over Theo's chair. Is that the best you can do. Come on, soldier.

Theo suddenly was angry and really poking with the fork, slashing. Colin laughed and dodged, whacked Theo again and danced behind the table.

Theo threw down his fork and walked out into the ballroom and toward the door, washed in sadness in the bright early light, in the silent house.

Colin called from behind, his voice echoing around the big kitchen. Hey, you can't depart the field of battle yet, we aren't finished.

Colin knew more about his dad than Theo did. It's not fair, Theo yelled, walking away.

Fair. Whoever said anything about fair – first rule of fighting.

Now down the stairs and at the first floor, his mother's hugging smell still in his nose, Theo hears clacking and buzzing, with a regular rhythmic beat, and some high whirring notes also, and beeps. He turns and follows the noise to what used to be a library, floor to ceiling shelves like ladders, built into the walls in dark wood. Some shelves still hold books but too high for Theo to see titles. The letters are dull gold, on fire when the sun's right. At the room's centre on an altar of overturned metal buckets, to amplify sound, sits a fax machine, linked by a long taut beige cord and a new orange extension cord to a brass outlet across the room. The cord hangs in midair and has flags and rags and police tape ribboning from it. The machine trembles on the bucket tower. Something is slowly being printed into its tray. Incoming, Colin usually yells, when he hears the machine begin to tremble and whine.

CONFIDENTIAL
TO: COLIN

The paper warm and smelling like chemicals. Theo lifts the slick paper and runs with it back out and down the hall, toward the rear of the house. Because it's from his dad, and Colin's disappeared somewhere, Theo decides to bring it to his grandfather.

Theo runs: he's a fast runner, and he's dodging things, feet slapping on cool marble, tile, wood, each a different feeling. Then he's on the terrace stone and bursting into the full sun now lighting the back lawn all the way downslope to the tree line. Gus's chair is empty.

Theo stops. He runs his hand through his hair, rubs his head hard, his fingers catching. It started hurting to comb so he stopped. Colin says they are shipwrecked, like Robinson Crusoe: no need to fret over personal hygiene, must survive, Colin says. Gus frowns when Colin says things like that. Gus is neat, he even lines his belt buckle up with his shirt buttons, which bulge over his big stomach – even when he's wearing shorts, which he wears with regular leather shoes and black socks. Gus tries to get Theo to wash and comb his hair, but Theo knows that if he waits long enough Gus stops talking about it.

Theo is brown everywhere except where his shorts are, the skin across his nose pink and peeling. His palms are much paler than the backs of his hands.

Mingus once said Theo was black, held out his own huge hands,

67

pink-palmed, and Theo's next to them. We look the same. You and me.

Then once when Mingus was wearing one of his costumes that had a visor over his face, he said, from inside, boy, you got so much you don't even know how much you got.

How much what.

What I mean is, I want to be on your planet. Help me get this fastened in back.

What do I do.

See the loops. Put the wooden toggles into the loops.

On one side were small brown wooden football-shaped buttons, and Theo threaded them into loops strung down the other side. Mingus grunted and began making sounds.

Mingus sometimes appeared in costume talking only in his made-up language. Theo sort of understood, sometimes, but generally didn't. When he was in a costume or talking his own language, he was not Mingus anymore, and people around him acted like he was someone else and they didn't laugh or make fun of him. After a few times Theo did too. He thought about how his parents were different people at different times and that surprised him. He saw new expressions on their faces, like strangers' faces: maybe everyone is like that. But he felt pretty much the same all the time. He wondered if that was normal.

Okay: Mingus was talking English again. I need to collect some artefacts – you want to help me.

Usually once he appeared in costume you couldn't talk to him, you had to wait until Mingus reappeared. But he flipped up the visor, which was a curved piece of grey plastic attached to ear pieces taken from a pair of sunglasses and glued to a bicycle helmet like an apricot pit or a brain or an insect head.

Okay.

The thready carpet at Mingus's room door reminded Theo of birds, how if you looked closely in the trees you could spot nests because of the red, blue, green they'd pulled from the old garden furniture. Theo felt calm when he watched birds, reminded of something he had forgotten, but something he didn't need to think about. He could just watch. There wasn't much like that.

Theo hummed, started whispering a story to himself as Mingus fussed with his clothes and a plastic bucket.

Okay so the path goes through that swamp and we know there are monsters in there. Yeah, but how can we get the treasure. We can try the magic salt again, it helped the last time. But.

We're not telling Colin about this, I just want to make a clean getaway.

Theo spent a lot of his time figuring out which of the directions given to him by adults to follow, as he frequently found himself told two things that couldn't both be true or both be done at the same time. He had learned to base his decisions on consequences: which adult would be most unhappy if Theo followed the other adult's instructions, and how would that unhappiness be expressed. Here Theo figured Colin was the bigger problem, although Theo was, as usual, uncomfortable making the decision.

I have to tell him. He'll be upset.

Mingus shrugged, a massive movement, and stared with his goggle eyes. It's your world, baby. I'm gonna keep walking, though. I need to get out there before the good shit's gone. Sorry, I mean stuff. Mingus shuffled toward the front hall.

Theo wanted to know what the good stuff was, but that would have to wait. He followed the noise, toward the ballroom. He stopped in the dark back of the house. He waited for a gap in the gonging sounds coming from Colin's room then yelled, Colin, I'm going to the beach with Mingus come and find us. Then he ran.

See, words have power, and if you control words you can control the world.

As they walked the beach, Mingus kept his plastic cartoon eyes fixed on the sand and his head not moving while the rest of his body jiggled and staggered, kicked up grains. He looked the way the dogs looked when they scented something. The only other time Theo saw similar expressions, not exactly the same but the same in the way it felt watching them, was when Theo watched people playing music. Some musicians managed to look goofy at the same time they looked like they were following a strong scent, as their faces twitched or tightened and loosened and tongues went in and out, or they chewed or made mouth shapes, the mouths disconnected from their bodies and even from the music sometimes. Getting something out musically meant squeezing something big through a small hole, it seemed. It looked painful, but Theo knew that couldn't be true.

Mingus jabbed down quick as a bird and plucked up something raining sand. It was a faded plastic green V, with little black magnets on the long parts of the V. Every morning in his class at the school in the city, one student was picked to spell out the day's weather and a quote from a famous writer on a white magnetic board that sat on an easel, using letters like this one, except smaller: the teacher seemed to think they were little kids. Mingus grinned, sweating.

Certain letters are the most powerful of all, and one day they're going to rise up and liberate themselves from the

European languages. The ones that go back to Greece and Egypt are just biding their time, waiting for people who understand to free them. Then their power can be unleashed for real, and they can change the world.

The letters, Theo asked, peering up at Mingus, who'd plunked the letter into the bucket and now shuffled off, his massive calves crusted with sand looking like the Snack Shack's breaded chicken drumsticks in the village. Colin ate them two at a time, one in each hand.

Yeah, the letters. I have to be careful. The government knows I know about this, and they'd like to steal what I'm doing. They want to turn these letters into weapons. They might just try to turn me into a weapon, or force me to work for them – Mingus wiped at his nose, churning forward – the beach is good because you got things let loose by the water that could be from anywhere, could have traveled thousands of miles, could have been floating for centuries, or just risen up from something sunk, just seeing the light again for the first time. But you have to get out early, cause there are lots of eyes on this stuff. Mingus pointed up.

Theo looked up –

No man, don't look. Satellites right now can see us. The eye follows everything. Then they swoop in.

Who does. Theo was half-running to keep up with Mingus, the sun hot on his back, his stomach growling, the low-tide ocean curling and hurling itself against the sand about thirty yards away. A couple of striped beach tents rippled nearer the water, and a stream of walkers moved there, all old.

Can we walk closer to the water, I'm hot, Theo said.

Mingus stopped and scanned things, big as a lighthouse. Okay.

They headed straight for the water. Is Mingus your real name, Theo asked.

No, it's a nickname because I look like a famous musician named Mingus. My real name is the same name as a line of kings of Egypt. My people. My dad wanted a powerful name for me.

You're from Egypt.

No. But real Egyptians, the first Egyptians, were black. The Greeks stole everything from us – all the shit they're famous for. The science and philosophy. Stole it from the first kingdom, my kingdom. Later, white people came along and called the place Egypt, but that's not the real name.

What's the real name.

Can't tell you, little man. Names are really powerful, and that name's too powerful still, even after five thousand years, still radioactive. It could blow up in your face.

How come I never heard of this in school.

Mingus started laughing, then coughing, still kicking toward the ocean, getting further away rather than closer: We don't have enough time for me to tell you why that is. Let's just see what's to see on this damn beach.

Theo now walked in Mingus's shadow, easier and cooler than trying to navigate beside him. Talking up at the giant.

How tall are you.

Six feet six and three-quarter inches.

How much do you weigh.

A billion pounds. I am the heaviest cat on this beach, baby.

I weigh ninety-six pounds.

Well, damn, you are the second-heaviest cat on the beach. Congratulations.

Mingus was huffing as he trolled through the sand, gleaming.

Theo thought of whales and the fact that they breathe, just like people, and sometimes you can hear them, in a boat. Sailors that hunted them said you could hear them breathing, and Theo realized right then: if you held them underwater long enough, they'd drown. He'd heard the dogs breathing, but he hadn't ever heard any other animal breathing. Did birds breathe. Squirrels. What does a snake sound like. He hadn't ever heard his mother breathe.

Are you an artist, Theo asked Mingus, standing now next to Mingus's bucket and staring down at the dry faded V.

Yeah. I make stuff. I play music.

That's not art.

The hell it's not. Why do you say that.

Art's pictures.

No, man. Art is ideas – everything else is just details, which tool you choose to use. And the ideas, they're monsters stalking us, drooling on us when we think it's raining. You have to pay attention. It's some crazy sh– stuff.

It's okay. You can say the bad words. I know them.

So your dad ain't an artist.

No. He says he's just a guitar player.

Mingus snorted. More like the man with the golden gun.

What does that mean.

It means every artist is a deadly dude. Some get rich off it, some get killed by it.

Theo collapsed on the sand and rolled over onto his back, tilting his head up at the hill of Mingus.

Are you rich.

I sure don't live on the beach. Let's go for a swim. Get some ocean on before I have to go back to the rats.

The air filled with the rough breathing of the water, in and out.

Were you a good student when you were in school, Theo asked.

Mingus laughed: I liked it cause I got a meal out of it. I liked math class.

I don't like it.

Math class or school.

School.

Hey, it's like dying, we all gotta go sometime.

Mingus smiled at Theo, but Theo stared at the sand, seeing the sleeping people he had to pass on the sidewalk to get to school, concrete wet at their heads and sometimes at their pants.

Bad joke: sorry – Mingus paused and stared at something, then grinned. For sure, most of what I learned in school didn't have much to do with school. But school's okay. I was valedictorian of my class in high school and I got a scholarship to Yale.

What's a valditorean.

It's a person who has to make a speech at graduation.

Why.

It's supposed to be an honour to be asked.

Making a speech sounds more like a punishment.

Most of the time, far as I know, it is supposed to be an honour. It's crazy, man, people are more afraid of public speaking than death. You can read surveys about it.

Are you famous.

The thump of waves made Theo talk louder. Mingus always talked loud. People turned and looked at him all the time even when he wasn't talking to them. Out here, the wind carried his voice away like sand. Theo wondered if words could blow away and still sound the same.

Not like your dad.

How famous is my dad.

He's famouser than all git-out. Mingus was talking in a fake voice. When Mingus got mad or wanted to make fun of something, he talked like that.

Why are you mad.

I ain't mad, man. I'm just angry that people like me, we have to scream to be heard. Plus he stole every good idea he had from black people.

My dad doesn't steal things.

Mingus began stripping off, first his hat, then his cape, then his shirt, then his shorts, flinging them all away on the sand, leaving him in ragged, saggy olive-green boxers that made him look like a baby in a dark diaper, eyes still hidden behind plastic shades.

Ask him about that: Mingus with a shiver began running toward the water.

Glancing up Theo saw a group of grown-ups spilling out onto the sand from the dunes, directly behind Mingus: from the house.

Theo watched as pale people in black pants and T-shirts and boots and chains stumbled toward the water: people who'd arrived in a van with his mother.

They began flopping, sand flying, kicking off boots, stripping off shirts to expose white ribby torsos and nipple rings, snakes and black bands and totem-pole designs tattooed on their arms and backs. One walked toward the water, then stopped to hop and yank off boots and then the man in his black pants ran toward the water and dove forward headfirst, arms at his sides.

Theo pushed out into the water. Then he lowered himself and kicked once, face down, drifting without paddling, away, the water suddenly cold.

So running back into the house now with the fax, Theo carries the secret code, warm on the slick paper, and he must bring it to the commander, but he can't find Gus or Colin and runs with the fax flapping in his hand, down halls and around rooms, bare feet muffled on musty carpet then slapping on slate, tile, wood. He runs.

He likes to run. He's good at running. He runs up and down any stairs, and adults always walk, sometimes even more slowly, when they go up stairs. But it takes too long if you don't run.

Noises come from more parts of the house now. Music starts to seep from different areas, different musics. Someone's screaming. Theo weaves among rooms, dodging and feinting, and hits a carpet and slips, feet pulled toward the ceiling, and slams against the slate floor, his head bouncing. Dark.

Now stars. Lights. He sees butterflies of light, lying on his back, and is nauseous. He rolls onto his side and gags up silver strings of spit. Nothing to throw up. He hasn't even had water. He shivers back down. He's trembling, he's underwater, everything fuzzy, blurred. Theo can't remember what he was doing before. He just woke up and now he's figuring out what he is, and where. It's coming back, drifting in. And he's drifting, the room moving, shifting. He closes his eyes but instantly opens them again: everything spins if he doesn't.

Staring at a point on the opposite wall, a target spray-painted in white that's the only sign the room is in use, besides the old rug on the floor, Theo slowly folds himself together and squats for a minute, arms around his knees, the fax crushed in his hand. The air sparks. He turns his head slowly, shakes it a little. Doesn't help.

What are you doing my love.

His mom, behind him, now downstairs, apparently.

I fell down. I feel funny.

Oh my god.

He hears her, feels the air shift, and then she's wrapping herself around him, touching his head, the back of his head, looking at her fingers, trying to hug him, but this just tips him over and he's on all fours.

I'm dizzy.

Oh my god. David Bowie. You've got the pupils. I'm going to find a doctor. Lie down, baby, and don't move.

She swirls from the room. Theo gets back to his feet, crouching. Then slowly he rises. There's mist in the light, and edges blur. He's goofy, loose. He walks, to the open door on the other side. The air pulses when his heart beats.

He wonders if this is what being high is like. Or drunk. Some parts of it are okay, some are scary and hurt. He's starting to feel a dull ache. He walks, for a while.

He walks. He sees Colin and a woman standing up, face to face, right up against each other. They don't have clothes on.

He walks past them and they don't notice. Their eyes are closed. Colin is brown. The woman is very white, and her hair is purple. Her neck is banded with what looks like a dog collar; Theo glides past them. He's gliding, not touching the floor. It's cool.

He glides and glides, touching the wall to keep from drifting too far off track. He glides through two more rooms and into a third one that's full of cushions and old newspapers and magazines. The seraglio, Colin calls this room, the cushions shiny and embroidered, scattered. People lie down in here. There is his mother, lying down, with the other woman from upstairs and two other people, one holding a tape recorder. They all look tired, sleepy. His mother sees him and he sees her face change. My god. I'm so sorry honey. Are you feeling better now, baby.

Yes, Theo said, dreaming and gliding. I'm going outside.

Okay baby, you go play. I'll be out in a minute and we can do something. Why don't we go into town and have a nice lunch.

Okay, Theo says, but his mouth is disconnected from his head, which is disconnected from his body. Eating seems a weird thing to do. He just wants to get outside and lie down in some shade. The air's not moving inside and it's hard to breathe. Breath. It's loud.

How does he get out of the maze, everything looks the same, same walls, same empty rooms, and he sees again the snow piled in the hall, feels cold air. Then he smells fresher air from his left and follows the hall toward light and he's back in the ballroom and someone is lying down on the parquet floor, arms spread wide. Eyes closed, resting on a cheek, mouth a little open. Did he fall. Is he asleep. Like in the city. No one was here earlier. He's a stranger. Barefoot. Theo notices his legs are tied together at the ankle with what looks like a twisted up T-shirt. Theo keeps walking, past the man. Outside. Must get outside.

Theo wonders if he should be scared. It's not getting better, but it's hard to care, because everything seems so soft and he just wants to sleep. It's the summer. Another day. He moves over the terrace, moving in a giant circle or stuck in a whirlpool, doing the same things he did earlier, walking the same places. How do you climb out. But Theo's just a kid. There's so much he has to wait on and depend on the grown-ups for. He makes sure the dogs get fed. He worries. He worries about his mother.

He worries about Colin and about Gus. He worries about his dad.

People talk about his dad a lot. People write about his dad. They say things about him that Theo doesn't understand. They say things that bother Theo.

Theo doesn't feel like a pirate. And right now he starts to cry. Because maybe he's dying.

Do people know when they're dying. His head is fuzzy, and he's dizzy. He wants to be somewhere dark and cool and away.

There is a moment of quiet, like the world is breathing. And from inside whatever room it's in, Theo can't remember now, comes the chiming. One. Two. Three. Four. Five. Six. Seven. Eight. Nine. Ten. Eleven. Twelve. Thirteen. Fourteen. Fifteen. Sixteen. Seventeen. Eighteen. Nineteen. Twenty. Twenty-one. Twenty-two. Twenty-three. There's shouting and a faint clanging crash.

The clock is broken. Theo remembers it sits on a mantel in one of the front rooms, close to where people usually start to congregate, drifting down from upstairs. The sun sits just over the bristly grey-green trees, and the earlier breezes are gone. The air hangs in curtains, and Theo notices Gus now, back in his chair, with a pipe. And a glass, his stubby legs crossed at the ankle. He is wearing a white T-shirt with a blue devil on it, from a college in North Carolina, Theo knows. Gus has on bright red socks and dark shoes. And a hat that says Jack Daniels. Why do pictures of the Devil always show him smiling, if he's supposed to be bad. And pictures of Jesus never show him smiling, and he's supposed to be good.

Gus is waving at Theo, waving him over. Come here, he's saying with his hand. Theo shuffles over the wiry grass and bumpy ground, so hard and dry that Theo's feet hurt. He floats a little but is feeling heavier, more connected. His head hurts.

Have you seen your mother.

I don't feel good.

Gus sets down his glass on the rusty wrought iron table beside his chair and stares carefully at Theo, curvy pipe smoking. Theo follows the smoke straight up but the light stabs his eyes. Ow. He ducks his head back, closes eyes, feels dizzy.

Here now, what's wrong exactly. Gus smells sharp and sweet, which is coming from the rum in the glass.

I guess I hit my head.

Hold on, son, how'd you do that. Gus is leaning forward, trying to focus on Theo's eyes but having to squint and then close one eye to see. Let me see your pupils.

Theo unsquints, but the light's still bright.

How'd you hit your head.

I was running and I fell down inside. On the rock part.

Christ almighty. Are you seeing lights at all.

No, Theo lied.

You sure now.

Yes. I just have a headache.

Gus collapses back, into the chair, rubbing his face up and down and knocking off the hat. Well, maybe you should take it easy for a few minutes, eh. Maybe get an aspirin. If it keeps up bad we'll make you up an icepack.

Gus struggles up from the soft seat and lowers himself to the ground beside Theo, stiff and sighing a lot. Whew. That's not an easy thing to do. Why'n't you take the chair.

Instead, Theo lays himself down, carefully, to avoid moving his head a lot.

So how do you feel now, son.

Fine.

That's fine. We can just rest our bones here for a bit, and go in and have a bite of something after a while. How about that.

Frieda said she wanted to go to town for lunch.

Did she. She came in like gangbusters last night. I'm surprised she's up.

Theo says nothing, but keeps his eyes open. In the blue high up flicker seagulls. The sky is close enough to touch.

Gus, when is my dad coming.

That, my friend, only he and the Almighty know. And his managers, I suppose. But it will be soon.

You said he was going to make a record here.

True, son. Soon as your da tells me I'll tell you.

Can we get a TV.

Ah, you know how your mother feels about that.

I just want to watch TV. I want to be normal.

Well, bucko. What exactly is normal, in your estimation.

TV.

Anything else.

I don't know. I don't remember right now.

Theo drifts with birds, hearing the low rushing of the ocean, and a bugle, and two people singing somewhere in the house, and somebody teasing the dogs, their snarls the kind of thing that happens when people are mean to them but think they're playing. Adults seem to do that to each other, too.

Theo is anxious to not be treated like a kid. But he wonders how many ways there are to grow up, and can you pick the one you want, or do you even get a choice.

Theo watches the gulls, hears the new sound of Gus snoring a little. Theo listens to the wind, the house, other stuff that must be the world. Then he closes his eyes to see if the spins come back, and when they don't, he leaves his eyes closed, watching fire on his eyelids and feeling really, really tired, suddenly.

He's in a boat, just him, on the water, a rowboat but there aren't any oars or a motor or anything. Or a life jacket. Just the ocean and the sun, and the boat, and whispering. *Hold on tight.* The waves get bigger, the boat starts to rock and jump, slow and low at first but then faster and higher, and it's a bucking bronco, like a horse, and Theo is lifting off the seat and slamming back down, going a little higher each time, and slamming harder and –

He opens his eyes. Sky birds snoring house sounds. He's on his back in the yard, where he was, next to the mound of Gus. The pipe is cold on the table.

Theo remembers little paper pills his dad sent one time that dropped into water turned into dragons and swans. From Japan. The day is unfolding. He wants to be in the ocean. Paper. Where's the fax.

Theo is not holding the fax anymore. Where is it. It was for Colin, but what did it say. Something weird, about a ship. Did he leave it in the house or outside. It's hard to remember stuff.

Theo wants to be responsible. He can be trusted with important things. He pushes himself up, and slowly onto his feet, and steers back to the house, which he just left. All day he's done nothing but circle around, in and out, up and down. He's getting dizzy. He wants to go in a straight line and not stop. Find Colin.

There's the lady from the car. She's out on the terrace now, drinking a glass of something, smoking a cigarette, sitting with two other people Colin doesn't know, two men. One has goggling eyes that pop out, and spiky hair. His clothes are all torn and both he and the other man have on long sleeves and long pants and hard, heavy-looking black shoes. The men sit propped on the stones of the terrace. All three are smoking. One is beating on the terrace with his hands. The others nod their heads to a rhythm they hear.

Hi Theo, the lady says. You remember me.

Theo does, but he doesn't remember her name. Sort of, he says, but not wanting to be rude. He's a little fuzzy.

I'm Gina. This is Richard and Alan. This is Theo, Frieda's son.

Hey: one speaks, the other nods and smiles.

Where's Colin.

Colin. Oh, Colin.

The motorbike's waspy whine echoed from the ballroom. I think that's him. He's inside, Gina says.

Thanks.

Theo walks around them and toward the open French doors. He can see the noise shooting out like smoke or waves. It hurts to hear, and Theo puts his hands over his ears. Ducking from the light into the darker ballroom Theo gets dizzy for a few seconds and halts, looking while he steadies himself, hands cupped over ears.

Colin straddles the lime motorbike wearing the towel cape, revving the bike, staring at the exhaust pipe and then at Theo. The towel says Welcome to Myrtle Beach, with a big seahorse on it. Colin also has on the goggles he wears when he rides, and a blue swimming snorkel strapped to his head. He holds a thumb up to Theo and spits out the snorkel and yells: what is up, white man.

Theo walks over with his hands on his ears as Colin stops twisting the grip throttle and the engine settles into a crackling and popping idle.

There was a fax for you, but I lost it.

Colin stares, his eyebrows angle down under the goggles: What did it say.

I'm sorry: Theo takes his hands from his ears. Something about an old-timey ship.

What. Sorry mate, what.

Something about a sail.

A mainsail.

I think.

Did it say something about reefing the main sail.

I think. I'm sorry, Colin – I'll try to find it. What does that mean.

Holy suffering nails of Jesus.

Colin guns the bike and skitters off down a hall toward the other side of the house, legs splayed on either side for balance as the bike totters. The noise splits Theo's head and he ducks, then isn't sure what to do. Is it something he can help with. He follows Colin, feeling bad. How could he know what it meant. But he could have made sure to deliver it. Theo's face feels hot.

Crows land in a noisy knot somewhere outside, sounding like angry babies, demanding and raw. Theo's been around babies and didn't like them much.

He hears loud voices ahead, agitated, but can't tell what is being said, the bike revving in the background, then the engine revs and grows a little fainter – Colin must be riding around to the front hall. Then the bike noise dies.

Theo follows the sound, coming into the seraglio and seeing his mother and the others up and rummaging through clothes and digging in pockets, collecting things lying around, yelling about where to put them. Theo's mother sweeps around angry and impatient; she snaps at the others, including the Marthe woman: My god, you act like children. Use the bathrooms or eat it. Seeing Theo walk toward her, she glides at him. My love, go outside and play.

What is going on. Why is Colin upset.

It's nothing, love. Go outside. We'll go down to the beach and spend the day. No, let's go into town and have luncheon. What time is it, Mark.

Eleven.

A.m.

Yes.

Good. Lunch would be good, no. We are going out for a while.

Frieda puts her hand on Theo's head and walks through the hall, gliding, in the direction of the front hall. She wears white fur and a very short skirt.

Mom, do you want to put on your shoes.

No, my darling, not necessary. Mark, Julio, find Richard and Gina and Alan and see if they'd like to come with. You too, for that matter, of course.

They're on the terrace, Theo says, to help.

The band is, Theo's mother asks.

Well, that lady named Gina is there with two men.

Let's get out of this place before I suffocate.

Theo watches the adults, unsure what to do. He puts his hands over his ears again, an ache returning.

What's wrong, love.

My head hurts.

What's wrong.

He looks at her closely, kneeling now in front of him. I hit my head on the floor.

Oh, no. Are you all right, my darling. She peers into his face, but seems not quite focused, and Theo figures maybe she forgot why she was looking.

It's okay, Mom, Theo says.

She smiles slowly, like the sun rising over the ocean: I love you, my love.

Others disappear through doors. Theo's mother still kneels in front of him, sniffing and smiling. She's just looking at him, and eventually she just sits down on the floor.

What are you doing.

Looking at you. You're beautiful.

Stop, Mom. He turns, angry and blushing.

Can't I look at my beautiful son.

I thought you said we were going to lunch.

Ah, so I did. When the others get here, we'll go. Would you like a hamburger. Yes, seafood, she says. She lies back on the floor.

Mom.

Mmm hmm.

What are you doing. Are you okay, Mom.

Mmm hmm.

Do you want me to sit with you.

Mmm hmm.

So Theo lowers himself to the floor beside her; her eyes are closed but she's smiling. He lies back beside her. Her head is lifted off the floor by the fur, like a pillow, but Theo's got nothing but stone under his head, surprisingly always cool. He doesn't want lunch. Where is Colin. Theo sees his chrysalises, glistening up under the attic eaves, gleaming lights in the dark. He wonders if they'll ever open.

Frieda. Come on, let's go for a walk.

It's the lady Gina, with the two men, and the short man with the baseball shirt who'd gone to get them.

Let's get her up and walk her around. Theo, what are you doing.

Helping her.

Okay, cool. Let's walk her around, get a little exercise, then we'll see about lunch.

The man named Richard says, dilettantes and parvenus.

Would you shut up. Gina glares at Richard as she bends toward Frieda.

Sorry man.

Richard's eyes bulge, a bright green, but the dark bruises under them get darker as he bends over. Gina isn't looking at Richard anymore, just lifting Frieda, limp but awake, staring, smiling from one side of her mouth.

I need a cigarette, Frieda says. Then she says, hello darling, but to whom is not clear.

Come on, show me your house, Frieda.

It's not my house, baby. It's Adrian's. He just lets me live here. He lets me live other places too. He's very kind. A kind of man. Frieda stares around. And my beautiful boy. His grandfather has custody. It's the only way Adrian can get a visa. Theo's mother says something else, in a language Theo doesn't know.

What did you just say, Gina asks.

The end of pleasure is pain, Frieda says. That was vernacular Italian, speech of the Roman street.

Really.

I forgot who said it. Not Dante, now that I think about it. Too Celtic. Must have been some Irish ballad. I can't remember. Shall we sing.

How about Nearer My God to Thee.

Ha ha. Frieda leans at Richard and kisses him, on the lips, Theo sees. Women and children first. Then we shall blow the iceberg out of the water with a big torpedo, we have learned our lesson, Frieda finishes.

Theo follows Richard and Gina, on either side of his mother, who is tall as Richard even barefooted, with Gina shorter; Frieda in her short skirt, and Gina in hers, Richard in his black torn things. A lot of people here look like they were attacked by something with claws. Theo has forgotten his head, concentrating on what the adults are saying. When he flicks back to thinking about his head, it hurts.

As a kid trying to guess what was important to grown-ups, based on what they said, Theo was almost always wrong. Theo figures maybe he'll try to find something to eat in the pantry because he is hungry. However, he follows the knot of adults, thinking about what to say if his mother wants to drive because that seems like not a good idea.

Theo was in a car wreck with her once. He was five, and his face hit the radio button on the dashboard, right next to his eye, on his cheekbone, and that side swelled up. The dashboard was made of wood and the buttons were silver metal, with a flat round top that made a circle bruise on his cheek, he remembers. He got to ride in an ambulance, and the ambulance doctors joked around with him, a lady and a man wearing yellow rubber gloves, the lady sat next to him, and the man sat on a kind of built-in chair. They called him a basketball because he had bounced around the inside of the car, but they smiled nicely when they said it. They talked to him about animals and his birthday, and food he liked to eat. His mother had been crying and yelling at him, he couldn't understand what she was saying after the car stopped and the police and ambulances came, but the ambulance doctors said it was okay and that she wasn't mad, that she was just worried about him and sometimes upset people get things backward, act angry when they're really scared and worried. We see it all the time, the man said. Theo had lived with his father in hotels for a while after that.

Now they are in the entrance, among Colin's chesspieces, and Theo's mom and Gina and Richard pass the open front door clogged with car and then someone is talking at them from outside, from the other end of the car. They stop. Theo walks up from behind but can't see so he moves to one side to see around Richard.

Two black cars out there on the grey gravel, three men in blue suits and one man in a blue police uniform. The cars have lights on top but no writing on the sides.

What happened here. There's no shortage of parking space, one of the men in suits laughs out.

Captain, or admiral. Sergeant. This is private property. We may certainly park wherever we like.

We're federal agents.

The men in suits were flanking Frieda's car now, on the steps, holding up unfolded wallets with gold badges on them. Behind them the police officer was looking up and down and around and at both wings of the house.

We'd like to talk to two of the people on the lease here.

The men mention Colin and Gus. They ask, are you – then they say Theo's mom's whole name, which is long.

Gina asks, what's the problem, officers.

We're not officers, ma'am. This is routine immigration procedure. We need to get some information.

The men ask if Colin and Gus are home.

Frieda says, we were on our way out for lunch.

Gina says, no, remember, we're going to eat on the terrace. I don't feel like messing with the tourists.

Staring at her, squinting, one of the men nods: yeah, summer people are a real pain.

Gina stares at him, the wind ruffling her skirt suddenly. Richard says, I'm hungry.

Colin and Gus are not here at the moment, they're in Manhattan at a meeting, Frieda says, straightening her shoulders.

When do you expect them back.

We don't know. They had a lot of business to attend to.

Busy guys.

The three men in suits look at each other. One shrugs. We could wait. Would you mind if we waited. We just need to get some information. If we wait we can miss rush hour heading back into the city.

Frieda sighs. Gentlemen. I think you might get bored. And you are trespassing. If you stay, please don't touch the grass.

Let's get back to lunch: Gina steers Frieda out of the door and she and Richard and Frieda move down the hall. Theo, will you shut the door please.

Theo stands alone now, the four men staring at him.

Hi Theo. Where's your grandfather.

Theo doesn't say anything. If he says he doesn't know, is that a lie, or would they think it's a lie. They walk up the steps closer to him, quickly.

I'm supposed to close the door now.

You're a good boy, Theo. You look like your dad.

How do you know my dad.

Everybody knows your dad, Theo. All four men grin. He's famous.

I have to close the door now.

Okay, son. We'll be out here not touching the grass. The men stand staring at him, now all on the top step.

Theo looks down and his heart beats hard. He goes to one door and swings it shut then walks to the other one, swings it shut. Ow, says one of the men, my foot.

Sorry, Theo says from behind the door, heart skipping again.

Just kidding, Theo. You're a good kid. Tell your dad we said hello.

Theo walks away from the doors, the big hall empty, the desert of statues to be crossed, voices now from a variety of directions, up and down, but no one near. Some of the voices again yelling, someone doing a football cheer, Theo knows, for Tottenham Hotspur – that might be Colin, it's hard to tell – an electric guitar drifting down from one of the upper floors. Theo remembers his stomach. Where is his mom.

Theo glides toward the kitchen and pantry, wondering if Colin knows about the men out front: is anyone telling him. Theo thinks maybe he should make sure Colin and Gus know. But how can he tell Gus if Gus's on the back lawn somewhere. Do men like that really wait around. They do on the TV shows he's seen in hotels and at people's houses. His mother says television's the crippler of young adults. Men from the government can do what they want, as far as Theo understands, so he guesses they will be around until Gus or Colin go talk to them.

Fucking hell. The words echo from somewhere ahead. Then louder: Fucking police.

Theo enters the kitchen and Seal sits at the scarred heavy table, wrapped in a blanket, with a sketchbook and scattered pens in front of him. He's drawing Colin, using both of his short, flipper-like arms to hold the pen. Colin sits in a chair, with his profile toward Seal, facing the door through which Theo entered.

Have you met Seal, Theo.

Yes.

The Seal instead of singing for his supper is going to make portraits of the residents of the house. He'll do you too.

There are police here wanting to talk to you and to Gus.

I heard. Ponces. They don't have a warrant. They'll need to come back with lawyers and catapults and –

Did you and Gus do something wrong.

No, my friend. One thing you'll learn is that one never has to do anything at all to attract unwanted attention from enforcement crotch-sniffers. They get bored, they're doing someone else a favour, they got yelled at by their wives, their bleeding feet hurt – they take it out on the poor citizenry, because they can. Like why does a dog lick his balls. Because he can. They're the ones with the guns. They're bullying gits. I will not give in to their intimidation.

What do they think you did.

I haven't the slightest idea.

Theo wonders if they're here because of Colin's day off last week, and asks, the words making his head hurt.

Every couple of weeks Colin said, right, I'm off for two days. Don't bother me. He'd take one of the cars and go away.

Last week, the morning after Colin left, Gus came up to the attic wheezing, and knocked on the door.

Theo, come on, wake up, son. I've got to go get Colin. Can't leave you alone.

Where is he.

Jail.

They drove down the beach to the town part of the island, a blur of low buildings with paintings and fishing nets in big windows, and hanging signs for doctors and lawyers and restaurants. Gus drove as always, slowly and deliberately, both hands on the wheel, not talking. Still can't get used to this bloody wrong side of the road business, he said, every time he had to drive.

Colin was sitting on a bench, legs crossed, smoking, in a smelly waiting room across from a man in a uniform behind a glass window with a hole in it. Colin had cuts on his face crusted with blood. When Gus and Theo walked in, Colin stubbed his cigarette out on the bench, saluted the man behind the window and said, later, Jackson.

What did you do, Colin, Theo asked as Gus and Colin walked without speaking back to the car.

Colin shook himself and said, I rode a horse into a bar. They arrested me for littering and animal abuse, and petit larceny of the horse, because the bar owner's a paid-up friend of everyone and a spectacular moron.

Why.

I don't know why, I presume it's something genetic.

I mean about the horse.

Colin exhaled smoke out the window, into the glittering outside and the people and things passing at a sedate pace, staring: when Gus drove, it felt like riding in a parade.

I got into an argument with some idiots and so at the time I figured the best way to make my point with them was to deliver it from the back of a horse.

Um. Where did you get the horse.

93

Borrowed it. Plenty around, favourite accessory of every bleeding debutante in this bleeding summer camp. What a country.

What were you arguing about.

Oh, man. It doesn't matter. I am a little quiffed at the moment and I think I'll just try to get some shuteye on the trip back.

Any other damage. Keep all your teeth this time, Gus asked.

We had a good spirited debate and all sides were aired, including the horse's. Some calisthenic exertion was involved, but that's good for the circulation and God knows I need more exercise. Plus I had a good jail breakfast this morning, they brought it round from the drugstore lunch counter, which luckily for me and the other residents of the big house also serves breakfast. It was greasy and hot off the griddle, served up on a paper plate in a glistening lake of fat. Runny eggs and some variety of sausage. White toast. Oleo pat. Colin picked a bit of tobacco from his lip. Oleo pat. I like the sound of that, should be the name of some obese prostitute.

I worried you weren't eating right, Gus said making a careful turn, hand over hand, like the car was a boat.

Colin tried to kiss Gus but Gus elbowed him. Hey, I'm driving.

Thanks, mate, Colin said after a minute, pulling out a cigarette.

They talked normally, mostly about names Theo didn't know and he stopped listening. Gus seemed to never get angry with Colin. Lots of other people did. He would have to ask Gus about it.

Theo watches Seal drawing, hunched over the paper and table, Colin shirtless and fingering a tooth in the back of his mouth, poking, saying, ow.

Colin glances at Theo narrowly, says, no, they're not here about my day off, and the fax isn't about my day off either. That's just a joke.

What's the joke.

Just an old joke between me and your dad.

But what's the joke.

Listen, my friend. In this life, it's just generally good practice to be ready to reef the mainsail at any time. Storms come up out of nowhere and it's easy for our tippy little crafts to turn turtle or get swamped out there on the great big sea. So semper vigilantus erectus. Keep a weather eye out for me and I'll do the same for you. Your dad and I like to remind ourselves of that periodically.

That's not a joke.

No, you're right. But don't worry. And let other people answer the door for the next couple of days, all right.

Why.

Just humor me, eh. Let a grown-up answer the door if anyone comes. And the phone too for that matter. And let us get the mail.

Why can't I get the mail.

Hon, don't worry. We just want to lie low for a bit.

Lie low. The Seal sketches. Theo's stomach growls. It's not really the stomach but the intestines making noise. That's the kind of thing Theo likes to know. He likes learning, but school was about not getting embarrassed, or hurt. Theo didn't really know the girls very well. Maybe they were different. There were other kids like him, a couple in the class, each eyeing the others; they knew, like a secret club, could tell, but they didn't really help each other or anything. Just noticed.

I want to know. Why am I not supposed to do any of that stuff.

Oh, Christ, would you give it up.

No. Theo's mad. He's not a kid.

Like a damn badger. Okay. Look. The police want a chat with your father. Immigration wants me and your dad. School wants you. Social services wants your mother and your dad. And you. They're lined up like planes at LaGuardia, waiting for their chance at us. Your dad thinks it's best if you are not put in a position where you have to talk to someone or see or hear stuff you won't understand that will only scare you. The place is gauntleted by lawyers so no worries.

What do they want my father for.

Just for once be a good boy and say, aye aye, sir.

No. I'm not scared. And I don't care.

Well, that's the end of the news, mate. No more. Just don't break my you-know-whats, eh.

The Seal stares at both of them. Somewhere upstairs is a saxophone, and where is Theo's mother. He wants out, he wants out, he wants to run, so he does, into the ballroom, in a circle, past the drum kit, the motorbike gone, the electric piano, the pile of shirts, cardboard boxes. Roller skates, his skates. He has two pairs. Where are the others. He likes to skate in the ballroom, but not now. Out. He needs out.

Onto the terrace, empty. Downslope at the end of the long ragged lawn, Theo sees Gus up in his chair. Why haven't the police out front found him. Theo worries. Should he try to get Gus inside. Is Gus in trouble. Why didn't Colin mention Gus.

Theo moves toward Gus, sun overhead a bright button on a blue shirt. He's over the terrace stone, air hot, the day a year old, and he still hasn't eaten. Can the police arrest Theo. Can they make him talk about things. Theo's stomach churns and sours. The dark humps in the grass near Gus are dogs. Gus waves. Theo hurries at him, watching the near wing of the house. There's a Brazilian flag now hanging from one of the upper windows on the other wing. His head hurts.

Getting closer, the dogs see Theo and wag but don't get up, tails just whapping the ground like a signal. Don't beavers do that.

There are police here.

What say.

There are police here. They want to talk to Colin and to you.

Gus straightens in the old chair he dragged here from one of the rooms. It has claw feet, with the claws holding balls. And the back is very straight. Beside the flowery white iron one with rust like blood, the wooden chair seems sad, away from home. It looks lonely.

Immigration possibly. Hmm. Where are they.

At the front door. They said they'd wait till you came back. Frieda said you were gone.

Where did she say I went.

She said you and Colin were at a meeting in the city.

Gus sighs. Bloody hell. Go on now, son, go do something fun.

Gus grips a white stein with a silver top on it that flips up and with snow and deer on the outside. He slowly rises to his full height, taller than Theo and shorter than Colin. The blue devil on his shirt looks Theo in the eye. The devil's eyes are white dots.

When will my dad be here.

Can't say yet, son, details still being worked out. It's complicated, like moving the prime minister, getting your dad from place to place.

Colin said the police were after him.

Gus frowns. That man talks too much. Your dad's fine. Don't worry about what Colin says.

The dogs still beat the ground, but much more slowly, like they have to suddenly remember and thump. Theo feels weird, weak, light-headed again, his head slowly aching, rings around things if he looks long enough. Okay.

Theo lies down in the shade near the dogs, under the umbrella curling and uncurling above.

Watch out for fleas: Gus is talking to him.

Okay.

Just a joke. Gus is further away, his voice quieter.

Everything keeps happening the same as before. Theo's back on the ground, the dogs are here, the sun's up, and Theo runs in circles, he's a dog too, checking on the cattle. He feels like the day has started over a million times. And his head still feels funny, and nothing has happened. Nothing any grown-up has said so far today has been true, and nothing has happened. Theo wonders about why. Theo figures it's because everyone is doing it: you can't say something real if everyone else is not. So they just keep pretending about everything. He guesses his dad does it too, but he can't remember.

Theo's stomach hurts. Theo pushes himself up; Gus is still visible, a slow walker. The dogs thump but lie on their sides, hoping they don't have to move. It's okay, Theo says aloud, and moves over to pet each of them. They wag harder, like they mean it, and push themselves up, panting, smiling. Dog smiles. Theo does a dog smile and pants too: he understands them. Then he turns toward the house, because he has to eat something. He can't escape, he keeps getting pulled back inside, the magic that won't let him leave. He steps over the motorcycle track: the border. Which side is madness. They say craziness in America. Mad is angry.

They're gone.

Gus stands far away at the edge of the house's right wing, yelling at Theo, now something about safe for democracy. Theo doesn't know what democracy means.

They said they would wait but they didn't. They wanted to talk but they didn't. School had opposite days, but it just meant putting clothes on backward. You couldn't talk opposite or do opposite things or you'd get in trouble. And it just made it easier for Theo's buttons to get pulled off, so his shirt flapped open and people snickered, even the girls, who squealed and tried to keep the boys from pulling their buttons, but some of them didn't try too hard, and some of the boys didn't try hard to pull, so it's already starting, the doing one thing and meaning something else.

Mingus is emerging onto the terrace now, carrying something in his hands. One of his cars. He makes things. They look like cars but he calls them weapons. He says they have power and value, and some people want to steal the power.

What's up, man. Mingus is looking up at Theo walking toward him, heading for the kitchen.

I'm hungry.

Me too, starving for everything. I am famished all the time.

What are you doing with your car.

I'm taking it outside. If the government finds out it's in here, the house becomes a target, because this ain't no car. It's power for the one who holds it. I'm getting it away from the house. Made it last night.

There were police here but they left.

See. See.

They were here to talk about immigration.

Of course, they always have a front, but that's never why they really come. They get their orders from deep in the tower, and sometimes even they don't know why, they're just following orders, man. But the real power's right in my hands and they know it.

Mingus hunched over the car, looking up, and started running toward the trees. I'll be back. Don't talk to them, okay. They can take stuff out of your brain before you even know it's gone.

Okay, but they're not here.

Halfway down the grass, hunched and running, Mingus yells back, they're never gone.

Theo keeps moving toward the opened French doors, the dogs trotting behind, wondering if it is true about police. Theo is afraid to ask too many questions, or even think them. Is that being superstitious: some people think that's bad. Theo can't help it, however. Birds, insects, when a shadow passes over and something you've never seen and don't understand attacks – superstition is what animals know. Maybe you called it to come, by saying its name.

Theo's eyes adjust to the dark inside and he walks toward the kitchen, empty now except for the dogs who hustled ahead and now lie on the cool terracotta. He feels better, his head feels better. Not hurting too much but things fuzz over a little at the edges.

He opens the refrigerator and has to pull hard because it's so big. Inside is a bottle of champagne and some kind of plant in a glass of water. And jars, sauces and things to put on other stuff, like mustard, mayonnaise, jars with Chinese writing on them. Some plastic packets of ketchup, duck sauce. A couple of big pale orange squash with green knobs. Theo knows there was cheese yesterday and yanks open the bottom bin, where sometimes apples appear and sometimes big deep green leafy heads that look like lettuce. Now it's empty except for three oranges wrinkled as old heads. They have faces.

Theo slams the door and moves to cabinets and shelves. The dogs aren't scrabbling on the tile so they must not be hungry. He hears noise now, from inside the pantry, and whimpering, then banging of some kind, thumping, rhythmic. Sex noise.

The door is closed and he keeps moving, his loose pants poking out. He feels his face flush, knowing someone else could see anything he's doing anytime, strangers, unless he's in his room. He hopes it goes down but hoping makes it worse. He hears whispers and mewing noises from the pantry.

Theo hums and sings, makes his eyes look at the wall of cabinets. On a shelf is gold foil, a tube of biscuits, which Theo grabs and runs with, a relay baton; but run which way. Is his mother okay. What is wrong with her. Do they want her too.

Theo thinks of his butterflies, of the birds outside, the dogs, the eyes of the birds and dogs. Theo sees the house full of people, people in every room, closets, pantry, storage areas, people everywhere, open drawers and there are people in them. Run. He sees his mother opening drawers, looking for something, not finding it. This big ship, and all these people, the crew. Where are we sailing. Are we moving.

Theo growls. He's wild. He runs into someone's stomach, soft. It's a lady, coming from a door. She's saying something but he's running the other way. Not a familiar voice.

Theo runs through squares of sun: for an instant he can't remember where, and how to get out, and feels a flutter of panic. There's a beach towel on the floor, and a football, not a soccer ball. He is in the back hall that connects in a curve a row of first-floor doors. If he keeps going this way he'll come to a heavy side door that opens onto the side lawn and the screen of wild scrub trees on the house's left side, on the other side of which but not visible is another hulking house. Theo's not sure if anyone lives there, but the same guy from the village mows these lawns and theirs. The man comes in a pick-up towing a trailer with mowers on it. He wears earmuffs, like the men who load planes at the airport. He always flashes the peace sign at Theo but never smiles, just cuts and leaves. He has a black dog with a grey muzzle who finds shade and lies in it, on a chain with a bowl of water. The man has to help her. She falls out of the truck when they come, and then he has to push her into the truck when they leave. He talks really loudly to her, sort of impatient, but he's nice when he helps her. When they first came, she didn't need any help.

When people die, do they look like the dead rabbit Theo found in the trees, flat leather with fur patches and teeth on one end. He wonders about mummies. He went to a shop in Paris full of skeletons and taxidermied animals with his dad and his dad's minders, and the owner led them to a locked room that was dark, even when they entered. He had mummies and you could buy them. A couple were children. Theo couldn't tell if they were boys or girls. He wanted to touch but the man said, *non monsieur, s'il vous plaît*. He dreamed about them still, every now and then. They were curled on their sides, nose to knees like dogs and cats. There were dog and cat mummies too, but only the people were locked up.

A bit morbid for my taste, his dad said afterward. A little too memento mori. One of the minders was holding the car door for Theo to climb in after his dad: the door shutting made a heavy sound, a thunk, and then, quiet, the high-pitched horns and cars engines and people talking all gone. Maybe that's like being in a tomb.

Dad, what do you think happens when we die.

His father turned slowly to Theo, behind sunglasses, and the rest of his face the same as it was: Those mummies get to you.

No. I'm just. You know. What happens.

Well, very fair question, and baby I ain't gonna sugar-coat it. I think you just saw one part of what happens. We're gone. Those things might as well have been shoes.

But not everybody's a mummy.

Well, my friend, I think we take all the beauty and love and joy we made in our life, and when our time's up, we ride that joy up in the air like a balloon, and our molecules all mix up with all the other molecules and all the other people and memories, and that's what the world's really made of, other people and memories.

What if you didn't have joy or love.

Adrian rubbed his eyes behind the sunglasses. That's the saddest thing, isn't it. I think everybody else, every thing, lifts those people up.

Is that like heaven. What about little kids who had bad parents. All they have is bad memories. Or babies. They can't even talk. What happens then.

Well, like, say you're a baby that's been treated badly, all it takes is maybe one second, a millisecond of happiness, or peace, like a flash of light – boom – that's enough if you're small, that power is so strong that's enough to lift you off, and once you're off, the others can catch you and – this conversation ain't helping my hangover, mate. Adrian finally smiled, his head back against the leather seats.

These seats could be made of people. People skin's, just like things are made of other animals.

You're a regular bloody cheerleader today, aren't you. Adrian slowly slid over and collapsed onto Theo, who laughed and

103

pushed him away: Cut it out, you weigh a million pounds.

Adrian's hair was brush stiff and stuck up everywhere, like Theo's when it was short, and Theo rubbed Adrian's head.

That's better, give your old father a massage like a good and dutiful son.

Theo rubbed both hands crazily all over Adrian's head and face and made himself laugh, knocking off the sunglasses and this roused his father – all right all right you win, I am retreating, like Napoleon in the face of Russian winter. Adrian on one arm groaned and fished for his sunglasses at Theo's feet and slipped them back on and pushed up to fall back into the big back seat's other corner. Christ, what's next. What else are you going to do to me.

Can we go to the Tuileries again for that ice cream.

Well, let's check with god here. Adrian pushed the intercom button: Brandon, what's the schedule.

Back to the studio, you've got bed tracks to finish – it's costing a thousand quid an hour. The sooner we finish the better for my blood pressure.

It's the room that makes a good record. This is one of the great rooms. It's all about the art, you philistine.

Oh, the bloody art. Tell that to Sir Michael and the board.

I feel a tantrum coming on.

Hold on, just wait till I can get the tape rolling.

Dad, the Tuileries.

Oh, yeah. Sorry, honey. I gotta go back to work. We'll for sure do that tomorrow. When I'm back at the hotel we can do the electric cars on the bed, okay.

Sure.

I want to fly a kite. Maybe we can do that tomorrow. For sure we'll play later, and then there's tomorrow.

Creeping at his petty pace. From the intercom.

I forgot about you, you parasite. Shut up and leave me alone with my son.

Adrian slumped and hugged himself. Don't let this happen to you son, he said, grinning.

What.

Everything.

Theo streaks through the house, biscuits in hand, crotch throbbing still. Where can he go. His head is a blur. He's passing a door.

Theo, baby. Don't hurt yourself.

Everyone moves in slow motion. Adults are so slow. And a lot here just lie around and sleep a lot. Are all grown-ups like that. He's approaching escape velocity and sees ahead one of the outside doors, the one opening from the laundry room. The big metal sinks sit scaly and grey now, with plugs on chains and thick slabs of wooden tables for folding, according to Colin, who led him around when they first moved in. Frieda was in the house then but tired.

He stops to wrestle with a latch and knob, then bursts into white light and he feels his head. He runs. He's eating ground and he's around the front of the house before he realizes it, and the men are gone, their cars are gone. And he runs across the pearls of gravel, small peas, paws soft and hurting, doesn't bother a real dog, and he keeps going, again behind the house, and there's Mingus and the Seal, and Gus playing croquet, something Gus likes, poor man's polo he calls it. Mingus and Gus hold glasses of something, the Seal clamps a long mallet between his seal arms. He's really good with them, he can draw and play croquet. Theo keeps running, his legs a little rubbery, dodging between things, and Gus yells, mind the wickets, son, they can sting you, and Theo dodges furniture, and keeps running, everything fast and dodge it and Gina and Frieda now stand at the terrace doors he circles and others loom behind in the ballroom dark like things floating just below the surface.

Theo, darling.

Let's go to the beach, he yells, his voice quaky from running. Let's go to the beach let's go to the beach, then beach beach beach and he keeps running, if he does that no one can say but or later or maybe or let me finish this first or tomorrow or no. He's past them and along the other wing, in the grass, grown-ups like to do things sitting down, like eating and talking and drinking stuff. Talking is what they do. Girls are like that sometimes too.

Theo's legs are getting wobbly and he's stumbling, exaggerating now, windmilling his arms and enjoying no control; he's seen astronauts floating in no gravity. Then back to the floor, back to earth. He ploughs into the ground, smiling and huffing. Lying there itching. Empty for a minute, still holding the magic baton in his hand. He made it. He's sweating.

Theo scrambles back up toward the wild land between the house and the neighbouring big house.

Theo, baby. Come here for a minute.

He doesn't do anything or say anything or turn around, keeps moving. If he can make it to the trees, he'll be safe. He jogs between trees toward one, circles around and plops into sandy ground with his back against the low, wide trunk. All the trees are short and flat, kept low by the wind that blows almost all the time, mostly in from the ocean but sometimes the other way. Sometimes it's so strong he can't stand up and he likes to lean, be held up by nothing.

He's breathing hard, hot, head radiating, throbbing, he has two hearts, he's an alien, sweating, picking at the biscuits now, tearing at the gold foil but putting the scraps in his pockets. He takes two biscuits and puts them in his mouth, but instead of chewing lets them just soften.

Theo.

At the edge of the trees. His mother following, not something she usually does.

Theo.

He closes his eyes.

Theo, baby.

He finally chews, the biscuit wet cake now.

Theo, darling. I need to talk to you.

Her just behind the tree now and moving forward, and now she's around the tree, barefoot and flushed. Frieda kneels and sits in front of him and he can see her underwear.

Mom – he turns his head.

Sorry, baby. She gets up on her knees. Ouch. Look, there may be school people coming about you. They tracked us down like criminals. And other people coming concerning other things that you don't have to worry about. But I don't want you to talk to anyone without me around, all right darling. They may try to get you alone, but if a stranger starts asking you questions about school, or about me, or about your dad or Colin or Gus, you don't have to answer them. This is your house and you don't have to answer any questions. They have to talk to us if they want to talk to someone.

All I ever talk to is strangers.

You know what I mean. Stranger strangers. Strange strangers.

What if they're normal.

Baby, this is important. Will you do this for me, will you

promise me. Don't answer the doors anymore, let someone else do it.

I don't answer the door.

You know what I mean. My god, it is hot. I am perishing and dry. Why don't we go in and get a cool drink and then go to the beach.

I thought we were going to have lunch.

We'll have something here, then go down to the water. How about that. We'll get a group and have fun. We'll play volleyball, get some exercise in the sun. Let's get the boat out, shall we.

Theo puts more biscuits in his mouth so he can't talk. There's no boat.

What. I can't understand you.

When is Dad coming.

Haven't any idea, darling, Frieda said, pushing herself onto her feet then standing unsteadily. But we can certainly have fun without him. Let's do some sports, my love, get some exercise. How would you like a –

I don't want anything, Frieda. Can we go to the beach.

Of course, let's get a party together and go. We'll take a picnic.

Theo's mother stands, swaying, smiling, long legs and warm fur. She must be really hot, Theo thinks. And when it's cold she wears less.

She wants to be called Frieda but he knows she likes to be called mom too: she just doesn't want to have to ask, and she doesn't like it in front of other people sometimes.

Can we just go, me and you. We don't have to tell anyone.

Sure, baby. You and me. Like when you were little.

She holds out her hand and Theo looks up from the ground. He pushes himself up, he comes up to her chest, and takes her hand, and she's holding on kind of hard. She's steadying herself against him, so he tries to be strong, hold her up.

They walk slowly from the trees, and there are people scattered around, the croquet players in back, Gina and Richard and another man with white hair but he's not old, and a man with no shirt has a guitar on the terrace, he's sitting cross-legged on the stones, and there's a tape recorder next to him, and a lady and a man, Theo has not seen them yet today, the lady has on black stuff and black sneakers and the man is wearing a 'staff' T-shirt and his underwear, boxer shorts Theo knows they're called: his are different, briefs like the bathing suit people sometimes wear here and Theo knows they're like the things ladies wear underneath, except his are hot so most of the time he doesn't wear them except when it's cold. The man and lady hold umbrellas over themselves standing near the orange Miami Dolphins cooler someone has dragged out, and the Seal now wearing shorts lies on a towel. Someone in the house is playing Theo's drum kit, which is under cloth in the ballroom. Someone else is playing the electric keyboard. It sounds like Colin, and they're playing one of Adrian's songs. There are stereos everywhere around the house and Adrian's records, and Colin likes to play Adrian's songs. Except no one sounds like Adrian.

Theo feels Frieda's weight, feels her stiffen as they get closer to people and – people start talking to Frieda.

There's nothing to eat.

This is not a hotel, you simpering parasite.

For some reason the adults all laugh but Theo doesn't know why.

My son and I are going to the beach.

Theo knows she's forgotten already, knows that's gone. His head aches a little in the brightness. She doesn't like being alone, and being with him sometimes is like being alone to her, he's not enough.

Mark, why don't you bring the volleyball things.

Volleyball. Why don't I just shoot myself instead.

Come on, it'll be fun.

Compared to what.

Come on, if you want to eat, you must play for your supper.

I'll play but I'm not moving.

Fine. You can hold the net up.

Theo and his mom are at the French doors entering the sound so loud it's a thing to press into, making the air even thicker.

A lady plays Theo's drums. She has on a shirt that says Bush Tetras.

Those are mine, Theo yells.

She stares at him, playing. Theo isn't sure that she hears. Or that she actually sees him. When people play music they get lost sometimes. Theo likes playing music, but never gets lost.

Colin stares too, but grins. He ends the song he was playing and starts playing an old English song on the keyboard, switches to organ. Not God Save the Queen but that other one. Theo heard it at some party for somebody's graduation at the Arts Club in Manhattan.

Frieda yells, it's too crowded. We're going to the beach. Did you shop yet.

No, Colin says, lowering the mix and volume. The lady on the drums moves one arm like a robot, beating a snare and kicking the bass drum like a march. One two.

Haven't had a chance.

The boy's got nothing to eat – come on, man. You're screwing up.

Fair enough, Colin yells, as Theo and his mom walk toward the kitchen and pantry. Colin reaches for a tall glass of beer perched on the keyboard.

Theo's stomach hurts. Mom, I want to eat before we go to the beach. His head hurts and he feels angry.

Of course, darling. I will fix you something.

They enter the cool kitchen. Usually there is someone in here, staring into the refrigerator or shakily trying to light a burner and make something like tea, eating something out of a jar or can, smoking over coffee or a glass of something else.

Theo remembers opening the refrigerator earlier and so goes straight for the now-quiet, open-doored pantry and the cans, while Frieda, cut loose, drifts like an unmoored boat along the cabinets, opening and staring, slowly.

Would you like some tuna, mom.

Sure, baby. She's sitting now.

Theo's out with two cans he found, and he goes to the drawer, yanks it open with a silvery sound, grabs out the heavy knife and begins stabbing at the cans. Stabbing feels good, but all he does is make a ragged hole in first one can lid, then the other. After widening, switching back and forth from can to can, he grabs two forks from the open drawer and walks to his mom and hands her a can and a fork and sits.

Thanks, baby.

Theo forks at the tuna, salty and pink. Water. Have to drink something or choke. Theo gets up and finds two glasses on the cluttered counter, now covered with plates and mugs and glasses and other things – a thesaurus and a crumpled T-shirt, empty cans – and fills the glasses and sets one down next to his mother's can and then plops down again and goes at it.

Eat. Frieda, eat, please.

Yes, baby.

She pats his cheek and gets some tuna shakily on the fork and puts it into her mouth and chews.

Theo's filling his mouth and chewing, and choking, and drinking water, and trying to swallow a wad of tuna, feeling like a boa, shovelling because he's hungry.

His mom sits chewing her bite, slowly, music overflowing from the ballroom into the kitchen.

They are so awful together, Theo's mom says.

Theo chewing, just keeps chewing. He drinks water. He bangs his can against the table to move the tuna from the edges to the centre where the hole is, so he can get it.

That certainly makes you appreciate real music.

Theo's finger is now inside, sweeping up whatever the fork missed. He's trying not to cut himself on the edges or the ragged burst of metal folded up from the can. Theo grabs the baton of biscuits that he carried in from outside in his pajama pocket and pulls more out, chewing and swallowing and drinking the last of his water and getting up and filling his glass again and drinking. Theo's mother has not eaten more than the first bite, but is no longer chewing.

You want more, mom.

No thank you, darling, I am not hungry.

Have some more, he says, eating biscuits.

Baby, I think I will lie down for a while. This morning has taken a lot out of me. Why don't you go down to the beach with Gus, he will go.

Theo crams in biscuits and leaves them without chewing, lets them soften. Runs again out through the loud ballroom, where Colin plays with one hand and with the other holds the glass to his mouth, and out the doors.

All the people are where they were, except the ones standing are now sitting or lying down. There is a pile of net and a volleyball, and poles on the grass beside the man who must be Mark.

Hey man, where's your mom at.

She's going to lie down.

Too bad. Let's go swim. Wash Manhattan off. Come with. We can play some volleyball.

Theo knows a couple of these people, others are new. Several are unsteady, several look bored, several frown at him. Maybe it's the sun and they're only squinting. The ladies don't seem to care. The sun is like the lights in Theo's attic. It isn't quite overhead but it's close, so it's – Theo assumes it's near noon and he's had some food. They're staring at him, dully, flat-faced. One lady waves at a fly.

Theo feels funny, says, I want to put on some different pants.

Sure. We'll wait.

Gus or Colin or even sometimes his mother usually is present when he's doing stuff with adults, but they think being there is enough and don't notice weird things or people or bad stuff until it's already happening. They're like lifeguards who talk to girls instead of watching swimmers. He likes it when they let him go, but also feels funny about that sometimes; like the way the dogs sometimes look back to see if he's watching when they run toward borders or edges or into the woods or toward the beach road.

Theo's scooting through the ballroom, awash in music still, the middle of something without words Theo doesn't recognize, the woman staring ahead, Colin focused on the keyboard with both hands, and Theo shoots into the dark hall along the panels that should be doors but aren't, to the main staircase curving up and he's running, jumping two steps at a time, from floor to floor to floor, sound now coming from each floor, voices and maybe radios, and what might be firecrackers on the third floor, loud sharp bangs from inside something metal – Theo remembers somewhere on the third level there's a shiny silver garbage can Gus bought for the garbage men who pick up on the beach road. One of the people last weekend dragged it up here to tape-record something. He had forgotten that until now. So many things and people disappear into rooms and he forgets about them.

Theo's puffing, at the mountain peak, moving through the door and up the narrow stairs weaving back and forth angling up to the attic. He pushes down on the handle to open the door and it creaks open. Theo shuts it behind him, making sure it clicks, before he takes off his pajamas and notices he's sweaty. He rummages through clothes on the floor, looking for his Hawaii shorts, the ones he got last year when his mother and he visited his father on Kauai. Theo really liked those shorts: he saw surfers wearing them and liked the dolphin pictures. His mother and father fought a lot then. She threw things. She tried to cut his father with his father's knife. Theo's father always carried a knife. He had a lot of them. Sometimes he had a gun. Theo had found it once in a hotel room.

Why do you have this.

It was heavy. Theo had to hold it with both hands. His father was in bed. The door between rooms was open, and Theo and one of the minders had eaten pizza in Theo's room and the minder left. Theo wandered around his father's room picking stuff up. And there was a gun.

Put that down, Theo. Don't ever pick up a gun that ain't yours.

Why do you have that.

The room was dark although it was afternoon. Rectangles of light around shapes of dark curtain. His dad's voice came from somewhere on the bed. Then Theo saw arms, one, two. Three. One of his dad's friends was here too. His dad had a lot of friends.

I wish I didn't have it, Theo. I need it sometimes. Sometimes I have to be in places that require a certain vigilance concerning personal safety, mate.

Why.

Comes with the job, my friend. Hand me a cigarette, darling.

Theo started to move but saw the arm swing toward the dark table beside the bed.

Music is dangerous, Theo asked.

Theo's father's laugh was really a cough. Well, yeah. It's life or death on stage, to me. It's funny because Alan always says he's just trying not to screw up.

Alan was the other guitar player. Theo liked Alan, who had two daughters. Alan lived in Ireland, Theo knew, and he had been to Alan's house. It had a roof made of grass. Theo remembered swimming in the pool and watching his breath in the air because it was always frigid on the old sod, Alan said. Too feckin cold to swim in me own pool that cost a bloody fortune.

You could break down and get it heated, you cheap bastard, Theo's dad said, splayed out on a chaise, in long pants and no shirt, tapping ash on the concrete beside himself.

And you could use an ashtray you unholy troglodyte.

I bet Alan doesn't have a gun, Theo said to his dad in the bed smoking, the cigarette's red tip making shapes in the air.

No, Alan stays on the sunny side of the street. He's a banker at heart, he just wants his tea and a warm bed when he's ready for it. We're different, all of us. That's what makes a good band. Otherwise it's like rubbing two pieces of flannel together. No sparks.

Is that why you and my mother fight.

Theo's dad exhaled a long time and the air got greyer. Theo, baby, I love your mother and she loves me. And we both love you. Your mother and I both feel things strongly, and sometimes it isn't about being different. Sometimes it's because you're the same. Your mother and I are too much alike.

Why is that bad.

It's bad if you don't like yourself.

You don't like yourself.

No, mate, sometimes I don't. And your mother's like me.

I don't understand.

Bloody hell, Theo, none of us do. We just try to keep loving each other and make sure the work gets done and the bills are paid and the kids kept fed.

The friend, Theo could see, was yawning, and she shook her head. She reached her arm out to peel back the sheets and Theo turned around and went through the suite door and closed it, his dad's voice following him.

Theo, give us a minute and we'll get some breakfast, eh.

It's okay, I just had some pizza.

Want to go to the studio.

Sure, Theo said to the door as he closed it and made sure it clicked.

In the bright attic Theo's kicking through clothes like surf, stuff flying, looking for dolphins. His cocoons dangle and his head's full of things ready to hatch; he wonders if the ladies will wear bathing suits. He thinks this is not really a bathing suit group of people. Often the people who visit seem surprised there's an outside and that it includes a beach. Theo strips down, noticing how white he is there. He wonders about girls. Theo sort of knows what's under their underwear but not really. He does know nothing dangles. But beyond that he's not sure. He starts to get stiff and now must find something to hide it.

Theo's nervous. He doesn't really know these people, but then he doesn't know most of the people who flow in and out. The house is a hotel, except without maids or room service – he likes hotels better, sometimes. Light from the windows blurs and shimmers, everything a little melting – maybe his head's not okay.

He sees a flash of orange and blue and, standing again, kicks through stuff to a pile – score. Dolphin shorts. Theo slips into them, folding his erection in and adjusting for it. He might have to sit for a minute, so he plops and waits, then gets up and walks around talking.

In the castle the wizard is trapped because the king wants him to find the crystal before he'll let him go. He's heard his dad and other people talk about crystal. But they stop when they know he hears, so he's not sure what kind of crystals they're talking about. Flake, brown, dosing. Theo hears words, a lot of words. Cocksucker. Fuck. Merck. Some of these he knows he's not supposed to know, and he doesn't know what they mean, not all of them, but he's heard them. They come closest to magic words of any Theo knows, the way kids learn them; but grown-ups use them differently He wonders if Chinese people have them too, or Africans.

Adrian and Frieda never told him not to use them. Don't believe in censorship, mate, said Adrian. They're just words. I use them so I'm not going to tell you not to. Frieda said, that puritanical conventionality and fear of the body and even language about the body, I can't do it. So sing out love, say what you want. You are free and beautiful. And everything about the body is beautiful. Shit and piss and blood and snot.

I think that stuff is gross.

Frieda and Adrian were lying on a bed, Theo doesn't remember where, a hotel. He didn't understand what they meant then, and they seemed drunk. He knew drunk.

His mother and father went to a party and he stayed behind with a minder. Theo and the minder ordered food and watched TV until it was dinner time, then they went to the hotel restaurant, although Theo wasn't really hungry. The minder was, so Theo watched him smoke and drink glasses of alcohol and eat. He was okay, but Theo couldn't remember his name. He told jokes, and even tried to read a book to Theo, but it was a book for little kids and Theo didn't say anything to hurt the man's feelings but it was boring. That was the last time Adrian and Frieda had lived together at the same time, when Theo had just turned nine.

In his room now Theo walks toward the window facing the castle's rear and the back lawn and the ocean. The man who invited him to the beach is at the rear lawn edge, a bundle of volleyball poles under his arms. One of the ladies carries the volleyball, throwing it up in the air and catching it, not throwing it straight but off to the side and too far in front so she has to chase it sometimes and it falls. Another man and lady walk behind carrying a cooler between them, and the dogs trot after them, tails up, then they streak into the trees after something, not barking.

Theo thinks about cocoons, and his attic, and about its coolness in spite of being closest to the sun of all the rooms, and he wonders if he should stay here for a while. Theo sees Mingus and Gus and the Seal walking from the lawn to the terrace, Mingus with an arm draped over Gus's shoulder. Maybe they'll come to the beach. Theo's actually scared of the ocean a little bit.

Colin is running toward the three men and suddenly throws himself at them sideways, bowling over the Seal and Gus but only staggering Mingus, who begins cursing at Colin, who lies on the ground under the others, laughing and groaning and hugging his ribs. Gus silently picks himself up while the Seal rolls onto his back and then onto his side and then leans up and folds his legs so he can use them to rise. He says nothing, at least yet.

From the mountaintop Theo hears only isolated Mingus words. Motherfucker more than once. Theo wants to know more about Mingus and about the things he makes. Mingus says the letters of the alphabet are vessels, they hold power. They sail.

Yeah, Mingus said to Theo, you are not a little kid. You understand.

Mingus says he's the goose that laid the golden egg that everyone wants to steal, sometimes he says he's getting bled dry by parasites. He can't say much about his ideas or his costumes or his art pieces, because if he makes it too easy, the government will just kick down the doors and force him to work for them. He says art is in the shapes of things, and that the ancient people knew art was everyday life, not something sealed up in museums, which Mingus always calls mausoleums, guarded by pall bearers. Mingus said most artists, the ones in museums, are undertakers.

Nothing ever changes. Below, the grown-ups are wrestling. Gina sits on the terrace edge, legs crossed, feet bare, skirt rippling as if underwater. Gina's hair blows sideways. She's watching the men roll around on the hard lawn. Then she's talking to the lady who was playing the drums, who's striding at Gina from the house with arms crossed.

Theo moves from the window and walks the room fingering his cocoons. Some look different. And in one of the last ones, near the door, something is moving. He almost drops it, it feels weird. It must be weird to have a baby inside you. He wonders why his mother and father still fight. He thought that when you lived apart things got better. His stomach hurts again.

Theo runs out the door, which he slams, and to the stairs and going too fast, almost falling on almost every step, he makes it to the first floor entrance hall breathless and dully headachy – he holds his arms in the air cheering to himself and yanks open the heavy double doors and is climbing over the car then remembers Colin and his mom saying stay away. He looks carefully around as he slides down the hot metal of the car, sticking to it – ow ow ow – but the police are gone and no one else is there. Cicadas are loud and Theo watches a little bird, a sparrow or wren, the tiny bright-eyed kind grown-ups think is cute, erratically following a cicada in the air, the cicada making a sound different than the usual rising, rhythmic call from the trees, with this one now constant and lower-pitched, in a straight line rather than a curve up like the regular sound. The cicada jerks and flits and the bird follows fast right behind, doing everything the cicada does, and Theo realizes the bird's trying to eat the cicada, and the cicada's screaming.

He runs, around the house toward the people, hearing crickets now.

What happens if those different police show up, the school ones and the other ones. When will they come. Will they come while his dad is here. Theo's thinking as he runs, stumbling but liking the air on his face. They don't have to answer the door. Theo won't anymore. He doesn't want anything to happen to anyone.

Around the back of the house and people are wandering, sitting; two have arms around each other. There is the big wide two-person blue and yellow inflatable air mattress, blown up out on the grass now and Colin bends over it. Theo slows to a walk, sees Gus's back disappearing into the house, and Mingus nowhere. Theo navigates, scuffing at the grass, to Colin, who's straightening up. Colin flicks his eyes left, then realizes it's Theo and holds his look, grinning as if he's embarrassed.

Hola, compadre.

Theo continues toward Colin, looking. On the big ribbed mattress, which Theo likes because in shallow water it's a horse or a shipwreck and requires gripping tightly to keep from getting bucked off, are a bucket and the two squash from the refrigerator, and a cucumber and two of the oranges – no, it's lacrosse balls that one of the guests brought and juggled with once.

The two squash sit next to each other with the knob-sides out and below them is the bucket, on its side, propped on the wire handle. Then next to the bucket, the two balls and the cucumber propped up over them, sticking up. Theo gets the cucumber but not the bucket.

That's dirty.

No, my friend, it's art. I'm going to put this on a wedding dress and a tuxedo and show it in Soho. Or maybe a mattress.

What's the bucket for.

Colin looked at Theo and said, let's say it's female parts.

A bucket.

Yeah. It's a joke.

I don't get it.

Right, young master sahr, there are just some things you've got to be a little older for. Not everything is for kids.

Can we go to the beach.

Absolutely, my friend. Let's go. Let's run.

Colin darts off, off balance, in long pants but no shirt. He is pouring sweat and his face is red. He's weaving in circles, jogging.

Gina is standing up, her boots on the ground, one up, one lying down. I'm coming too, but I'm not running.

They are watching Colin ahead, streaking toward the beach walkway.

There used to be a real walkway there but it's gone, Theo says.

You mean like a boardwalk.

I found old pictures. Colin and Gus said famous people used to live here.

Do you remember any of the names Colin and Gus said.

Gina is wearing sunglasses. He has to hurry a little to keep up with her. But he doesn't mind. He wants to tell her things.

Not really. They said a rat pack.

Ha. Really. Gina is smiling hugely. Your house has quite a pedigree. Do you like it.

It's okay. I like it better than the last one.

Where was that.

I lived with Frieda in Manhattan. Before that in Connecticut and a lot of places. My dad thought it would be good to be away from Manhattan. Gus and Colin are supposed to mind me.

122

They're also supposed to watch out for my mom. That's what my dad said. He's coming here. He's going to make a record.

That's cool. What's he like. Does he hang out with you.

He's usually busy. There's always people talking to him or calling him. And he gets really tired. Sometimes he's in bed for a whole day. Once he was in bed for three days.

Yeah, I'll bet he gets tired. Do you like his music.

Most of it. He always takes me to shows and to recording things. Once when I was little I got to sit under the piano while they made a record. It felt really funny and he played me the record and you can hear me laughing. It's near the end.

That's kind of famous, did you know that. You're famous, too.

Theo smiled, his face hot.

What's your mom like.

Theo thinks about his mom. Frieda reminds him of an animal, protecting something. He's not always sure what, but she gets really upset about things, and then can be really happy. She gets madder than his father, and she's sick more than his dad. Sometimes she forgets she's a mother, Theo thinks.

She gets mad a lot, but she's funny too. She likes to go to parties. She usually takes me. She sings to me.

What does she sing.

She likes to sing old songs in German and French. She says they're what her nannies sang to her when she was a little girl. She gets mad at my dad.

She does.

Yeah, and he gets mad back at her. That's why they don't really live together. Frieda says she and my dad are like two tigers caged together. If the world let them have more room, they'd be fine.

123

Gina and Theo are among the dunes now. Dry sand on the wooden cross-ties squeaks under their feet.

Do you know my dad.

No. Only by reputation.

Is that good.

Yeah. Among musicians he's a popular guy.

How did you meet my mom.

She was at the club last night. I realized I'd met her before. She is a really good connector. She's always going, hey, you simply must hear this band, or you absolutely must see this painting, or you two absolutely must meet.

What do you play.

Didn't we already have this conversation. She's smiling.

I don't remember what you said.

Keyboards.

Do you like the beach.

Yeah, I just never get to see it. I'm too broke.

Does it cost money to go.

It does if you don't already have money.

I don't understand.

It's the way the world works. It's only the poor people and the schmucks who pay for things.

What's a schmuck.

A schmuck is a, um. A schmuck is someone who doesn't know he's a schmuck.

What.

Sorry. Never mind.

Am I a schmuck.

She stops and stares at Theo, wrinkling up nose and mouth, one hand on her hip. Then she stares back where they came from, at the top of the house visible over the dunes. Then she puts a finger to her mouth and goes: Hmmm, I do not think you qualify as a schmuck.

All right, Theo says, and starts running on the squeaking sand through the last few feet of dune and down onto the beach, wide and dry, tide still out, his head ringing so that he shakes it, a dog. Sun on sand hurts eyes.

Ahead he can see the volleyball stuff up, a few people from other houses. The volleyball people don't look like the ones from the other houses. They're animals in fur when it's hot; they're from a cold place. Theo watches them in their long pants. Now one man is taking off pants, hopping on one leg, and he's in his underwear. Boxer shorts. He's very white. The others don't say anything, just plop on sand with no towels or blankets or chairs or anything. Just the cooler. Coolers.

Scattered up and down the beach are colonies of sitters under striped umbrellas or tents. Air ripples and shimmers, and people walk on wavy legs and a golden retriever has none at all, just brown gliding over wavy air.

The man in the boxers is thumping his chest with his fists, and the others on the sand are pushing onto feet as Theo slogs toward them through snow. He twists around to see Gina – smiling and stripping off her T-shirt on her skinny white chest and a black brassiere. Theo knows about brassieres but tries not to. But he can't help it, he's looking. Her chest in the bra, it's bouncing a little as she walks.

Theo turns and the other ladies are tugging up shirts. One has on a flesh-coloured brassiere so it sort of looks like she's naked and one has on some other kind of chest underwear that Theo doesn't know. He stops looking.

One of the men flips up the cooler lid and pulls out bottles and passes them around. Theo can hear the hiss of the tops

125

being twisted off and the men throw the caps at each other and all tip them up and drink at the same time.

The man who carried the equipment, Mark, gets onto his feet but he's weaving a little.

Full contact. Shirts and skins. Mark grins.

Hey, we're in too. Let's put some money down on this contest.

Colin's voice cuts even through the beach wind. Behind him on one side is Mingus and on the other, the Seal. Further back, Theo sees Gus, carrying a folding chair.

Theo wants to swim. He doesn't want to play volleyball; the grown-ups mostly aren't noticing him, except for the ones who have to, Gus and Colin, and Colin seems wobbly. Gus is planting an umbrella, stabbing over and over at the sand until he stops, then shakes the umbrella. He opens his wooden chair by flipping it, and then lowers himself into it, one of the sling chairs, and Gus looks like a baby in a cradle, his legs barely on the sand and him sunk into the cloth with a floppy hat like babies wear and sunglasses. And he has his bottle.

Even Gina's not paying attention to Theo. They just want to meet his dad. Or sometimes his mom, but a lot of the time that's just to meet his dad, too. To talk to his dad or give something to him. Or to ask his dad for something.

Stay where I can see you, okay, mate. Gus is talking, his voice thin on the wind, to him. Theo just walks ahead, toward the water, not looking back.

Theo's chest hurts. Somebody slams into him from behind, and he spills forward, half turning as he falls, his head feeling cracked, a sharp pain in a line, but then it dulls and disappears. One of the men he doesn't know, with no shirt and bumps on his chest and shoulders and back, is sitting on him, the man's arms holding Theo's shoulders down. Theo is mad and pushes at him.

Get off me.

Didn't want you to feel left out.

Theo's hair on the left side is crusted with sand, and there's sand in his eyes and nose and on his lips.

Left out of what, being stupid, Theo asks, straining but the man grins, pushes, sits. He lets Theo struggle for a while that feels like forever, sun knifing into Theo's eyes.

Get off.

Theo's feeling smothered, a little panicky, frantic; trapped. In the middle of everybody and everything still alone. No one home. The staring man with hands on Theo grins then springs up and spins away, back toward the others. Theo pushes up fast and kicks sand toward the man's back, the sand not even close and the man turning once to look back, pointing at his eyes with two fingers then pointing the forked fingers at Theo.

Theo looks at Gus in his sunglasses and shade, not moving or saying anything: he might be asleep again. People are running back and forth, ducking under the volleyball net, knocking into each other, even the ladies. Someone is throwing the volleyball at people. Theo watches for a few seconds, then he sprints over and flings himself at Colin.

Bouncing, rolling, knocking people down, Theo ducks and runs at bodies with his face down between his outstretched arms, trying to avoid elbows and knees, he's slammed and bounced hard, this isn't a game. Theo's head is now in a lady's stomach and it's Gina, who goes over backward with him on her, his face now inches from her chest. He can see drops on her skin, between. She smells like soap: she pushes him off, grinning.

Get out of there.

Theo's up now and hopping around, flinging his arms and kind of dancing, his body's just on its own; he's spinning and spinning until he's dizzy and collapses. Woozy and hot and sweaty and now powdered with sand and grit, he's panting. Gina is standing in front of him, legs apart, hands on hips, as people unknot and bend over, or sprawl in sand. Colin's on his knees.

Okay, let's play.

Colin gets up, staggers near Theo, and then he makes motions with his hands like he has the ball, but he doesn't. Colin pretends to toss it in the air and hit it, and Gina on the other side pretends to hit it too. Her arms look strong: Theo can see the muscles move in them. She stretches her arms in front of her and pretends to bounce the ball off her wrists.

Colin turns and looks at Theo: Don't let it hit the ground, mate, dive.

So Theo dives with his arms out, sliding on the sand. Brilliant, mate. Colin stares up in the air and his head follows an imaginary ball, falling near Mingus, who stares too, then draws back a foot and kicks at the air.

Colin leaps with arms stretched, although he's only a few inches off the sand, and Mingus dives. Gina says, our point, didn't make it over.

Colin says, un-bloody-likely. That was just a killer block.

When something needs rules, adults don't use them, and when rules are stupid is when they add them. Theo just wants to play. He wonders who is at the house now, who's left. What are the dogs doing, as someone walks a setter on the beach. Theo sees two boys on all fours, digging at the sand, breakers washing over them. No adults are around them.

Colin's leaning on his shoulder: Hey, stop mooning about. I need my teammate focused here.

Why does his mother take the stuff that she does. Gus is stitting up now, scratching under his shirt, yawning, holding a cigarette low in his other hand, hanging at his side. All these people are. All these people are strangers. Theo thinks maybe something is wrong with him. He feels funny.

I don't feel good.

What's the matter, mate, the heat. Why'n't you just sit for a bit.

No, I want to get in the water.

Theo thinks this would feel better. He can walk past the boys, see what they're doing.

Colin's reaching for something from the cooler. Gus always brings things wherever he goes: he's like a turtle. Home and hearth, Gus says, just in the middle of anything. He and Theo will be sitting on the lawn, or watching 'Wheel of Fortune' on the old TV in his room. There's not supposed to be a TV in the house, his mother said no TV, but Gus said, I'm a grown man. Home and hearth. Theo knows hearth is a fireplace. Gus talks to the lady on the show.

Theo without thinking starts walking at the water, the low roar like people, the white fringe on the green waves, the same colour as when he had a sinus infection and stuff came out of his nose. A big brown wood boat churns from right to left offshore, its cabin white, ladies in bathing suits on the front part of the boat and the roof of the cabin, some men in the back part, holding glasses. The ladies are all lying down. Theo shades his eyes, can't see much.

Theo's stomach's growling. He remembers the biscuits and tuna, the lunch his mom promised. Or she didn't promise, just said. Theo feels regular vibrations in his feet. Gina's beside him.

Where are you going.

Swimming.

Can you swim.

Yeah. I'm a good swimmer. Sort of.

Okay. Mind if I come with you. I'm tired of these people.

They're your friends.

We're on the same circuit, I see them too much. We always end up at the same parties, same clubs. Same mansions. Gina smiles.

Theo looks back: everyone's flat on the sand. One lady and one man lie on top of each other. They all look shipwrecked, ragged and wet, pale, except for Gus under his umbrella staring down the beach.

They pass the two boys digging at sand with bright red and yellow buckets, making a trench around a raised place that looks like a castle. Theo looks, they look at Theo and Gina. They seem his age, blond, long hair in their eyes, long surfer shorts like Theo's. They must have been to Hawaii too.

Nice castle, Gina says, smiling.

Nice tits, one of the boys says, grinning, and the other one laughs.

Gina turns on him. Little boy, she leans down close to him, that's rude. But you're so young you don't even know what you're saying. So I won't punch your fucking little boy face out the back of your head.

Theo stares. Gina's staring at the boy, who's staring at the sand, shrugging, digging, grinning, as is the other digger.

Gina straightens up and sighs, walking away and leaving Theo standing staring at them. The two boys look up at him. Fuck off, the other one says.

Theo kicks him in the chest, the sound like a drum, and yells.

Then Theo stands still, panting, his heart pounding, head pulsing. Two hearts. Gina's beside him.

The two boys are standing up now, one with a red spot on his chest that he's rubbing.

Run to mommy, pussy.

She's not my mother.

Still a pussy.

Come on, Theo. Gina's pulling him toward the water: What happened.

I kicked him.

Why.

They made me mad.

Yeah. Gina sighs. She turns, as does Theo. The two boys stand and look, one with arms crossed, white flowers on their long shorts. One has a big portable phone on its back in his hand and jabs at it with a finger. Theo's seen these before, but mostly in limos. People around his father sometimes carry them, and parents of kids in his school. He's seen them in Manhattan, men in suits usually but once a tall lady in a short skirt and a see-through plastic coat.

Let's cool off in the water.

Green surf, and the sand's sinking. The brown boat's down the beach. In the shimmering air, figures move, fly kites, play paddle tennis, sit under awnings and tents. Where the land curves like a big jaw to the right are houses with walls cutting off the beach.

Gina wades out in her skirt. Theo tries not to watch as the cloth floats and swirls, sticks to her thighs. She dives.

Theo pushes against the water, then dives in a shallow arc, just under, eyes tight shut, a hand on his nose, then shoots up sputtering. Gina's not anywhere.

Theo scans in a circle, standing, the water just below his waist, not as deep as he thought. Back on the beach a phalanx of Colin and the other people is stumbling toward him, the two kids are squatting on the sand, Colin's stopping to talk to them, or talk at them, he's kicking whatever they're building, he's backing up, he's running through it, yelling, pointing at them, laughing, now he's dancing in a little circle, the others are staring at him, some keep walking, the boys are yelling at him, one's waving the big phone, which is almost as long as his forearm. Why do they have that.

Mouthy little prat: Theo hears Colin, who's now on a line toward the water.

Theo spins to check the water – Gina's there, floating on her back, paddling, skirt billowing, her pale skin blazing in the sun. She'll get sunburned, Theo thinks, and dives but keeps his head above the water, and tries to swim like he learned in lessons; putting his arms over his head and pulling down, the freestyle or crawl, he can't remember, but it's hard and after five or six strokes he decides to paddle like the dogs, lifting his head out just in time to get a face full of wave. The salt burns in his nose and throat and he stands to spit and shake, then jumps forward, frog-kicking.

Gina's turning over and bending to dive: her rear sticks up in the air under a skin of wet skirt then she's gone. Theo stops and stands, water just below his chest. He looks to the shore. Colin's rolling in the breakers pretending he's dead, he always does this, and the Seal is walking up wearing pants with the legs cut off at the knees, talking to people, who are looking at him and talking, smiling. Theo doesn't know anyone. He turns and dives.

The ocean's hissing and churning, and muffling like in

a bathtub when you're under. Theo tries opening his eyes: brown-green blurs and shadows. How close in do sharks come. Crabs. He closes his eyes and comes up, huffing.

Gina, now on her back, floats. When Theo took swimming lessons he just sank during the survival float. His teachers said it's because he's skinny. Colin said, it's because you're so dense, mate, and laughed. Like a brick.

Theo's up and watching everyone, and Gus, way up on the beach, under his striped umbrella, and there's a jeep driving up the beach with two men in it, in uniforms and sunglasses, and it's driving from the high dry strip where Gus is to the low wet band the waves reach. And it's stopping where the two boys are, who are pointing at the ocean. Maybe the jeep will sink.

Theo sinks, into the water, hands on nose, until only his eyes are showing. The two men are talking down at the boys, and the man who's not driving hops down and walks around the jeep and toward all of the people wallowing in water and sand, or floating, the Seal somewhere, Mingus forming a big T on the sand and Colin now standing with two men and a lady in the water, talking and hitting the water with their hands, backs to the beach.

Hey.

The guy from the jeep has sunglasses and a gun. He puts his fingers to his mouth and whistles: Hey. You. Yeah you. The man crooks a finger at Colin, gestures at him. Come here.

Why. Colin's yelling back.

The man stands with hands on his hips.

Colin's slogging through the water now, others following, some others on the sand converging at the uniformed man.

Colin and the guy are talking. Colin puts a hand on the guy's shoulder for an instant then moves it off to gesture back

133

toward the house, then out at the ocean. Then he turns and points directly at Theo. Theo hadn't realized Colin knew where he was. He stands up.

Colin's talking still, and smiling, and now the guy from the jeep is smiling. Then the two of them shake hands and the guy walks back toward the two boys. He talks to them for a minute, then gets back into the jeep and it drives away, down the beach, spraying sand. One of the boys holds the phone to his ear again. The other squats with his back to the ocean and Colin and Theo and the sun.

Theo closes his eyes and falls backward just as a wall of heavy wave hits: it thumps him and he spills sideways and under.

Dolphin, diver, moving, moving – up for air, blowing, hair over eyes, seaweed, a spy, a diver, back down into cool rushing and the hum, no thinking, everything behind. Eyes open an instant, then closed, no looking just swimming, pulling hard, bumping the bottom, his chest on the sand, pulling, the ceiling of water over, then up and through it to something new.

Theo's moved just a few feet from where he was last, and Colin's thrashing at him, head down, spraying; not even knowing, just automatically there, wherever Theo is.

Nothing's different. Theo dives. Swim on, thrash through the water. Struggle, fight the waves, shipwrecked, battered, jump and spit. Ride. Theo's going to ride a wave, body surf. He needs to be a little closer to shore, the water's at his chest. He's lifted up and in on a swell, sort of thrown toward Colin, churning and spouting. Other heads bob or talk, two wrestle, the guy in the underwear is trying to run, his saggy briefs embarrassing. He has to hold them on. Someone further out, a head, holds up an arm – someone else yells. The arm holds some bright orange cloth, a lady's suit maybe, yelling more. Theo doesn't want to look.

134

Isn't this brilliant.

Colin's here now, blowing, grinning, paddling. Shaking gleaming drops from brown skin, bursting up shattering the water, ribs a ladder, like Theo's. Colin's white under his arm, tanned everywhere else. Looks like a mouth.

Hey, mate. Your mom left. She said to tell you goodbye and give you a kiss. Colin leans down, eyes closed, puckered up. Theo throws himself backward: Gross.

Colin opens his eyes, smiles, then reaches out, puts his hand on Theo's shoulder.

Your mom's going away for a bit.

What do you mean – on a trip.

No, she's going someplace she can rest. She's very tired.

Why can't she rest here.

Well, Colin grins, this isn't the most tranquil environment in the world. She needs a little peace and quiet right now, and this just isn't the place for that.

Is she sick.

Sort of, Colin says. She just needs some time and some looking after.

What's wrong with her. What does she have. I could look after her. You and Gus could help.

Colin narrows his eyes a minute to look at Theo. You're a sweet kid. No. She needs to be away from us.

Maybe away from you.

Ha. She'd agree with you there.

The two of them ride up and over an incoming swell. Splashing and wrestling further inshore. Theo's hit by a wave, too quickly, and he's off-guard, a stream of them, slapping at him, and he wants them to stop. And they don't, they just keep coming. Water's too deep. Chest compressed, feels hard to breathe. Why did she leave without telling him. She's tired and worn out by waves, too. Theo thrashes, panicky a little, the bottom gone from his feet as he's lifted and set down. What makes waves: you can't see it. They just come. Keep coming.

Theo's sputtering and struggling inshore more, to shallower water. Colin's following.

But. Big change of plans. Your dad will be here tonight. Case was bloody thrown out and visa was granted.

What. What case.

Colin's grinning lopsidedly. Doesn't matter. We got word from the office he's on his way from Perth. Good news, eh.

Theo's grinning, jumps backward and sinks, to the bottom, sits for an instant with arms around his legs, eyes closed, cheeks bulging, holding air in his mouth. Letting current wash over, hearing the sound of waves breaking themselves.

His lungs. He blows out and shoots up, splashing. Colin's staggering in toward the others, yelling something.

Colin. Colin.

Colin turns finally away from the others: What, mate.

What happened with the jeep.

Colin smiles and staggers as a wave slaps him: The spoiled little toffs mouthed off. But we have juice too, and I know the cop, he's a good monk. This is the playground of the beautiful people, and the beautiful people have to be able to play. So we play on.

The two boys, Theo notices, now just sit and watch all of them, not talking. Maybe if he hadn't been with Gina, if it was just them, maybe they could hang out some. Theo stares, hands shielding his eyes. He sighs, slapping at the water, hard, over and over, seeing how far he can spray. Watching the two boys get up and walk, then run, pushing each other and laughing, away. Watching until they dart right toward dunes and disappear, presumably going home.

three.

*It costs too much to shine
in this world.*
– Jean-Pierre Claris de Florian

Theo wakes to the sound of water, splashing. Where is this. Eyes open, in his room, in the attic, the dark space full of sun from the old windows at both ends, three on each side. But barely there, the water; somewhere below. Theo yawns, scratches, pushes hair away from his face. His dad. He remembers: his dad came last night.

Theo's up and off his big mattress. He smells himself – yeah. Stuff needs washing. Gus bags up clothes in big white bags and a truck comes and takes them. Colin calls it the diaper service. One time last winter they burned all the dirty clothes in a fireplace. Colin was drunk. A car came the next morning and the three of them rode into New Jersey and went to a store and Colin walked around pointing at things, Gus and Theo pushing carts and throwing the things into them. When they got back to the house and tore open the bags they found women's clothes and some sports uniforms, along with replacements for burned things, and two toasters and rugs and tools and toys and something called a Cuisinart, in a tall box. Colin kicked that box to the back lawn and shot at it over and over with his silver pistol. The box still sat outside somewhere near the trees, the colours on the cardboard faded and the box shredding. Pieces of it ended up in squirrel nests.

Colin called it an experiment. He said they were in Eden and their job was to classify everything, figure out what to call it.

Gus said, for once in your bleeding life, would you shut the bloody hell up. Too much jawbonin, Tex: Colin talked like a cowboy. But he was quieter for a while, a day or so.

Theo's at the attic's front windows now, hands spread on the splintery ledge, the glass Xed by iron. In the spaces between the iron lines he sees the front, the cars, the long van that is the mobile recording studio, black cables strung umbilically from it and running up the steps and in windows and two red metal boxes on the ground outside, humming and smoking. Generators: the electrics in the house would go up the spout without them, one of the sound guys said. The RV arrived after dark yesterday, just before his dad.

Sound, faint, from inside the house; new sound, something Theo could feel in his feet and his hands on the window ledge. People playing music, different than records. A guitar snarling up. Sounds like his dad.

A butterfly. A butterfly at the edge of his eyes in the attic. He turns and follows it, a monarch, bobbing. From his cocoons. He walks, looking at the hanging cases, looking for anything moving. Here and there, like an eye behind a lid, there's stirring. He can't wait to show his dad. What else does he want to show. His drums. Theo wonders about his mom, wonders will she come. Where is she. Colin just said in a place like a hospital, just a place where people will take care of her for a while, help her feel better. Theo didn't know she didn't feel well.

Theo jams a hand in his hair and it's stuck, fingers catching on tangles. He has a brush somewhere, in the bathroom he uses on the fourth floor. He runs around the attic, both hands in his hair, a bubble ready to pop. No words. Theo's famished. He wants to see his dad.

When Adrian strolled in last night, Theo was asleep on a pile of towels in the ballroom, the adults scattered in a variety of rooms, a net of smoke hanging just under the ceiling, the ballroom doors open and the dogs lying half-in, half-out, under a bright moon. People were out on the terrace, some in the grass. Moaning. Theo woke, his stomach hurting, heard moaning and laughing and then lots of noise, shouting. He pushed up from the towels, forgetting where he was, then adjusting, remembering. He shook his head. All the lights were on in the ballroom, but only he and the dogs and Colin's motorbike were there. Theo got up and slipped on a drumstick, which rolled out from under him, and he lost his balance. Ow. Hurt. He hopped for a minute, the dogs alert now, watching. The air was hot.

Theo wandered toward the noise from the house's front, through the back hall, and in all the voices he heard him. His father. Theo bolted, and under the dim hall lights there he was, surrounded by people, arms around people, wearing big square sunglasses, with his satchel slung over his shoulder. He didn't have on a shirt, but he did have a Rangers hockey jersey tied by the arms at his neck, like someone choking him. Adrian leaned hard on the people on either side of him, a lady taller than him and a bald man in a suit. So many voices, and the chesspieces a forest to weave through, upright and prone. Theo pushed a little, slipped between and hesitated at the empty space around his dad. All the adults talking. His dad swaying.

Here's who I want to see: his dad noticed and bent a little scarily, the woman still holding on to help him keep his balance. Hello, sweetheart.

Theo's dad was on his knees now, arms wrapped around Theo, hugging back, swimming in smells that made him dizzy,

145

sweet and odd, things he only smelled around his dad. Theo's cheek felt Adrian's sunglasses, pressing, and Adrian said bloody hell and tossed glasses sideways and off. Theo looked at his father, sunburned, unshaved, his eyes black dots. His breath. Maybe his dad was sick.

Theo, baby, I missed you, mate. I love you.

Hi, Dad. Theo, a little groggy, just held on for the moment. Waking up.

I brought you some stuff, mate.

My butterflies are hatching. Theo rubbed his eyes, looking at the lady, standing and smiling down at him. She had on furry pants and a football jersey.

That's brilliant, mate. This is my friend Shelley.

Hello, Theo, I'm glad to meet you. She held her hand down, had to stoop a little. Theo noticed her shoes were really thick. She was a giant.

Come on, mate. Show you something.

Theo's dad moved, stood up, but then he squatted again, as if his legs weren't working right. Fuck it, Adrian said, and flopped over and on hands and knees began crawling over the black and white tiles.

Maybe it was a joke; Theo hoped it was a joke, so he got down on hands and knees too, and then so did Shelley, and then everyone else started dropping, following, except the man in the suit, who talked to another man, both looking and smiling but not crawling.

I like my suit, the man shrugged, smiling, and Theo realized the man was talking to him. Because Theo was looking back. Theo turned and crawled but his dad was up ahead somewhere and Theo was crawling and jostling among other people, like in a herd but not funny with people, just weird, and why were

146

they doing this. Theo stood up, scooted to the side among the crawlers, and the bald man in the suit and Theo walked behind along the hall. Lit camping lanterns glowed along the way – one of the things they bought on the trip to New Jersey after they burned all that stuff. Colin bought a tent and lanterns, and a bow and arrow. And bags and bags of candy. Theo had forgotten. His dad really liked candy. Chocolate. Dentists came to his hotel to fix his teeth. Theo was there once when his dad got a haircut and a dentist came. His dad said it was an emergency and he couldn't go to the dentist's office. Too complicated, mate.

Are you glad to see your dad, Theo.

Yes, of course. Who are you. Theo was tired and agitated now, his dad swept away.

My name is Silvio. I work with your father.

What do you play.

Silvio laughed. I don't play anything, I'm pretty useless that way. I am president of the company that puts out your father's records.

Is it like being president of a country.

A little bit, except without the army. I wish I had one at times. I help people hear your father's music.

How do you do that.

Ah, my friend, that is a very tedious and long process I don't want to bore you with. Let us just enjoy each other's company. I believe your father has some surprises for you.

They were leaving the hall and entering one of the big down-stairs rooms, the one Theo's mom had been in when she was here. In the centre of the room was a Christmas tree shooting almost to the ceiling, completely covered with tinsel and lights, and wrapped gifts circled its bottom, enough to build a

147

wall. Theo's father sat on his knees and everyone else scattered around, some standing again, but Shelley sat cross-legged beside him, holding his hand.

It's not Christmas, Theo said. The lights in the dark dazzled, hurt a little, the tree a shape made of light. Where did you get all the lights.

What do you think, eh. Looks like a miracle to me.

It's summer.

Yeah, but I thought we could have Christmas. The presents are for you. There's a couple for you, baby: Theo's dad leaned toward Shelley and she kissed him.

And of course some coal for Colin and a few things for me dad, who I hope is snug in his bed right now, dreaming of sugarplums.

The other people in the room milled around now. Theo was not sure what to do.

What do we do.

What do you mean, mate. It's Christmas morning. Dive in.

Theo felt sad, and then felt bad for feeling sad. People looked at him. Some frowned, yawning. Others paid no attention.

What's the matter, love. Every day's Christmas when I'm with you. Why don't you see what Father Christmas brought.

Theo walked toward the tree, flopped beside it.

When did this stuff come.

While you were asleep. Surprise, mate. Father Christmas managed to miss the expressway traffic. Found his way to Gatsby's mansion. Did I tell you about this place: Adrian turned toward Shelley.

Theo sat, holding a wrapped box. Glitter on it fluttered off so the dark air sparkled. Adrian whispered into Shelley's ear, his hand on her leg. Theo ripped at the paper and peeled to get at a brown unmarked wood box about the size of shoes. It had a lid and he lifted it. Inside was tissue, and in the tissue, a knife. A curved one with a handle that looked like an animal's horn.

Hey, that's what they give to young men in Tanzania when they come of age. It's a symbol of manhood, made of oryx horn.

Theo laid it down in the box, put the lid on. Thanks.

Keep going. Happy Christmas, mate. Shelley helped with some of the presents.

Open that gold box: Shelley smiled at him, pointing at his feet, where a box in gold foil glowed. Theo reached down to grab it. It was heavy.

What is it.

Well, open it and find out. Shelley smiled at Theo, and Adrian grinned, looking at Shelley. Her teeth were really white. Theo felt funny when she looked at him, and he wanted to look at her. She looked like a movie. Lots of other people were looking at her too.

Theo opened the box, hard cardboard, the wrapping thin and tissuey, and it had Japanese or Chinese characters on it. Korean ones looked different, he knew. In the box was a doll or an animal, Theo wasn't sure, and it was plastic.

Your dad said you like animals: Shelley was looking at him again. Her eyes were far apart. Turn it on.

It could be turned on. Theo lifted it, having to shake off the tight ribbed brown box with purple paper inside, more tissue. The thing had big eyes and a tail; it was white and had a black face that was round, and round ears.

It's a monkey.

Theo saw that now. He turned it, looking for buttons: at the bottom. He pushed a small switch to the side and the thing squirmed in his hand. That tickles, it said in a high voice in English, and then it made a noise like a fart.

Theo was ready to like it and looked at Shelley to say thanks. She was kissing his father. This was his third Japanese robot from one of his dad's friends. At least Shelley didn't tell him how expensive it was like the last lady. It would make his dad happy if he acted happy about it.

Great. Thanks a lot.

Theo's dad's eyes were closed, then open. Hey mate, Shelley went to a lot of trouble to get that.

Thanks, Shelley.

So open some more. Happy Christmas. Adrian stared around at others, saying stuff, laughing. The man in the suit moved closer to Adrian, leaning to whisper. Both smiled.

Are there presents for you, Theo asked.

Sure, mate, seeing you is the best gift I could possibly get. Go on, tear into it. Santa really took a shine to you. He knows you been brilliant.

It was hard to hear because someone turned on a radio or tape player and now there was music like you hear in Jamaica; Theo knew his father liked it. People laughed and pointed, poked and punched, wrapped arms around each other, some others were kissing, somebody was always screaming or yelling, Theo stared around, at the pile highlighted in the dark, shiny paper catching light as if it were wet. Would his father notice if he left. Colin's voice lifted angrily, then it laughed. Where was Gus.

Can Gus help me open stuff.

Adrian now standing had an arm looped around the necks of two men, and his other arm around another lady, not Shelley, and in one hand a big black bottle. Theo's dad always picked

Theo's voice out of the sounds: yeah, son, sure. It'll give him a charge. Where is he.

I'll go find him.

Theo got up and pushed through the ring of adults until he reached empty space and ran. It was dark and he bumped into Mingus and two ladies standing close together. Mingus had his arms around them and he was wearing his pants and a cape and the ladies were touching his stomach.

Hey, baby. What's your mission.

Do you know where my grandfather is.

No I do not.

Theo ran on. He was not sure of the time; maybe Gus was asleep, like Theo had been. Gus slept more than Colin or Adrian. His dad sometimes didn't sleep at all. Sometimes he just stayed up talking, or Theo would hear music when he went to sleep and music when he got up. How do you make a record in a house. The big camper thing out front. Theo wanted to toss a ball. He wondered if his dad might tomorrow. His dad liked to kick more than throw, and Theo tried to remember where a soccer ball was. Theo called it soccer and Adrian called it football. So did Gus. There was a team in New York that he and Colin and his dad had gone to see play, the Cosmos, when Theo lived in Manhattan. There was a minder too, one he never saw again, and a driver. Colin started yelling at some men and he took his shirt off and tried to fight them and they had to leave before the end of the game. In the car afterward Colin stuck his head out the window and screamed until his voice was hoarse; his dad pulled him back into the limo's back seat. Then Colin crawled out the window and over the roof and knocked on the other window, while the car was driving. Adrian laughed but was really mad, it seemed. The minder checked the door lock and opened the window and reached out to hold Colin, who was yelling, and when his legs were in Adrian grabbed and yanked: get your bloody ass in here. Before the game Adrian bought Theo soccer jerseys and a ball and some kind of flag. They were in the attic somewhere.

Gus hadn't been in his room. It was starry outside but Theo ran back toward Adrian through the ballroom. The dogs had disappeared. They got shy sometimes. Maybe they were outside.

Back in the room with all the people, the music was louder and people had dragged in cushions and cloths; Theo saw some towels and piles of clothes, pillows collected from other rooms. People scattered in the dark; he heard voices in different places along the halls. In the big room with the tree and the presents his dad now had a guitar – and there was Gus, sitting against a wall talking to a lady. Gus was smoking his pipe. He and the lady each had a bottle.

Theo ran up to Gus. Will you help me open presents.

Gus's eyes were halfway open and slow, and it took him a second to swing around to Theo. Of course, son. Excuse me a second, darling.

Theo waited while Gus slowly got his legs under him and stood, reaching out toward Theo, who grabbed Gus's hard hand. Gus's hands were different from anyone else's in the house. Standing, Gus winked at the lady and let Theo lead him.

A man aimed a microphone at Adrian, and another man Theo didn't know had a guitar too. A lady was pouring her drink into her hand and a man was licking it from her palm. One lady had her shirt off now. Some of the people from the beach were sitting in a circle, leaning over something Theo couldn't see. The tree lit up backs and halos of hair; someone pounded on Colin's congas, dragged in from Theo forgot where. Standing next to the tree, Theo sat down and stared up at Gus, who breathed deeply and lowered himself slowly, dropping hard the last few inches.

Hard on the bum. What have we here.

Presents from my dad. Help me open them.

Theo picked a large box and pulled it toward him. Some man sprayed something up in the air from his mouth, and people were laughing or yelling. Somebody was mad. Somebody was telling Colin to put his fucking clothes on. Music was louder. Theo's ears rang a little. Gus was holding a package, staring at it.

Open it.

Reminds me of holidays when your dad was a boy. A bright-eyed little bugger. Just like you: Gus reached over to rub Theo's head. Theo let him.

What have we here, eh: Gus was ripping into paper, and Theo was too, then into a white box, inside of which were cars, electric cars for the electric track, like the one Theo played with in the hotel room when his father had to go to court. One was a Batmobile, one a Ferrari, Theo knew, because of the black horse on the yellow shield on the car's hood. Theo's box said Macy's. Gus's said something in German. Gus struggled with the tape.

Theo remembered the hotel when his father came back with toy doctor bags, a lot of them. Theo saw them in Adrian's room. Adrian said he liked to play doctor, and laughed. Theo didn't understand.

There's tape on it, Theo said to Gus still fussing with the same box.

Right, Gus said, and stared at one end, then slipped a

fingernail in and slid it. The tree shook. Someone fell or was pushed. Singing. Popping sounds Theo knew were champagne cognac, which his dad liked, and which sounded different than other pops. Adrian cross-legged held a dusty black bottle, his other arm protective around the guitar, Adrian's hand on its neck, the way he had put his hand on the back of Shelley's neck, light and warm, Theo knew, because he'd had the hand on his neck. Never cold. Adrian always had warm hands. Frieda called it one of his redeeming qualities. What's a redeeming quality, Theo asked. A reason not to kill him, Frieda said.

Gus held a mask with horns and a snout like a dog or wolf – gold, snarling with red lips and white teeth. Hey, that'll be great for Halloween, eh. Gus lifted the thing and put it on his face, holding a hand at the back of his head.

Use that to keep the wolf from the door, fight fire with fire – Gus stared at the mask, said: from Tibet, probably a bloody antique, some kind of museum piece. All right. Gus set it down: That just wet me whistle, now what else did Father Christmas bring.

Someone had a camera: flashes. The man with the tape recorder walked now, looking down at his dials. Theo's father was talking to a man in sunglasses and cowboy boots, who was laughing hard. Shelley sat between them, leaning on the other man. Theo saw his father, grinning, swivel around to the bottle and his eyes caught on the tree, then Theo. He grinned, blew a kiss at Theo, yelled: I'm glad you're here, buddy.

Theo waved across the floor and reached for a box: Gus bent for a package out of the landscape of presents, reminding Theo of his kindergarten, the blocks teaching shapes and colours. Some things here were wrapped but not in boxes. Who did all this, Theo wondered, looking around at the adults. Who wasn't drunk. This was someone's job.

Music. Somebody slid on the wooden floor without a shirt, on his stomach, on something spilled. Got up with lines of dark on his chest, blood. From the edges of the wood tiles. Parquet, it was called. Or nails. Theo turned to a box, ripped, opened. It looked like a necklace. Was that for him. He picked up something wrapped but not a square or rectangle, a big shape. He ripped: someone screamed. Theo peeled back the paper on a football, but it was too big to throw; it said New York Giants and had writing on it, names, signatures. Theo put it down and stood up. He wanted to feel happy. Adrian was playing the guitar with his eyes closed.

Gus wore a black pirate hat and held a shiny metal folding telescope to his eye and squinted, swinging it around at the ceiling and the adults. Can't tell if it's a kaleidoscope or not: Gus laughed, swinging the thing toward Theo to look at him – now there's a rum face if ever I saw one.

I'm going to go to bed, Theo said.

What.

I'm going to my room.

Gus focused on Theo through the telescope; Theo could see him wrinkling his face, really looking. You sure, mate. A lot of booty here. But all right, we can open more tomorrow.

Gus tried to give a pirate salute, Theo thought, then Theo walked toward one of the hall entrances behind the adults, pushing his way through and away.

Now, next morning, Theo is starving. He hears low sound getting louder as he goes down the waterfall of stairs. Real drums. Maybe someone's playing his in the ballroom. His dad's making a record.

He's hopping down the stairs, passing upstairs halls like

a slow elevator moving through sounds on each floor now, voices, clanging, singing, rhythmic banging, some kind of whistle, and the music rising up through the well of space the staircases wrap around. Theo likes to drop things from the top floor and watch. Sometimes he spits. He tries to hit Colin's chesspieces, a couple of which can be seen all the way from the top. Christmas. Theo's head floods with last night. He wonders what else is under the tree. He wonders if there's food. He wonders if his mother is okay. He wonders about the butterflies in his room. Will he have to see anybody before he sees Adrian. Did the man in the suit stay in the house. Did he sleep in his suit. Space – what would it be like to swim through stars. Why do adults drink so much coffee, or drink it at all. Why do adults like alcohol. Adrian and Frieda both have given him alcohol. And cigarettes, they let him try. Both things felt like torture, or a test. And dogs, school, boys like him, girls, about girls. His cheeks feel hot. Damn. He softly says the words sometimes, when no one can hear. Where does air come from. He wonders if dogs burp. Do girls burp. If spider silk is strong as steel, how can he break a web with his hand. People say he's lucky. If so, how can he tell.

Theo's almost at the bottom now and the music is loud. In the entrance hall Colin's chessmen lie in pieces, jumbled. Theo wonders if Colin did this. Theo can't see any people. Could he live outside and never have to come in. Is his dad okay. Can he find something to eat.

Theo smells food. He moves toward music, which is where the smell's also coming from. In the ballroom Adrian and three men Theo doesn't know are playing, and there are microphones and a man with a beard and headphones. Adrian's eyes are closed. The air is foggy and smoky, and there's a cloud up at the

156

ceiling. Theo feels the air in his lungs. All the men are smoking. On the other side of the room is a wooden picnic table Theo's never seen with alcohol bottles on it and trays of food, and a lady with pink spiky hair in an apron, dishing something out of cartons.

Theo's drums are moved over to the side, everything draped with towels, his bass drum stuffed to keep from making noise on the tape, he knew. The drummer's on a different kit, old and wood. The French doors are open. Adrian's leaning now to say something to the other guitar player, and he looks mad. Both stop playing but the drummer and the bass player don't, they just watch and bob, playing, both chewing gum. Vamping, it's called, Theo knows, which makes him think of vampires.

Adrian shoves the other guitar player with a hand to the chest. The bass player rolls his eyes. Come on, man.

Adrian turns on him but sees Theo and his grey face lightens. He smiles: Hey mate, are you hungry. There's dinner here.

It's morning.

Well, it's food anyway, tuck in. You are looking ribby. Is Colin not feeding you.

Sometimes.

Bloody hell.

Theo walks to the table and the lady, who smiles at him: Hello. Would you like some couscous.

We went Moroccan, Adrian is saying, a cigarette on his lip that he squints through. You remember when we stayed at the Mamounia. You liked the couscous, you couldn't get enough.

Morocco Theo remembered because of camels and people yelling at them, kids younger than Theo outside staring up at the hotel windows and calling whenever anyone looked out of the suite windows or went on the balcony: asking for money,

Theo could hear, in English. One of the adults threw coins. It's a very poor country. The kids chased down the money and pushed and shoved over it, like seagulls fighting over food and men scrambling for foul balls at Yankee Stadium. Theo had seen five Yankees games and three games in Los Angeles. His dad bought him a hat and jersey each time, and they never stayed past the seventh inning. Theo wanted to see how the games ended, but Adrian couldn't sit that long.

In Morocco ladies ran next to the car and held up babies. Theo remembered a girl crawling, with sticks for legs. What's wrong with her, he asked Adrian, who had his eyes closed and was leaning on his friend Rob. Theo's dad didn't open his eyes but Rob said, bad luck. She lives in Morocco.

Why doesn't anyone ever explain anything, Theo thinks now. Everyone always knows more than he does, and won't tell, and he just has to live with it. Kids just have to. When do you get to know.

Theo says, sure, to the pink-haired lady, and she takes a plate, a real plate not a paper one, and scoops out the couscous, which has chunks of meat in it and, Theo notices, yellow raisins. He hates raisins.

Adrian's drinking from a bottle and he's got sunglasses on now: What's it sound like, Don.

The man with headphones shrugs, smoking. It's a warm room, not bad. Definitely need to close the doors. We might need to swap you and Kit.

The drummer spits over his bass drum and onto the floor.

Good christ, this is my home. You're a goddamn animal. Clean that up.

The drummer stands up from his stool, stumbles, then

walks around the kit and lowers himself onto his knees, and then onto his hands. Then he sticks out his tongue and licks the place where he spat.

Thank you. We do need to maintain a modicum of decorum. There are children and ladies present.

The woman is busy with the food, staring into a pot. Theo's just staring at his father and the drummer.

I'm going to go outside, Theo says, walks with his plate toward the doors and the bright outside. The drummer is now lying on the floor.

All right. There's a sign from god. Let's take five, Adrian calls, and pitches his cigarette toward the food. Whose idea was Moroccan.

Theo looks at the bass player as he passes him. The man's grey, too, his face dotted with little hairs. It's funny to think of hairs growing out of a face. Wolfman. Humans are animals but pretend they're not. The man's eyes are bright blue, and he's wearing a shirt without sleeves, and his thin arms strain as he does something with his instrument, squatting, reaching to lock his hand around a bottle and bring it to his mouth. He has arms like a lady, Theo thinks. Theo is thirsty.

Hey, sport.

Adrian's voice, echoing a little: at the French doors, Theo turns to look back.

Let's have a little breakfast together, eh. Adrian's grinning, the words a little slurry. Adrian's wrestling out from under his strap and another man with a moustache is helping him. I'm going to do a fry-up. How about that.

Theo stands, thinking it might upset the lady, who stirs vigorously with her back to the room, silent.

This'll just be another course. I need some grease.

159

Theo hopes there isn't a fire: he remembers last time. Adrian's talking to the guy holding his guitar, and he's lighting a new cigarette, and he's barefoot in bell-bottoms and walking across to the man in the headphones.

Hey, pal, come here.

Theo walks back from the outside door, holding his plate and not wanting to hold it, but not wanting to be mean to the lady. Theo notices now, he hadn't before, there are other ladies lying around in the dark corners, two asleep on each other, on piles of pillows and with one of the Oriental rugs over them.

This is my friend Don. He's the best sound man in the history of sound men. He is a very sound man. You're adrift in the ocean and you need a solid bloke to hold onto, here's the guy.

Don is smiling, reaching a hand out toward Theo, which Theo holds and shakes.

Good morning, Don says. But I can't swim.

Theo says, I got my certificate last summer: I'm a Dolphin.

Theo took lessons at the 92nd Street Y, hating them, in a cold pool that burned and with a woman teacher who yelled, a short woman with short yellow hair. But Frieda had the driver take him every Saturday, and the driver sat at the pool edge, trying to smoke and being told he couldn't by the instructor every Saturday. You can't smoke in here, sir. So he sat with an unlit cigarette in his mouth, staring at the instructor and the girls in the class. The instructor spent a lot of time talking about swimming for her college, and racing, and the Olympics. She seemed angry. There were four girls and four boys, and Theo saw other kids were shivering too while the lady stood on the pool edge and talked at them. Frieda asked Theo whether there were men in the changing room: They didn't talk to you, did they. Nobody talked to him in the changing room, the men in there in the early mornings were old as turtles, with skin like wrinkled sheets and weird hair in weird places. He didn't like to look but sometimes he couldn't help it.

A dolphin. I am sticking with you if we get shipwrecked.

Come on, Don, I'm making breakfast. Sunny-side up. It's a beautiful day, mate.

Don stands from behind the table with the recording equipment as the lady puts aluminum foil over trays and containers, really fast and sharp, ripping the foil like she might be mad.

Where did the lady come from.

Adrian says, Manhattan. She's staying with us. We need decent food. Colin's useless. That's a cool sound, Adrian says, turning to watch the lady rip sheets of aluminum foil from the roll. Darlin', would you mind if I taped that.

The lady kept working but said: That's fine. Todd Rundgren did it last.

Oh well, forget it. Adrian grinned. Thanks, baby, we'll need something later – can you set up a buffet.

Certainly. How about pasta with an omelette option, spinach salad, baguettes. A tort.

Pasta's fine. Come on, Theo.

Adrian's sunglasses were on, and Don and Theo followed him toward the kitchen. Wind now blew through the open doors. Theo remembered the other guys and turned around. Now the drummer sat behind his kit again, draining a beer and squinting into the light from outside. The other guitar player sat on his case, rubbing his eyes, yawning. He looked up and yelled.

So what's the plan, Adrian.

Taking five, Adrian said, not turning around. First, sustenance. Should I make enough for you.

161

No, man.

Later, then. Adrian put both hands on the door for a few seconds, standing still, shook his head. Whew. Okay. We're open for business. I'm thinking bangers and whatever. Candy canes.

Adrian's at the refrigerator, and Theo's now behind him, and it's full of leafy things and fruit, and packages with meat. Potatoes, cheese. Colours invading that usually grey-white space like one of the empty rooms.

Where did all this come from.

Father Christmas, Adrian said, bending and squinting with a hand in the back. I talked to Colin about this. No more Wild West.

What do you mean.

Aha. Adrian's pulling out a sealed package of meat. Sausage.

It looks funny. Weird. Like the old men at the Y. Will Theo look like that.

Brilliant. What would you like with them, son.

Um. Nothing.

How about toast.

Okay.

Don, can you see about toast.

Sure.

Don's smoking and he's just twisted open a beer. He's looking around, Adam's apple bobbing as he drinks. The bass player wanders in, sits, smoking. Tear me off a hunk of that beast, eh.

Right. A successful hunt. The village will eat well tonight.

Arista wants me.

When.

L.A. tomorrow.

Fuckers. Blow them off.

Can't. They're paying me better.

I'll top them.

The bass player snorted, inhaled and exhaled cigarette. You're cheaper than Bowie.

Hey now. Them's fightin' words.

Look, man. I don't know what this gig is. I do know what Arista wants. Bird in the hand.

Suit yourself. I won't beg. Sausage.

Yeah, I'll take two.

You're a wanker.

Yeah. Still want two. Car's coming later.

What about you, Theo.

I'll have one.

Don.

I'd be grateful for two.

Let's see if we can get some tea going, eh.

Adrian faced the stove, cigarette smoke twining up above him. Theo looked at his back, scars, and ribs, bruised arms. His dad was thin, like Theo.

You're a quiet one, Don is saying to Theo, draining the beer.

Theo looks at him and at his dad. I guess.

You are not exactly Oscar Wilde yourself, mate. At least in Theo's case it's just him not wasting his pearls on swine, Adrian says. Where's the tea, I'm dying for it.

The bass player is bent at the open refrigerator with his arm in up to the shoulder, pulling out two beers.

Theo, can you make some tea as these animals don't seem to speak English: Theo's dad's drinking from a glass, brown stuff.

Sure: Theo hops up and goes into the pantry, trying to remember where tea might be. He knows Colin and Gus both drink it. He doesn't understand it. He likes Coke. Most afternoons, no matter what, Gus and Colin have tea, and usually some kind of biscuits. Theo eats biscuits with them. Sometimes Colin wakes up just in time to have tea, or appears while Gus is sitting outside under a tree, or in the kitchen, with a cup in front of him. Gus says tea is a chance to stop and catch your breath, like when boxers take a break to get ready for the next round.

Is life always fighting. Right now Theo's wondering if the tea is up near the ceiling, and pulls over the old dark stepladder on wheels and scrambles up, holding on to the pole it has on one side. Colin won't touch the stepladder or use it. He says too many ghosts have had hands on it. It is worn, the wood darker from hands on the pole, some of which Theo thinks must be kid hands because it's worn where he puts his hand.

Shit. Bollocks.

There's crashing and a whoosh from the kitchen, the sound of chairs pushed back and one banging on the stone floor. Cursing. Holding the pole Theo jumps from the ladder, thinking stove and Adrian.

Something's on fire, a towel or – his dad's pants, and the other two are spraying him with beers, him holding his hands out of the way. He's always careful with his hands, even in his sleep, Theo knows. Theo knows one of the minders' jobs is to make sure he doesn't sleep on his arm wrong. Once his dad fell asleep on a plane leaning against the window and hurt his arm because the circulation was cut off. Adrian had to stop working and a lot of doctors visited. Adrian doesn't like to shake hands, and he lets other people open and close doors, and he never touches car doors. Theo's seen his mother yell at Adrian to close a car door and his father ask a stranger to do him a favour and shut the door for him. His mother drove

164

off with the door open and it hit a light pole and another car. His dad yelled a lot then too. That was one of the times when Theo stayed with his dad for a while. Or really with minders in hotels, while his dad worked. That was on a tour in Europe, Theo remembered, after he turned seven. Lucky seven, his dad always used to say. Lucky seven. He would always shake Theo's hand, no matter what.

His dad was saying bad words, and the other two were laughing now in the hazy kitchen. Polyester will go off like a rocket, man. You should wear natural fibres to lower your combustibility.

You could also stay away from open flame. You're a menace to yourself.

Adrian was walking around the kitchen in circles, bumping into things, yelling. Then he veered into the open door to the ballroom and wove toward the glass doors. Gonna go for a swim, wash off. Theo ran after him, past the two men, into the ballroom. The pink-haired lady was smoking a cigarette, the drummer and other guitar player gone, but Theo could hear their voices down a hall, yelling.

Theo ran up beside his dad, who looked down and put an arm around Theo. My friend, let's go for a swim in the beautiful. Then his dad started singing an old song that Theo had heard him sing before, from way back in the olden days. Gonna dust my broom.

What happened, Dad.

Ah. I spilled some oil in the wrong place at the wrong time, which is just the kind of thing fire likes, waits for those little moments, sneaky bastard. We'll finish the job when we get back eh. Just want a little air and to get the smell of melted plastic out of the lungs.

Feathers of black ran down the front of Adrian's pants, which were loose and purple and tied with a string that had burned through, so he had to hold them up with one hand. The legs were bell-bottoms and he kept stumbling over them. Christ. Bloody hell.

His dad stopped and bent and tugged down and kicked out of the pants and left them. He had on underwear, black and shiny like it was wet already, shorts.

I've been practicing the drums. I'm pretty good.

I'll bet you are. Play me something when we get back, will you.

I think my butterflies are hatching. You should come up and see them.

I would like that, mate.

You gave them to me.

I did. Right, I remember. How about that. Glad you like them.

Are you making a record here.

Doing the preliminary work right now. Seeing how it sounds. It's tricky business, and the space has to be really right. It's more important than the musicians.

Are you going to stay for a while.

That's the plan. Are you glad.

Yeah. How long can you stay.

Forever and ever. Never leaving. We're going to have some fun. I need a vacation. I've been working like a slave.

How long is that.

Adrian grinned down, and then looked up at the sun, a white circle on his black sunglasses. Until you get tired of me.

Are all these people going to be here.

Some of them will, yeah.

Will my mother come.

Depends on if she gets better.

166

She's sick.

Yeah. We want her to get better, right.

Yeah. How is she sick.

Oh, she's – you know how if you eat a lot of candy, too many sweets, you get sick and your stomach's upset.

Yeah. She just ate too much.

Well, she just, she's doing too much stuff that's not good for her and we need to help her not do that.

Are drugs like candy.

In the dunes now, they kick through the sand toward the sound of the sea, their feet hot. Adrian's looking ahead, but his hand's back on Theo now. No, mate. They're drugs. You want to steer clear of them. Some people can handle them and some can't, and they can certainly break your back.

We had units on drugs and how bad they are. The teacher said they can kill you. We learned all about them.

Yeah, what is that, fifth form.

Fifth grade.

Grade, right. Yeah, that's true.

I don't want that to happen to mom or you, Dad.

Adrian stops, and slowly kneels down and puts arms around Theo, swaying a little. Don't worry, love. That's never going to happen. I love you too much to let that happen. Okay.

Adrian looks at Theo, but Theo's eyes hurt from the glare of the sunglasses and he turns away. Okay, mate, Adrian asks.

Okay, Theo answers.

Race you, Adrian says, and stumbles running toward the ocean breaking now ahead of them, dotted with people and seagulls like things growing up from the sand, all facing the same way, a crop.

Theo takes off fast as he can, then looks back. His dad gets up off the sand, his chest white with it. Theo turns and runs unsteadily backward, raising his hands over his head. I win, he yells.

Fair deal, you sure did. Tortoise and the hare, you run circles around me right now. I'm a little short on wind, a little off my form. But I'm going to get some rest here, some healthy living and we'll see what's what once I get my blood up.

A big wave crashing, Theo hears behind him.

Did you know that butterflies migrate.

Do they.

Some go all the way from here to Mexico. They're called monarchs, the ones that are orange and black. And it takes so long that no butterfly makes it all the way. They fly and then lay eggs along the way and the new ones hatch out and fly and lay eggs and they keep doing that to follow the weather and the food, back and forth every year. And it's a really long way, like five hundred miles.

More like five thousand. Where'd you find all that out.

I read it in one of the books you gave me.

Isn't that bloody amazing. So here's me trying to migrate to the beach and you might have to carry on for me, make it to the water.

Now Adrian's coughing, clutching at his throat, go on without me. Go lay your eggs. Keep the species going, baby.

Theo laughs, his dad fake swimming in the sand now. Come on, Dad, let's finish the race.

All right matey. Adrian pushes up. On your marks get – Adrian takes off running, and Theo goes too, catching up with his dad and bumping into him, and his dad grabs him and keeps him from passing, oh no you don't, taking advantage of an old man, and Theo fights a little but not too hard and they run together into the first water, the low backwash draining out, the sand getting sticky and thick and they keep running until both stumble and fall into a few inches of water. Theo sputters up, his dad on his side, and Theo is back up and keeps running into the low waves, the ocean flat and glassy, a couple of boats plowing across, one with a skier kicking up roostertails. Theo dives into the face of a wave, he's a fish, opens eyes an instant, blurry, shuts eyes tight, flails, tries to stay on bottom but is pushed up.

Theo sputters for breath, pushes hair out of the way and turns to see where Adrian is. Nowhere. Then he feels something and squeals, feeling fluttery and excited. It's a hand. His dad's tickling him, Adrian's pale body in the water split in the middle by the black of his shorts, two separate white things. Theo's pushing away, kicking and laughing. His father comes up, spluttering, his streaked hair shaggy, amnemone anommne anemone – Theo remembers the waving. Ow, Adrian is saying, his lip is bleeding. You caught me a good one, grinning. Then he lunges at Theo, who squeals again. Sea monster, Theo yells, and dives under, swims, a dolphin, no hands, just legs, but isn't going anywhere. Adrian's hands are grabbing his kicking legs, and Theo flails with his arms, up to air.

Breathing hard, not seeing because of hair, Theo ducks under again, just the cool water and the grinding surf and churning. Inhales water, coughs, stands up, water at his chest, starts spinning, slapping at the water, jumping up and down, waving his arms and kicking, spinning in slow motion because of water, not thinking, hair whipping around but stuck over his eyes, not seeing, moving. Adrian's on him now, pushing him under and laughing; looks like I caught myself a crazy seal. Theo's fighting, his dad's lifting him back out, both sputtering, his dad yelling, blow me down, it's the white whale I've been hunting me whole life, Moby Theo. I thought you'd be bigger.

Theo's laughing, you didn't catch me. And diving backward into a wave, pushed forward sideways toward the beach, heart pounding, and blurry everything, he's wild, hair over his eyes, can't be caught.

Do I have to go back to school: Theo suddenly thought of it, with his dad here.

Adrian squints at Theo – sunglasses, where'd they go, Theo didn't notice when they came off. I suppose you do some time. Can't really avoid that now. You've got to be tamed, you little savage. Adrian lunges again, grabs Theo around the waist and both sink, Adrian trying to tickle. Theo's pushing and coming up for air, out of the water.

I don't want to die.

Hey, I'm the one in danger here, you're a menace. Look at my lip.

I don't want you to die.

I'm not going anywhere, you're going to have to put up with me for a long time.

I don't want my mother to die.

You're mother's strong as a bloody ox, I wouldn't want to be the grim reaper that comes for her. What's bringing all this on here on this lovely and amazing day here on planet earth, the most amazing place I know of. None of this now: Adrian tickles again, Theo squeals and ducks.

Is it school. We'll figure that out, mate, the three of us. Your mother let you stay away for a long time. We'll need to come to a meeting of the minds, you and your mother and I.

She's sick. And you're always gone.

170

Sorry, love. It's tough to hang on for the ride if you're a family in this band.

Adrian reaches out to rub Theo's head. Theo barks, dives and swims away, a dog, a seal. An eel. He wriggles in the cold water, which feels good. He's a diver, he tries to stay in one place but the water moves him. He pushes up.

Adrian stands staring out to sea, watching a boat with a lady skiing behind it on a rope. She's wearing a bikini. Adrian's splashing water up on himself now, on his face.

Well this woke me up all right. I feel invigorated and full of sap now.

Theo's father dives under, while Theo watches waves, looking for one to ride.

When his father's head floats up, slowly, and the head shakes and looks around, Theo yells: Let's ride waves.

Sure, mate.

There's yelling. A group of men and ladies on the beach charging into the water, Colin and the bass player and the sound man and someone's yelling Adrian. A couple behind lug an umbrella and tug on the wagon from the gardener's shed. Somebody's pushing a wheelbarrow with a person in it over the sand, and someone else is pushing a wheelbarrow with a person. Maybe they're racing, but they're hardly moving and one spills sideways.

Colin's holding up a bottle. He's got a cigarette in his mouth, one of the ones he makes himself.

Adrian's staring at them, head barely above the water, and his face is weird. He looks angry. Then he shakes his head, flings water around and stands up. Adrian yells, but not words, his head tilted back. Then he looks at the beach and the people and smiles, looks at Theo, smiles, looks behind him as a tall wave curls. This might be the one, Adrian yells. He begins swimming, more like thrashing, and Theo does also, his head down, trying to get on top of it, holding his arms out straight and feeling it lift him, the feeling when you get it right and he rides over the water pulling at him but not sucking him down and then it bends like it's diving and crashes and he's tipped into the sand on his shoulder and turned over, and he's struggling up and into a crouch and sputtering and stumbling onto his feet and in shallow water and his dad's nowhere and then Adrian's poking up much further in toward the beach, crouching and sputtering and laughing. Good one, eh, Adrian's saying back at Theo and Theo's grinning too.

His dad up now and slogging through the water, toward Colin, and others move their way, and Mingus is there now, digging: he's got a shovel and wood and steel pails; Theo remembers them from the gardener's shed, full of spiders, the shed and the buckets, the shed wet and dry and dark.

Theo's dad drinks from the bottle now, someone brings him sunglasses, and along the water men and ladies wade in or plop in the shallows and let the water wash over their legs. The lady Gina bends with Mingus, they're piling up sand, Mingus using the wood and a ball of twine to measure something or straighten something, and it's hot now that Theo's kicking out of the water. He thinks about turning and jumping back, at a desert and has to cross and there are giants to avoid, and his dad laughing really hard, and the bass player's there now, and they're passing the bottle and a cigarette and starting to walk up the beach, away, Colin with them wearing one of his skirts, it wraps around and has flowers.

On the desert Theo kicks past the men and ladies and there are chairs and towels, and a rug from somewhere, and an umbrella and a cooler and giants, and Theo on a quest has to be invisible, he moves through them and no one notices, telling himself the story *past the guards and at the castle* and Mingus is there guarding it with a lady guard, and they're the enemy but they're secretly good and Theo's moving over the sand, letting his hair hang in his face, kicking up to Mingus and Gina, and they're building a tower that spirals up, it has flat parts that circle up, and it's about knee-high on Mingus and he's really sweating in a cape and one of his helmets and wraparound glasses, and Gina's in someone else's bathing suit, it's too big and Theo doesn't look but he can't help it, and she's bending over to dig.

Hey, how's the water.

It's good. What are you making.

Mingus looks up: Stick around and find out.

It doesn't look like anything.

Not yet. We're going to make a fountain.

A fountain.

Yeah, you can help.

How are you going to make a fountain.

Well, stop asking so many questions and help.

It's too hot.

Suit yourself. You can cool off in it later then.

Theo wonders what he should do. His dad is here, but. Is the house empty. A lot of people are here. Where is the Seal. Is he in the house. Does he have clothes on. Theo walks on the desert, the sand scalding his feet, squeaking so dry. Air watery when he looks to where the land disappears. Both directions.

Theo is a spy. No one knows who he really is. Two people squeeze something from an eyedropper onto their tongues, a man and a lady, tilting their heads back, tongues out like dogs, eyes closed. Another man plops beside them. Theo hears something about Adrian, see if he wants in on this. They laugh.

Theo runs, down to his dad, thinking about kicking a soccer ball. Maybe his dad will play football. Adrian holds the bottle by the neck, at his side, and lifts it between his fingers like a cigarette, spills some on his face. The label is black.

Theo's standing there and looking up, kicking sand on his father's leg. Adrian notices eventually: Hey, mate.

Can we play soccer.

You mean football.

Yeah, football.

Right now.

Yeah – I'll get a ball.

I'm trying to figure out some work things here, love. Maybe in a bit. Adrian puts his hand on Theo's head, fingers still warm even under the sun, warm enough to be warmer, his father's palm like a hat.

You're making me hot, Theo says, and spins out from under it and runs into a lady who bends in the middle and backs away, hey, easy, you might make me miscarry, and Adrian and the other man both cough out laughs. Theo keeps running, being chased, has to get away or he'll get caught and then the rescue will be ruined, *have to get the golden owl from the dungeon* and he's dodging and running, away, and he wonders if those two boys are somewhere, maybe.

He remembers a tyre swing, he doesn't know where it was, a big tyre on a long chain under a giant tree, with plastic around the chain so you could swing and hold on to it, and swinging back and forth, the wind, and looking up through the branches where the sun broke in and right into your eyes and you had to close them and just swing, feeling weird and dizzy and warm, no earth down there, just air and swinging and then a voice, and he remembered where it was, at the house in Jamaica and it was Ada the housekeeper saying, Theo, your father says to come inside now, it's time to go. Go where, Theo said, eyes closed. Ada laughed: Time to go home, boy.

This is home.

Child, you going to New York and you got to get on a plane to do that, and planes don't wait. So come on now.

I'll do it if my dad tells me.

Theo, your dad cannot come right now. He loves you and wants you to be happy, but he cannot come right now. You need to get down and get ready to leave.

Theo opened his eyes, the tree like an umbrella keeping the sky off, and at the tree's edges was everything. The house was blinding white, the shutters blue, a red roof made of tiles. Flowers big as plates, red and white and yellow, and a lady inside with his dad. The air smelled like salt and something sweet. Last night the house was singing, men with really long hair they called locks – dread was what the Europeans called them, dreadful-looking locks, so the men called them locks but dreads sometimes and his dad and a man with a tape recorder, and one lady singing. Theo went to sleep hearing them, the singing like when you don't quite run and you don't quite walk, like a dance. The house cats trotted with tails in the air, only their legs moving, like bumper cars with the rods at the back that ran to the ceiling and sparked, and the birds sounded wild and angry, and crickets and tree frogs. Outside the gate, from up at the road, came high horns of motorbikes and jitneys.

Ada, will you be here when we come back.

I don't know, Theo. Maybe.

Theo swung, not pulling or pushing the chain anymore, just hanging on, swinging lower and lower, slower. She stood with arms on her hips, and he looked at her, back and forth.

You want some fritters before you go.

Theo loved conch fritters, loved tearing at them with his teeth. Even his dad told him to cool it. The clean strong taste and the rubbery toughness. He thought about animals, and eating them. Sometimes it bothered him. His mother was a vegetarian for a while, and in the hotel they only had vegetables and fruit. Then one rainy Sunday his mom finally came out of her room and called room service and asked for a steak, and said, I need blood. Yes ma'am, Theo heard from the phone, him holding on to her leg.

Ada stood until the swing slowed and became completely still. Theo hung for a minute, not moving, and then hopped down. Okay, he said, giving up.

Theo now kicks sand on the beach, thumping among people, pounding the sand with his feet, stomping. He's flattening; he stomps over toward Mingus and Gina, and others now there, digging and piling sand.

It looks like a cake, Theo says.

Mingus wrestles with wood planks he's brought in the wagon, along with some stepladders, stuff from one of the rooms full of junk, Theo figures. Mingus is sweating and drinking from a big glass bottle – Olde English 800. Mingus says it clears out the poisons, drinking that. Mingus drinks a lot of them. Sometimes he brings bottles in a suitcase, along with the arrows.

Gina's burying one of the other adults in the sand so only his head and shoulders stick out of the cake.

Mingus laughs, gleaming. Everyone's gleaming, or dull with sand. Theo's feeling dizzy. His stomach hurts.

Mingus and two men are setting up stepladders to hold planks flat, four that stick out like helicopter blades. Two ladies sit on the first two planks, and two men are struggling up onto the other two.

There's a trench around the cake with pail-shaped mounds of sand at its edge. Mingus and Gina are giving out straws and bottles of beer and Olde English. One man has one of the black bottles his father likes.

Some strangers not from the house now stand watching, old people in big hats and shirts and shorts, but not too close.

Make a wish, Mingus says to them, smiling big. It's a fountain.

Mingus stands in front of it and lifts his arm like an orchestra conductor, and moves his arms, and the people suck liquid into their straws and spit it back out, up in the air, on each other, on Mingus. One lady squirts toward the people watching; it's not close but they still move backward.

You people are at the wrong beach, one man says.

Baby, you are so right.

Mingus takes a big swig from his bottle and walks toward them, holding his cape out with his free hand. They stumble backward but not fast enough. He sprays Olde English, them swatting at the air as if it were insects, and he drinks quickly and sprays again as they stumble and back away. The fountain whoops and yells, some spray from their planks toward the old people.

Alcohol's illegal here. We'll be back with police.

Mingus waves his bottle around, points down the beach at tents and chairs. Yeah, nobody drinks on the beach here, they serve cocktails. Mingus points the bottle at one of the ladies.

Come on back when he gets in his coffin for his nap, baby. Mingus winks. I bet you looked good when you were alive.

Adrian's here now, grinning. You're the reason I pay a fortune for this place.

Mingus turns, spits at the sand. He grins, then guzzles and spits at Adrian, who ducks: Bloody idiot, and runs at Mingus and staggers him, both are grinning, Adrian shorter and skinny getting pushed around by Mingus, Adrian in his underwear and Mingus under his cape. The bottle hits the sand and spills, a spreading brown.

Adrian, huffing, stumbles over to one of the fountain people, takes the black bottle. He has something in his hand that he swallows, then he takes a big pull at the bottle. Then he seems to notice Theo.

Hello, mate, what do you think of the fountain. We can cool off in this.

Adrian walks closer and everyone sprays him, and he shakes like a dog. Come on in, he grins. Theo moves over, into the sticky warm spray. He's next to his dad, who's got his mouth open, like catching snowflakes. Theo closes his eyes, and he's hot and his stomach feels like something sharp's poked into it.

Dad, I don't feel good.

Well. You don't feel well. Good is an adjective and well is an adverb. Let's do something about that, eh. What have you eaten. You look a little shaky.

You were going to make me something and you forgot.

Sorry, love. I'm falling down on the job. You need a better dad, or at least a better cook. Let's get Leslie in on this, come on.

Theo ducks away from the people still spraying, which is weird. It's spit. His dad's wet and greasy-looking. Theo notices he needs to shave and he looks tired and patchy. His dad motions at one of the other adults, a man with a cigarette and shades and a mohawk, who slowly gets up from the sand and tilts his head. Theo thinks a mohawk would be cool but his mother keeps saying no.

Dad, can I get my hair cut like that.

Sure, mate.

Where's Shelley. Theo remembers the presents. He wants his dad to kick a ball. Maybe if Theo played music more and got good at it his dad would listen to him more.

Theo's dad's grinning and slapping hands with the man with the mohawk, talking low, ducking heads together. The fountain people are all spraying the man who's buried up to his chest, and he's gleaming now and the sand's chocolate-brown, and Mingus sits cross-legged talking to one of the ladies, he's touching her hand, reaching over to do it. Theo hears the words miracle and interval. The lady is nodding. She's pretty. Theo feels funny.

Colin runs over wet, and he's got a hunting knife stuck in the waist of the thing he's wearing, and his eye-shadow is smeared down his face so he looks like a zombie or some of the people who come to the house sometimes who've just played a show, they wear make-up around their eyes and –

Where's Shelley: Theo asks Adrian.

I hope you like her. I do. She had to go to work.

What work.

She's a model. It's sort of like acting, at least if all your character ever has to do is make faces. Anything beyond that gets dicey for most of them. Shelley's not like that, though.

Let's do it, Colin is saying, and the mohawk man is smiling.

Dallas is in town, he's falling by later, Adrian says.

Outstanding, things are slowing to a crawl otherwise.

Adrian looks at Theo funny, and says, I gotta make sure Theo's taken care of. I'm on me own here.

We can get somebody, Colin says.

Later, maybe: come on, son, Adrian says, let's go eat.

Theo thinks, why do they talk so much. Why did Adrian say he was on his own if Colin's right here. Why can't they leave his dad alone: someone's always pulling at him, wanting his attention or asking for something. And –

Come on, chop chop, my friend. I'm famished, let's get those bangers, maybe Gus'll join us. This walk is killing me. I feel like Lawrence in the desert.

Who's Lawrence.

He was an Englishman who made a career in Arabia, marching across the burning sands dressed in curtains to ensure that Europe could have all the gasoline it needed. Let's take a rest here.

Adrian sinks into crossed legs next to a cooler dropped away from everyone up the beach, opens it and clanks around in sweaty bottles, grabs something, a beer, rummages until he finds a bottle of Coke, a small bag full of powder, a sandwich, which he hands to Theo: Allah be praised, it's a miracle.

Then Adrian coughs and coughs and keeps coughing until he's gradually bending over the sand and Theo sees Frieda's face.

Are you sick.

No, it's just the cigarettes. I should cut back, shouldn't I. Maybe you can help me.

Okay, sure. What do you want me to do.

When you see me getting ready to light one up, just say, memento mori.

What's minto moray.

Memento mori.

What's that mean.

It's Latin. It refers to the grinning skull always breathing down your neck.

What's that mean.

Adrian laughs, coughs a minute. It means, my friend – Adrian pushes his sunglasses up his face, and Theo notices he's still holding the small bag full of powder, which is kind of brownish white. It means, don't smoke. Adrian laughs again. So, right, you see me lighting up one of those death sticks, just say memento mori, Dad.

Adrian's still in his black underwear, his legs thin like Theo's; piano legs Frieda called them.

Eat up, eat up, we've got to keep you fed, you're growing like a weed. Adrian stands up on his spindly legs and moves back toward the water, tips the beer up. Budweiser. Adrian doesn't like American beer but does like Budweiser. It's tastelessness is distinctive, he says, like fugu or tofu. He calls it the pick of the litter.

I thought you were hungry, Theo says.

I don't like to get filled up, have a pile of heavy food sit like a rock in your digestive system for hours. I like to eat but not a lot at a time, I think it's healthier; it passes through you faster, doesn't stay in one place too long. We'll get something later. Where's Gus, do you have any idea. He should be looking after you.

Theo's chewing the sandwich, which is warm and just a slice of bright cheese on the white bread, no mayonnaise or mustard or anything. It gums up in his mouth. The Coke needs an opener, but there's not one in the cooler.

Adrian, away, walks a little faster, bent over now holding something up to his face: the little bag, Theo remembers.

Theo bends over the cooler, full of beers and bags, but no ice. Everything's warm. Little bags, and some have pills, red and green ones. Theo sees carved boxes; he's seen these before, from North Africa, when they went to Morocco. Theo picks up a small box and opens it on pills that look like aspirin.

Theo closes up the cooler, stands. Adrian now sits in a circle of people under an umbrella, pink and white stripes, the edge rippling and whipping. The wind is stronger, and gulls stand on the sand, flock around the people, some of whom throw things at them or to them, hard to tell which. People walk on the beach and Theo sees a jeep coming, the same one as earlier with the two police officers. One of the men in the circle under the umbrella stands. It's one of the minders, Lev, he's stepping over people and walking fast but casually toward the jeep, heading it off. He's walking in front of it, so the jeep slows and turns; it has big eyes that stare at Theo, unblinking. A uniformed man gets out from behind each flapped door, and Lev smiles and holds out a hand.

Theo turns and runs back toward the house, over the desert, sharpness in his stomach now. He's been around a lot of police at different times. Theo's read about jail and seen movies and TV shows – one of his classmates waved around a magazine article about his dad. The article said a lot about drugs. Let's bet, the kid said, and other kids started in on Theo, or on his dad, rather, saying, I'll bet he's goes to jail this year. Then: Let's bet on when someone will like you. Nobody likes you. Why doesn't anybody like you. Something's wrong with you. You're like a girl. One kid's father ran a bank, one took pictures of models. I want you to have a normal life, his mother said, go to a public school.

Theo grabbed the magazine and ran back into school from

182

the hot black playground, past the monitor lady always looking the wrong way and never seeing anything that happened. The teacher would be in the classroom at her desk, she never came out for recess, and Theo streaked to the janitor's closet, where kids only temporarily hid things because the janitor drank alcohol in there and he wouldn't tell but the thing would just be gone or thrown away, and Theo decided not to hide it there, and he started walking fast, in and out of other kids lining up in the hall and teachers counting and he walked close to the sign-in desk at the front door and kind of ducked to go past and pushed on the big bar of the front door and went down the steps and to one of the big prickly bushes next to the sidewalk blooming with empty cans and bottles and greasy napkins and platanos bags jammed in, and pushed the magazine into the bush, more weird fruit it produced, and then turned around and went back up the steps and kind of ducked again and ran this time down the hall, a couple of teachers saying no running, and Theo passed his class where the teacher was eating and reading, carefully not looking up, you could scream and yell or bang and she still wouldn't look up during recess, and he went back out past the monitor lady and ran toward the monkey bars and found a spot where there weren't any kids and pulled himself up and climbed until he sat at the top, next to another kid he didn't know, from a different class, and the two of them sat up there not talking, on top of the tower, looking out over the chasing and playing and huddles of kids, the swirl and churning, waiting till someone made them come down, back to the planet earth.

Walking back toward the house under the beach sun, Theo broils impatiently. He's not a kid, and a lot of things he didn't notice before he notices now. Or maybe he did notice, he thinks, as he remembers when he was eight and seven and six. He thinks maybe it's just he knows more now, he knows what to call things, and before, when he didn't, he saw and noticed but didn't know what things were. He knows about drugs, and that adults do dumb things that even they know don't make sense. That's one thing he didn't see before. Theo wonders if he'll do weird things that don't make sense too when he's a grown-up. He wonders if he'll hurt things or people. He tells himself no, but thinks of times he's maybe done it already. He's Lawrence now, at the edge of the desert, and he's climbing to a dune's top, pulling at the sea oats and trying not to pull them out but he does and feels bad, he doesn't like killing things, even plants. It seems unfair that some random creature can come along and pull a thing up or kill it, he doesn't like that now that he is old enough to think about it. He likes meat, however. So he stops thinking about it.

Theo on the dune, wind pushing his hair from his eyes. Theo's arm is shiny, jewelled armour – he lifts and looks and can see flecks of light, the salt that he knows from class is a crystal, which means it has a shape – he thinks he can see it, maybe, but can't remember what it's called. He's a lizard with a crystal skin, he lies on the sand, on his stomach, rubbing against the sand, wriggling. It feels good and he closes his eyes, watching enemies lazy and vulnerable and not knowing they are being watched. The ladies sit and the men flit around them, bring them things, touch them, push them over, and the ladies just laugh. Sometimes one gets up and walks toward the water. A couple of the ladies are standing up with men. The men lie on the sand alone, or squat; a couple are throwing something, a bottle, back and forth like a football but they keep dropping it or missing it, throwing badly. Mingus's fountain is just a weird pile of sand, everyone gone from it. They probably didn't want to waste the alcohol, Theo thinks. Theo can't see his dad – where is he.

Theo lifts his head, scans: Adrian's lying on his stomach and a lady is smearing something on his back. Adrian's still wearing his underwear. Theo wonders if Adrian remembers. Adrian flips over and the lady's rubbing his stomach. No, Theo decides. Theo rolls over and down the dune, rolling over sea oats stiff and dry, cracking. They keep the dunes from blowing away, Theo knows. His dune's not that big and he has to push himself to keep rolling. At the bottom he stops on his back, squinting up at gulls fighting over something that looks like a sandwich, chasing the one with the white square in its beak. Maybe it was his sandwich. Theo can't remember if he finished it.

All is dry on the beach, and then there is all that water, a country of water. The people that live there are fish. Sharks are out there, and dolphins and whales. What else. Submarines and octopuses. Treasure somewhere. Theo is tired of being alone. Shipwrecked.

Theo slips through the sand behind the dunes now, the sound muffled. Now there are birds and wind in the stiff branches of the trees at the back lawn's edge, the trees old creatures ready to fight if they have to. Theo's army – *wait, I'll go and check, this house looks deserted.*

There's no one outside that Theo can see. He moves quietly, wanting to get inside the castle without the guards knowing. He moves along from chair to chair, toward the gazebo, which he runs up into, keeping an eye out for the Seal, and through and down the other side. Better to go in back or front. Back maybe; but they'll be expecting that, it could be a trap, the glass doors are open and it's dark inside. He'll go to the front side. He slips carefully around the house's right side and flattens himself against the wall, inside the row of bristly green bushes, and moves to the grey corner and takes a quick look around: the front doors are open, folded inward, maybe another trap, the mouth. His mother's car left with her. He has to be careful. Theo slips away from the bushes, where there are always sharp things and spiderwebs, which Theo hates. He likes spiders but hates the webs.

The best strategy is to run fast up and roll, so he streaks up and in, the stones cold on his feet slapping, and he hits the black and white tiles and rolls to the side and knocks into the pieces of Colin's big chessmen and makes a lot of noise, hitting a metal trashcan that had been a bishop's head.

Theo hears hooves clopping.

A man on a horse emerges down the hall, the horse brown and the man with long hair and a suit with a big flower on the flap of the jacket. He is holding a black bottle and has yellow gloves on. Theo notices the man's feet in the stirrups are in sneakers. The man's head is near the black ceiling.

Is this Adrian's house.

Yes. Who are you.

I'm a friend of his. You look like him – are you his son.

Yes.

Nice to meet you. My name's Barry. I'm in the house up the road a couple of clicks. I heard he was camped here too. Where is he.

He's on the beach.

Which way is that.

It's around the back of the house, where the ocean is.

Ha. Right about that. What's the best way to get there.

Follow the hall to the kitchen and then go through the ballroom to the back lawn.

Right then. Thanks, be seeing you. Hey, you want to ride out with me.

The man smiles and looks kind of familiar. Theo figures, famous too. He doesn't know where he would sit. Theo notices his big watch.

What time is it.

The man lifts his wrist: two-thirteen p.m. Eastern Daylight Time.

Um. I have to find my grandfather.

Fair enough. Ah domanee, then.

What.

A domani. It's Italian, it means may the force be with you.

Okay.

Theo had gone to this big deal New York premiere of Star Wars with his mother and some of her friends. They left before it was over to go to a party in a tall building next to Central Park, and then another party in a warehouse somewhere. Theo slept in the car with a minder and woke up in a different hotel than the one they were living in. His dad was maybe on tour.

Theo hopes the horse doesn't poop in the house. The dogs do sometimes and Colin doesn't notice. Gus sometimes does. Theo tries to clean it up. When do people learn to do it in bathrooms. Theo tried to remember: what was it like. How do you teach that.

Theo'd learned to watch carefully where he walked, the outside was mined with it. Ladies would notice and say something, and sometimes Colin became agitated and did crazy cleaning with buckets of water and soap, just throwing it at stains and bad places and swirling mops and towels over floors or walls.

Once in a while Theo came on Gus with sleeves rolled up and scrubbing at something that bothered him. He liked things shipshape, he said: But my back won't let me do a lot of washing up.

So it's a good thing the house is dark, Theo thinks now. He hopes the horse hasn't.

But it has. In the room with the Christmas tree and all the presents. Even from across the room the air's thick with it, a kind of green-brown odour, not like dog; or people. It's a pile of black apples beside the presents. Theo wonders if the man did it on purpose. Sometimes his father's friends do weird things and call them jokes.

Theo remembered when he and his father were checking into a hotel and upstairs, walking down the hall to the room, they heard muffled screeches that got louder. His dad was walking very slowly, behind Theo and the minder, carrying his doctor's bag, and his guitars and the luggage were in the elevator with a hotel guy and another minder, and Theo and Tony the minder reached the door and that was where the screeches and squawks were coming from. Tony frowned as he put the key in the door and put a hand on Theo's shoulder and gently moved him back so he couldn't see as Tony slowly swung the door open. Theo followed him in anyway.

Birds blurred through the air, shrieking and chirping, perched on lamps and curtains and fluttering and fighting for high places to sit. Theo and Tony just stood for a few seconds looking around: a million of them, blurs.

Adrian reached the room and frowned, then grinned. Then the phone started ringing and Tony picked it up and answered, and then he handed it to Adrian, who listened and burst out cursing and laughing, talked, hung up.

Jimmy and Calvin. They paid the concierge five hundred to let them in and the birds cost them a thousand. Said I'm not worth it. Certainly correct on that. I like this, let's leave 'em in here.

So Adrian went to meet Jimmy and Calvin for a drink and Theo and the minder ordered room service and ate in the bedroom watching television while birds flew in and out and screeched and chattered. The TV had to be loud. The phone rang once and the minder answered and said into it: Adrian wants the birds to stay.

Other people are complaining about the noise, the minder said after hanging up.

Will we get in trouble.

The minder laughed and ruffled Theo's hair. Why did adults always do that. They did the same thing to dogs and dogs didn't like it either. No, the hotel will keep everyone happy – we'll just have to pay more money. That's the way the world works, my friend. The universal solvent is money, and there's nothing you can throw it at that it can't at least slow down enough to let people get out of the way, or just plain escape.

The minder took a long drink from the tall glass of alcohol he was drinking and put it down, then stretched out on the huge shiny grey bed, on the other side of which Theo sat cross-legged, with a big black plate of French fries in front of him. He could see his face in it before ketchup. The minder still had his shoes on but fiddled for a minute and kicked them off onto the floor, startling a couple of small yellow birds. Maybe canaries.

His dad came back the next night while Theo and the minder were having a pizza and watching television. The birds were pooping everywhere, and Theo draped a towel over his head while he sat or walked around. He kept thinking about the birds, about what would happen to them. Maybe they could just be released somewhere. Theo knew some were not from America – would they be okay.

Dad, can we catch the birds and let them go outside, maybe in the park.

Adrian lay on the floor, eyes closed, a dark acoustic in his hands, grey chalky drops all over it, trying to find the chords for the way things are, he said. Well, Adrian said, I suppose we have to do something, and that seems like a natural solution, doesn't it. I'll get Ira to come and clean up.

Ira was Adrian's manager, his personal manager. The band had managers but they were different. Everyone in the band had his own manager: the managers talked to each other when the band members didn't want to talk to each other. That had happened a few times that Theo knew of, because it meant Adrian snapped and snarled at everybody, even Theo. He got more upset than when he and Theo's mom had arguments. Nothing bothered him like the band. Or sometimes if he was working on a song he got really angry, throwing things and yelling: once Adrian yanked out a fistful of his hair and didn't even notice. Theo saw bleeding scalp.

Why do you get so mad, Theo asked once in Jamaica when his dad threw a bottle of alcohol across the sunny living room, and his mom screamed at his dad; she was nervous and jumpy that day, for a couple of days, and everything seemed to make her mad. Both of them spent a lot of time being angry on that trip, like a kind of hobby, something they chose to do, and other times, and it was hard to tell why they liked each other. The house in Jamaica had white walls and paintings on the walls, and wood everywhere, wood furniture and tables, and a lot of plants, and a saddle on a sawhorse. One room in the house also had guns; lots of guns, pistols, on the wall, all kinds, old ones and new ones; his dad collected them. The room had a special lock that had numbers you had to know, a combination lock. Theo's father would open the room and take Theo in and show him guns, just taking them off the wall and saying, isn't this a pretty one, and telling the history and facts about the guns from Germany and Czechoslovakia and Russia and England. There were empty places on the wall where guns used to be: Where is that one, Theo would ask. Closer to home, Adrian would say, I have to go places where the people aren't very nice.

Why do you have to go places like that.

I just do. No worries, though. I take care of myself so I can be sure and take care of you, okay.

Why would his dad have to go to bad places. Was he doing something bad. Could Theo help. Should he try to stop it, like with cigarettes. When do you stop trying to help people who need it.

Adrian got up from the hotel floor, leaving the guitar and his alcohol, and wandered around the room for a minute, staring up at the birds and brushing things off of tables with his arm; drink glasses, dishes, books, clothes, pizza boxes. Then he walked through the suite to the front door and kicked it open all the way and walked back through the suite, clapping his hands and saying, let's go, let's go. He entered the bedroom and picked up room-service dish covers and began banging them like cymbals: Theo jumped.

Dad, what are you doing.

Solving the problem.

Birds scattered and screeched and flew and bumped into things and found the door.

What will happen to them.

They're free, that's what'll happen to them.

Adrian stared at Theo, his eyes on Theo but not really, Theo knew – he was thinking about something else.

They'll be okay. And we'll remember them, they'll bloody live forever. We'll burn bloody candles for them. Maybe heaven is just God remembering. Heaven: Adrian snorted, weaving a little.

Ease up, Tony said, lying on a couch with his boots on, reading a magazine.

Fuck you, Tony, don't ever tell me what to do. Adrian pulled out a knife handle and flicked it open. He always carried a knife. He stood swaying beside the sofa staring at Tony, who stared up at Adrian.

Suit yourself. His eyes flicked back to his magazine.

Adrian in a weird looping blur that surprised Theo swept out his knife hand and caught the magazine and spun it flapping like a bird across the room. Tony rolled off the couch and knocked Adrian's feet out from under him and Adrian fell forward still holding the knife, which stabbed into the carpet. Tony had pinned Adrian on his stomach, Adrian's head mashed up against the bottom of the sofa, which was covered with flowers, pictures of roses on the fabric.

Let's take it easy now, just slow it down: Tony was talking, his arms pinning Adrian's. Theo was able to speak again – but he didn't know who to talk to. The word that came out was: Dad.

Get off me you goddamn eunuch. You're fired.

You're not going to do anything else –

Yeah, yeah, just get off.

Dad. Dad. What happened.

Red on the carpet red hand prints.

Cut myself, thanks to James Bond. I should sue you. Maybe Lloyd's will sue you.

Sorry, Tony said, and in a quick motion was back on his feet and between Theo and Adrian, his big back there. Theo started toward Adrian but Tony stuck out an arm.

Give him a minute, son. Hang on.

Adrian glared up, staring at his right hand, bloody, poking at it with his left hand.

I've had worse. Adrian struggled getting to his feet, and Theo ducked and ran the couple of steps and put his arms around Adrian to lift.

Thanks, mate. I'm sorry for the mess.

Once he was on his feet, Theo felt his dad lean down and kiss the top of his head, and then Adrian was walking through the outside door and gone, followed by another bird.

Christ. Tony looked at his watch: Theo, lock the door and don't open it. If you get room service, just tell them to leave it outside and look through the peephole before you open the door – use a chair to stand on. I'll be back.

Tony was in the doorway saying this, a hand on the door frame, looking down the hall, then gone, closing the door.

Tony came back when it was dark.

Where's my dad.

He's okay.

But where is he.

He went to visit some friends. Mark's with him now.

Aren't you fired, Theo asked.

Tony smiled: He didn't mean it. He bought me a drink. He's okay. Tony kicked off his cowboy boots and flopped onto the couch. Did anyone come by.

Some people knocked but I didn't know who they were.

You didn't open the door.

No.

Good man.

Theo didn't see his dad again on that trip. Tony took Theo in the car back to his mother's hotel in Chelsea and handed him over on a bright afternoon. Frieda was sleepy, Theo remembered.

Now in the Christmas present room, gloomy even in the daytime, Theo wonders if a grown-up will notice the horse stuff and clean it up, or if he will have to. Heat makes the smell heavier, you can almost see it. Theo looks at the presents and thinks they look like something laid in a pile by a big animal. Theo hums a song, one he heard on his radio, don't you want me, baby, don't you want me. He remembers the band is called Human League.

His dad hates that kind of music because of the synthesizers, and for other reasons, too, but Theo stopped listening to why he didn't like it. Theo likes the song.

Theo keeps humming and rips into shiny paper but gets hung up on ribbon, and starts hitting the gift on the floor. Then he stops. Theo fingers off the ribbon and finishes: whatever it was, is in pieces of glass and glitter.

Theo picks up another one, long and slender, flat, not square, in paisley paper – he knows paisley from India. Very light. No sound – he rips in and opens, and it's a feather, two feathers, nestled in tissue, white with gold glitter and gold veins, the feathers long, black and blue and green, with eyes at the end. A peacock; he knows peacocks. What kind of a present is that. Theo tips up the box, black in the black of the room. He sees nothing, but an envelope slips out, heavy as the feather, cream-coloured with gold ink, curly handwriting that says Theo.

Theo tears into the envelope and unfolds a note: 'Theo – we know you like birds so, when you're ready, we've got a peahen and a peacock for you. They make good guard animals, and when you need to wake your dad up, they are loud enough to do the job! Love and kisses from your friends Gram and Vida.' And then below the printing is ink that's maybe initials, and a heart.

Theo doesn't know who Gram and Vida are. But peacocks are cool. What do you feed them. Where would they sleep. If they build nests, how do they get their tails into the nest. What do their babies look like.

Theo drops the feathers and looks at the other presents, the tree glittering alive in the dark, and he wonders how grown-ups think. He starts to hum again, and stands up and wades into the presents like water, moving them around with his legs, and then he falls onto his back like he's been shot – ow, box corners hurt – dumb. Theo thinks about other kids, remembers Morocco and India and the kids there, asking for money on the street. He remembers seeing them from cars, playing soccer with a rolled-up ball of cloth that had string or rope around it; it had sleeves hanging off like a little round person getting kicked around. They yelled and smiled. He wonders if Gram and Vida are a man and woman. Do they have kids. Theo wants to talk to somebody.

Theo's up and humming, out of the dark room and winding his way through the secret passage toward the wizard. He must defeat the snake-dragon, and he's got to find the golden knife with the poison blade. Only he can find it. He's in the kitchen and there's the lady, the food lady in an apron, with pink, and she's tall. The kitchen smells funny. Theo realizes it's cooking – shiny steel pots cover the stove.

She notices him and smiles: Hello.

Hello, Theo says. Is this your job.

Yes. I am a chef.

I thought chefs were men.

No – chefs are women, too. I go to people's houses and cook for them.

What are you making.

A meal for everyone.

Is it lunch.

It's just a meal – I give people different options so whatever they feel like eating, whether it's something light or something more filling, they have a choice. I make things that are good any time.

Okay. Can I ask you a question.

Sure, honey. She was stirring, moving from pot to pot.

Theo doesn't know her and doesn't think his father knows her, so it isn't like she's a friend. He cannot remember the last time he was somewhere where there were more kids than adults. He wonders if people from other countries feel this way when they're in America. Except he does speak the language at least.

Can alcohol make you sick or die. Not like just being drunk. I know about that.

The lady turns to look at him holding a big spoon. It's shiny and has a yellow handle. It's new-looking.

I have a son who's about your age. Are you ten.

Yeah.

She turns back around to the pots, pushing the back of her hand against her forehead to move some pink hair out of the way.

Why do you ask. Are you worried that you're drinking too much.

She's not looking at him but Theo knows she's making a joke. No. I just wanted to know. Why do people drink alcohol.

Can you help me here for a minute.

Okay.

Can you go over to that warmer on the table and lift out the pot with the orange tag on top and bring it over here.

Theo scuffed over, tugged out the pot with the orange tag – others were green and blue and two were purple – and walked it over to the lady: What's the purple for.

Eggplant. Thanks.

Theo stood beside her, looking. She didn't have polish on her nails and no jewellery. He thought if he only saw her hands he would think she wasn't a lady; her hands looked like his dad's, with veins and bones and thick fingers. Can fingers have muscles.

Why do people drink alcohol. It tastes terrible. It's worse than coffee. Can't they be relaxed without that. Is that why they take drugs, to be relaxed.

Theo watches her hands, like they're separate from her, they're like birds on strings. One flies past to pick something up and then it's over a pot doing something. The other's fluttering in the background.

The lady's reaching into her apron, which is folded up, and she has a towel over her shoulder and one folded over the edge of her apron: I would say so. Some people who take drugs are unhappy about something. Some people just like the way the drugs make them feel.

How do they make you feel.

Hmm. Like you're not yourself anymore.

What are you when you're not yourself.

Good question: she smiled. You're like a little Zen monk.

What does that mean.

She made a soft face at him: It just means you're asking questions people have thought about for a long time.

What's your son's name.

Marco.

What's your name.

She smiles at the pot. Leslie.

Theo thinks about outside, sees the green-brown lawn rolling toward the grey trees and the white dunes and the blue-green ocean.

Maybe your son could come over and play sometime.

She looks at Theo for an instant and turns back to her stuff. That's very nice. Maybe he could. What kind of things do you like to do.

Theo's scratching the middle of his back, flicks his hair out of his eyes, remembers Gus, he wants to find Gus.

I'm good at soccer, and I'm growing butterflies up in my room.

Oh really. How do you grow butterflies, what do you plant them in.

Theo knows she's joking. Grown-ups are so corny. My dad gave me chrysalises. He got them in England and mailed them to me. They're in my room and you could see them if you want.

Maybe when I finish my work we could go look at them.

Have you seen my grandfather.

Which one is he.

The lady is looking at her watch, big under her right wrist; the dial is black.

Theo thinks of ninjas or spies. His dad has sent him comic books from Japan that have ninjas. If there were ninjas in the house. Or if he were a ninja.

Bye.

Theo runs off, and as he runs he kicks and punches, stopping sometimes to flip hair from his eyes. He moves into the gloom, the house dark at its centre even on the brightest day, just a place light can't reach. Theo likes that sometimes but not today – he punches and kicks his way through it, connecting with shadows that run away. They'll still be waiting for him, he knows, he has to stay alert. They're after him and he's got to get to Gus. Save the prisoner. Move toward the light.

Theo thinks maybe Gus's back in his room, with his TV. Frieda always says the same TV things, which Theo repeats to her as she's saying them, and sometimes she smiles at this and sometimes she doesn't. Television is a desert where the brain goes to die, or something like that. Theo can see her standing in a hotel door she's just come in through, arms crossed, smoke ribboning up from the cigarette at her elbow, as Theo and a minder watched something called Joanie Loves Chachi, which Theo thought was stupid but couldn't stop looking at, and Theo said, I asked him to, it's not his fault.

Who's the adult here. My god, I'm sounding like a PTA mother. She waved her hands and swept through – she was wearing a jacket with fringe on it and a cowboy hat – and back out and down the hall to her room. Was that in New York. Theo couldn't remember. Hotels are hard to tell apart.

The heat hits him a couple of feet before the glass doors and then he's out in it, sun full on the terrace, so he steers toward the tables with metal umbrellas, and the glider under the awning, where he can sit and not sit, keep moving, sliding back and forth, kicking his feet. No adults around. Where's Gus.

Theo hears sex noise from one of the windows. He knows one of the voices but he can't hear the words. There's moaning. Men and women both do it. His face gets hot and he knows where Gus is. He doesn't know where to go. Maybe the trees, where there's shade and no one will find him. No one looks that hard anyway, the grown-ups always get distracted, even when they play hide and seek with him, they give up and laugh and he can hear the ice in their drinks.

Theo's now running, just running, in a wide arc, a plane sailing toward the trees and then in, circling. Where can he land. Nowhere. He'll have to crash, so he prepares for impact. Runs in, catching his crotch on fingers of bush and tree, the sand under his feet prickly – sharp things in the softness.

Hair in his eyes, panting, no people. He hears faint music from the beach – a radio or tape. Something loud is happening, voices yelling, laughing, yelling. Theo finds a sightline back to the house, the lawn empty except for overturned furniture and the scattered remnants of other days, and in the woods, the remnants of a fence.

Theo hears voices, now a little louder. And people are streaming out of the dunes onto the lawn, stumbling and pushing, a wide ragged line of them spreading across the lawn and then narrowing again to go through the glass doors. No Mingus. And Adrian and Colin last, pushing at each other and bumping into each other, Colin with one of the beach umbrellas folded under his arm. The gauntlet has fucking well been tossed, Theo hears.

Adrian and Colin go to the gardener's shed as Theo stands watching, and then they both come out pushing bicycles, two ladies' bicycles that are the only ones not too rusted to ride. Adrian's carrying a beach umbrella now under his skinny arm. And they're pushing in opposite directions over the lawn, wrestling with bikes and umbrellas. Then, far enough: each turns his bike to face the other, and Adrian's balancing his umbrella on the handlebar and pushing the bike and hopping on and trying to pedal, and wobbling hard, but by standing on the pedals and straining, Theo can see his legs and arms, he's still only wearing his black underwear, and then Theo sees Colin up and coming too, Adrian and Colin riding at each other holding the umbrellas and then they're passing and each is poking at the other with the umbrella, jousting. Adrian's off and over in a blue of bike and arms and legs and umbrella, and Colin is whooping, calling Adrian a foul varlet. Adrian's still on the grass.

Theo's not thinking, just running from the woods as Colin's off the bike, stumbling but upright, oh hello, mate, I wondered where you'd got to.

Theo is at his dad's side, Adrian with a red circle in the centre of his forehead.

Are you okay, Dad.

Don't know yet. But I want a rematch.

Adrian's sunglasses are in the grass, and he is struggling to raise himself onto elbows. He's fine: Colin's voice, behind.

Bastard. This affair is not ended.

Hey, mate, my steed is still fresh. Care for another.

Adrian is smiling now, but his eyes are closed. This will not go unavenged. Just warning you.

Colin is riding around on the bike and singing. Adrian is up and running after him with the umbrella, swinging it at Colin's back, then stops and collapses with his head in his hands. Oww fucking hell. My head is splitting. What did you fucking do to me.

Lucky you were so numb to start with you bloody sponge.

Can't feel the tips of me fingers, you bloody fuck.

The man with the horse is here, suddenly, Theo concentrating so hard on his dad he's not noticing anything else. The man is galloping, the horse circling Adrian and Colin, and Adrian is hitting Colin, punching him on his stopped bike and Colin's ducking away.

Can't play without fingers, you lousy cunt.

His dad's always told Theo that sometimes you have to fight, if something's important enough. Nothing makes his dad madder than music. Is this important.

Peace, gentlemen. The man on the horse is moving his horse sideways against them, pushing, so they have to pay attention to the horse and let go of each other.

Get that fucking animal out of here.

After the riot's over. The man on the horse is pouring something on Adrian and Colin. It's a beer. Theo notices bottles tucked into the pockets of the man's black coat, which is probably hot because it's really hot right now.

Get off my lawn. Adrian is hitting the horse with the umbrella. Colin's pulling him away as the horse shies, and the man is putting his hand on the horse's neck and trying to calm it.

My head is killing me, Adrian's screaming.

Mine too, Colin yells. We need medicine.

Theo's standing behind them, saying Dad. His dad's not hearing. Adrian pulls out his knife again – Colin knows and Theo knows and Theo grabs his arm from behind: Dad, no.

The man on the horse holds a pistol in one hand now. It's a big one, with a long barrel. He's pointing it.

That better be a fucking cigarette lighter, you poncey cowboy. Adrian, staggering, pushes Theo off and runs at the horse's rump and gives it a slap that echoes. The horse moves but doesn't jump or go crazy.

There's a shot. Theo sees the ground jump hear his foot, a little bit of grass and dirt in the air, the horse is neighing and the man is circling and laughing, and Colin is standing with arms crossed and Adrian is lying on the ground with an arm laid across his eyes.

The horse man stares, holding a hand in front of his eyes, the long gun hanging down in the other hand, pointed at the ground. Then he raises the gun and sights along the barrel, aims back toward the house. The red end of a car is sticking out at the house side, from the front lawn and driveway. The man shoots and there's a loud ping.

Theo's suddenly back in himself: he realizes he'd sort of gone away. His dad is smiling under his arm across his face, saying, I need something. I need a better class of guest. And sorry, Theo, love.

It's okay, Dad.

My head's not right. I need to get out of the sun for a bit, man. Let's get some chow. Where's Gus.

Theo perks up – I've been looking for him too. I think he's. I think he's doing something with a lady.

Sometimes Theo's able to imagine what happens besides noise, but it's only with regular people, not old people. Does it still work the same. Now he tries not to.

Others wander out of the glass doors now, toward Adrian, who's on his feet and with an arm on Theo and an arm on

Colin. The man with the horse stands off at the lawn's side, the horse's big neck a ramp to the ground where the big head is cropping at the short grass. Theo can see the horse's pink tongue. There's a high whining and someone's riding Colin's motorbike out of the ballroom across the terrace and onto the grass, two ladies, and they've taken off their bathing suits. The back one spills from the seat onto the grass, laughing.

Shit, man, I haven't slept since Monday, Adrian says, shaking his head like a dog. Where are the dogs, Theo wonders. He can't remember the last time he saw them.

Adrian's shaking his left arm, touching the tips of his fingers to each other, a fingering exercise: I think I'll live, unfortunately, but I need medicine. My head's a mess.

The fallen-off lady is standing, without clothes, red-sided. The other lady is at the far end of the lawn and turning, sending up chunks of dirt.

The naked lady is now walking toward them, looking at Adrian. She is pretty. Theo's heart is pounding and she's looking at Theo now, and at his shorts.

Oh, honey. I guess he's growing up.

Theo's face is burning, he doesn't know where to look. Adrian claps him on the back: Beautiful, Theo, it's okay. And you: Adrian's reaching for the lady and putting an arm around her. Help me with my headache.

Colin's shouting in the background, climbing on another man's back and then struggling, trying to get on the man's shoulders but the man can't hold Colin's feet and Colin can't get his legs over the man's shoulders. Colin's yelling: Theo, bring me a stepladder. In the carriage house.

Previously Theo's only been inside the carriage house when the heavy doors were already swung open. He remembers rusty pitchforks and shovels and other tools he didn't recognize. And an old piano, except rotten and spotty, with the wires inside rusted and broken: an upright, not the flat kind.

Colin had been in the carriage house that previous time. He was swinging a shovel at the old piano.

Why are you doing that, Theo asked.

Theo sidled into the dark place wispy with cobwebs and a giant spider of webby chandelier dangling. Long-handled tools lined the wall, hanging. A cigarette burned on the piano's lid and Colin picked it up and took a deep breath from it. He left it in his mouth. Then he bent over, looked up at Theo with crazy eyes: Beware beware, his flashing eyes his floating hair weave a circle round him thrice. Colin grinned: and close your eyes with holy dread for he on honeydew hath fed and drunk the milk of Paradise.

Colin looked mad, angry mad not crazy mad as they used the word in England – beware beware – and now he was spinning around in a circle, holding out the shovel.

Theo fell backward and then scuttled out the door, hanging off its hinges, followed by Colin's voice – Theo, my lad, never underestimate the value of a classical education. Theo turned back to see Colin pounding on the piano with the shovel, yelling.

Standing outside the carriage house now, Colin and others wrestling on the ground, Theo wonders what a classical education is. Does he have one. He tries not to think about it but sometimes he can't help it – school. He likes to learn things, he wants to learn things, and he has a lot of questions. Like now about his dad, if his head's okay.

Sometimes Theo thinks he can see the skull under someone's

skin. Not see see, but just be reminded it's there. One day his dad's head'll just be a skull. His heart flutters, suddenly, like it's trapped; his mom's got a skull too. Ladies, everyone. Him. Dogs. Where are the dogs.

On the lawn between the house and the shed wanders a woman in a big white wedding dress, with red sneakers on and a red bow in her hair. Her stomach is big: she's going to have a baby. A man with long hair is crouching in front of her, taking pictures with a black camera. Theo's own hair is in his eyes. He blows it out of the way. He doesn't see anyone he knows, his dad and the naked lady and most of the others inside now. Theo doesn't want to be in there.

Theo shades his eyes with a hand, tries to guess what time it is – just a little later than when the horse man said it was two, so it's probably three. Theo is in enemy territory: he must be careful. Theo sees a bear emerge from the trees, and the bear is Mingus, walking with the Gina lady. Mingus holds one of his Olde English bottles, and he's waving his other hand around and pointing up at the sky. The lady is laughing, now she bends over to laugh. Theo runs at them.

Mingus is saying, the first time all the stuff's been together at one time – Gagosian saw it and wanted to do it at both his places. First time he's done a show like that.

Gina is chewing gum and blowing bubbles. Both of them are wet, Gina's seal-sleek, still wearing her skirt, her legs smooth and she has painted toenails. Mingus' big stomach uncovered, big as the lady in the wedding dress.

You look like you're going to have a baby, Theo says, hopping around.

That, my friend, Mingus says, is what survival looks like. When the revolution comes and food's scarce, all you little

206

skinny people'll be dropping like flies. Theo, you need to get you one of these, Mingus says, patting his stomach. This is my friend.

And it's so sexy too, Gina laughs, winking at Theo. Her smile makes him feel funny. She's really looking at him. Theo turns away and starts jumping around, to distract himself. He sees animals; he's a cub.

I have large appetites, Mingus says.

He's now wearing unlaced high-top sneakers big as boots, scuffed white, and he's shuffling over the grass, his yellow cape and shorts like a signal. Theo thinks he's big as a fire engine or police car. What would cars be like if they were people. Maybe they are already and we just don't know it.

What's your real name, your Egypt name, Theo asks, following them over the lawn back toward the terrace, and Gina peels off toward the men she was talking to earlier – are they in the same band. Theo can't remember.

Already told you, I can't give that up.

Why.

'Cause it's giving away power – names are powerful, and most people just throw all that power away, spraying their name all over the place. Mingus leaned down, like a cloud, making shade.

Names are like fate. In lots of cultures being named is considered the most important part of your life. The name tells which way your life will go, what kind of person you are. They call in their shamans to pick a name when a baby's born. The Jews keep the name of God secret, and the Muslims have ninety-nine names for Allah because one isn't enough for such an almighty dude. Ha.

Mingus reaches out and grabs Theo around the neck in a boa-constrictor arm, and Mingus is reaching for Theo's waist and hoisting him up and through the air and tipping Theo over his shoulder so Theo's hanging down Mingus's back and his legs are flailing and kicking beside Mingus's head.

Upside down Theo's feeling dizzy and his head feels huge and throbby as he strains to lift it and look back, watching the earth bounce, smelling Mingus.

You need a bath.

Yeah, I know, I been working hard today. We're going to get some lunch now – you need fattening up.

The lady in the white dress and her red sneakers are upside down, and next to her a man in what looks like a black dress, or a robe, Theo can't tell, thumping along, and the man in the black robe is holding a big orange ball and he's putting it up under the robe or because he's upside down he's dropping it down into the robe, which is like a bag with his head at the bottom and it makes his stomach big and round like the lady and there's the photographer hanging by his feet taking pictures of them hanging by their feet, and them kissing, Theo thinks, at least their heads are together, and the man's hair is long and the woman's is very short because she's taken off her veil. And her red shoes, and the photographer's wearing blue overalls with one red shoe and one blue shoe and a red sock with the blue shoe and a blue sock with the red shoe, and Theo's just hanging and watching but Mingus is grunting about him being heavy. They all are skulls. Where is his dad.

Mingus slips Theo off his shoulder and again Theo's stomach flips, then Mingus is lifting him straight and over his head and setting his legs like a wishbone around Mingus's neck. And the pregnant lady and the man with the basketball and the man in the army uniform are all swapping clothes while the photographer takes pictures, the lady's big stomach in the sun and her big breasts. Theo sees nipples like eyes looking at him, so big and round. He pokes Mingus in the back of the head and he's burning up all of a sudden, so embarrassed.

Hey, monkey, Mingus snorts. He turns so they're facing the ocean and away from the people and then lifts Theo off his shoulders and sets him down.

Why'n't you go play a little before lunch. Somewhere there ain't women.

Theo's so embarassed. Should he say sorry or thanks, or just nothing. Why didn't it happen to adults. And he wanted to look, not not look. But.

Natural as water flowing, man, nothing to sweat. It's the body just letting you know you're alive. It'll calm down.

Theo doesn't know where to look or not look, and the birds whirling, and he just doesn't want to be confused anymore, he feels always like he's swimming and he doesn't know if that's an island or a whale or a sea monster and if when he's standing on it he'll be safe or bucked off and swimming for his life. But he's a pirate. Frieda keeps saying that anyway.

Theo's bouncing, looking back now at the house: the man and lady and photographer and the army man. The lady's wearing the uniform with the coat open, her stomach sticking out like a white dome, one man in the dress, one man in the tuxedo, all barefoot, the men looking alike, Theo can't tell. The photographer lying on the ground taking pictures of them; now rolling over so he's upside down taking pictures.

At the side of the lawn Colin on someone's shoulders is wrestling with a lady on another man's shoulders, then they break apart, tottering and screaming and laughing, then the carrying men move apart and somebody counts and then they run at each other and thump, Colin and the lady.

That's not fair that you won't tell me your name, Theo says.

Mingus flips a stick: Sorry, man, I gotta know you better.

How much better. You come here a lot.

Look, there are a lot of people who would like that information, so they could control me. And if you said it to somebody and they said it to somebody, and it got out on the web, and that web's vibrating, then some spider's going to pick that up. And I don't want that to happen. I got about eight thousand strikes against me as a black man already, I have to hold on to what little I got left to me after I been scraped and peeled.

Theo peers up at Mingus, flipping, plastic eyes shining and black in the light, beads of sun on his face.

Adrian's outside again now, walking toward Colin on the ground, with the president in the suit from last night who now has shorts and a shirt with flowers all over it. He has a glass in his hand. He's the only person in shoes. His dad has a pair of white pants on, almost falling off; they hang way down, and the suit man has an arm around his waist. Theo wonders where the naked lady is. His dad frowns, whistles: Colin.

Colin on the ground yells: Yeah.

Quick meet. Roger's on his way.

Theo sees, as he and Mingus walk, heads on people everywhere turn toward his dad like deer hearing a stick crack.

Adrian notices the ripple of attention, shakes his head, laughs harshly like he doesn't think it's funny: Bloody hell. Let the games begin.

When Roger comes it's always a big deal. Theo likes Roger, but his dad gets crazy when Roger's around. There are different kinds of famous. Theo's dad is one kind, and Roger's another bigger kind.

Of all the people around Theo's dad, Roger's the hardest one to figure out. Theo can never tell if he's joking or not, or if he's mad or not, or if he's mean or not, or if he's nice or not. It does seem to Theo that Roger is laughing at everyone all the time, in his mind, like an alien observing Earth. He even looks like it: Roger has really big eyes but they remind Theo of a snake or a lizard, because he blinks really slowly and stares all the time, and they're bright green, really light, and it's almost like you could look into them and see what's in his head, but instead it's the opposite.

Roger and his dad fought a lot the last times they were together. They make the songs for the band and so they have to work together, but lately Theo knows they've been doing it all by mail. His dad sends tapes and Roger sends tapes back.

The last time Roger came, in Jamaica, he brought Theo a bird, a green cockatiel with red cheeks. Theo named it Mo because it looked like it had a mohawk. But you can't keep it in a cage, Roger told him.

But you brought it in a cage.

Only because I had to get it here – now it's free.

Theo worried about the bird, watching its wings whir and hearing it shriek around the house over the heads of guests. Theo followed it around until it came to one of the open windows – all the windows and doors were open – and was gone. He ran outside into the garden; do cockatiels know how to live in Jamaica. It was dark, but moon and stars spotted the sky and the trees rustled with other birds. Maybe it found some friends; maybe they'll show it how to find food. Maybe it was really a gift for the other birds. But why did Roger bother to say it was for Theo. He stood outside listening, to the birds and the people, and wanted to lift the house and let the people out.

Theo went back in to tell Roger about Mo but Christina said Roger was outside with a reporter. Theo walked out the front, past the big jacarandas waving in the dark, and saw two people in a jeep. He walked toward them, and saw the two shadows blur together. Theo stood for a second.

Roger, Mo flew away.

The lady and Roger pulled apart, and Roger's voice came at him.

That's a happy ending.

Is that why you gave him to me. So he would fly away.

I gave him to you because I like you. I give presents to people I like.

Theo knew Roger was staring at him in the dark, he could feel it. Then a little orange coal moved in a curve up and brightened, and Theo saw Roger's face, squinting at him. Theo heard a sigh and maybe a whisper. He turned and walked back toward the house, the bricks warm under his feet and the air thick and sweet from the cigarette smoke in the house carried out by the breeze. Theo breathed deeply.

Theo now leaves Mingus, a shadow on grass. If Theo were a minnow he'd be hiding somewhere away from the big fish.

He runs over the hot green bristles of grass. Music booms from inside the house – what doesn't Theo know about everything, why is there so much. He's tired of being a kid.

He's shooting past the people on the terrace talking, from bright into dark, the ballroom floor gritty and people sprawling everywhere with plates and the air rich with food smell. Theo is hungry again: where are the dogs. They like people and food. He wants to show his dad the butterflies. Where's Gus. There's someone taking pictures. There's always someone taking pictures. Theo makes a face and runs into the kitchen. People stand around, and Leslie is behind the table with a spoon putting food onto plates. A vase of flowers sits on either end of the line of warming things. She brought flowers. She's now wearing a white jacket and her pink hair is candy. She's smiling. Theo wonders what his mom is doing.

Bloody leaches and parasites, Theo hears Adrian's voice. Roger's something you can feel in the air, something coming. At least to his dad, but Theo feels something too, everyone a little louder. Maybe it's just because they're inside and sound's got nowhere to go. Where are the dogs.

Theo winds through people, squinting in a stab of sunlight through the stained glass at the side of the kitchen, people occasionally rubbing his head or pinching as he passes. He ducks.

Dad, you want to see my butterflies.

Adrian's got an arm around a man and a lady, one on either side, and the bald man who's the record president holds a plate and feeds forkfuls into Adrian's mouth.

Is your head okay. Why is he feeding you.

Because he can, Adrian says. And I'm busy holding these people up. They're both train wrecks and they'd lay waste the crockery.

The man looked familiar, from TV or a magazine. The lady reached out to push the bald man's glasses back up his nose.

We need to nail this down, the bald man says.

Yeah, yeah. I know, Adrian sniffs and looks around, chewing.

Dad, I can't find the dogs.

They're okay, mate. They're the only ones with enough sense to escape this asylum. They're probably outside somewhere.

No they're not. They're not anywhere.

They'll turn up, pal.

213

How is my mother.

What, Theo. Adrian's actually looking at him now, he sees his father focusing.

How is my mother. Theo wants his dad to listen and thinks he'll hear this.

She's fine, mate, she's okay. They're taking good care of her.

Can I see her.

Sure you can see her, we'll figure out a time and go, eh.

What's wrong with her.

She's just sick.

Will she get better.

Adrian lets go of the two people and bends over and steadies himself and kisses Theo on the forehead and puts his hand on the side of Theo's face, the hand hot. He feels the callouses on Adrian's fingers as Adrian tucks Theo's hair behind his ear.

I love you, mate, and she does too, and we're all going to be fine. She just needs some rest, mostly, and some medicine, a little fucking peace and quiet.

Adrian usually doesn't say that word when he talks to Theo. Therapy medicine or medicine medicine, Theo wonders.

Do you want to see the butterflies.

I promise, mate, soon as we get things Bristol fashion here, I want to see butterflies. You find me wherever I am and we'll go see them.

Is your head okay: does it hurt. Theo's looking up at him.

No more than usual: Adrian straightens again, smiling down in his goofy way, and tilts his head back and laughs. Ah, it is great to be alive, isn't it.

First. The bald man is raising his eyebrows at Adrian, the plate elsewhere now.

Yeah, yeah. Let's go find the phone.

Adrian lets go of the man and the lady: You're on your own. Adrian takes their hands and puts them together: I now pronounce you. Then he walks down the back hall with the bald man.

The man and lady wander toward food, not looking at Theo, who doesn't know where to go, in trees again, unnoticed. Until someone notices him and looms up at him or swoops down on him to rub or pat or poke or ask a weird question breathing on him. Or try to tickle. Where's Mingus. Where's Colin. Where's Gus. It's crowded and loud. Music kicks up from a tape player in the ballroom: old-time music Theo knows is jazz, with a clarinet. Who put that on. Colin's in the ballroom yelling now, in from outside: I want a cup of tea.

All the voices: You just have to tighten up and get through it Some parts of it are okay Anything you like Okay so there's police Don't want to have none of this down below zero any more and then there are their bosses And there's juice And if there's a rule But not always I love the ocean man I have a bra but I forgot to put my glasses on A lot better since I got out of the joint Terrible eyes one four five progression two tone suede and she put it in her mouth Got anymore Say what Let's go take a taste and you can tell me that again Pretend he's dead and you've never left I just need a thousand to finish this I need ketchup Tell you what I'm flying there's only two ways to leave And she gives it one of these –

Theo's trapped, the kitchen crowded, a tide of people finishing first platefuls and back for more, more people because of Roger. He doesn't know how many are in his house now, and it feels weird to call it his house because he can't even see anything familiar, everything covered with bodies and where are the dogs.

215

He hopes they're just shy – and someone saying police. What about police.

Theo pushes through and out the back end of the kitchen and past the pantry and down the hall, the welter of sound following him down the narrow channel of the hall like water in a tight chute.

Gus's at the front door in a towel, like a sheet-draped chair, so wide and stable, bottom heavy, with legs sticking out and long feet on the ends. Two ladies and a man Theo hasn't seen before are behind Gus, the ladies and man in bathing suits, the ladies both wearing cowboy hats, just standing and scratching themselves and staring at the men in suits at the door. Immigration, Theo hears. Documents. Status, confirming, probation. Who do they want. Visa. Resident. Do they want him. His stomach. Who's in trouble.

Theo thinks of school, of desks in rows, kids with heads bent over paper, the teacher at a desk, bent but looking up every now and then. The weather board with sun and numbers on it. A girl scratching her leg without looking. Windows tilted inward, and outside, steady low hum of traffic, birds.

Theo walks up to Gus and stands a little behind him and touches his arm. Gus looks down to locate what touched him – Theo thinks of the horse and how automatically it twitches, without thinking – and, focusing, notices Theo, then winks one eye at him but he's not smiling, and swivels back to the men in the door, who are sweating. Gus's moustache is wet and he's smoking his pipe. Theo looks through the men at the light brown gravel circle and the big horseshoe arms of the long straight driveway, and the cars, the black car they must have come in, and the mobile recording truck, its main cable up the steps and off through the hall somewhere to the right, the other side of the house. And a new one, a long red vein. Where does it go: Theo decides to follow it, the black cable snake. Maybe it's got the dogs and they need help. He weaves off, leaving the voices.

He follows the snake into the hall, dark, then there is stained glass, an angel, and the seraglio, full of cushions, near the Christmas tree room, and his dad's in there bent over on a cushion with a lady rubbing his back, his head's hanging, and the bald man is talking to another man, a young one who might be a musician, Theo's seen him somewhere, both with arms folded, and the snake disappears here into a soundboard and a small city of equipment. His dad's head. But there's no phone in here. The bald man notices Theo and walks over.

Your dad's not feeling well. Let's give him a chance to rest for a minute.

Is it his head. What's wrong with him: Theo's voice rises. His mom and his dad resting. Is it his head. We need to get a doctor or take him to a hospital.

The bald man smiles down at him. He's fine, he's just taking some medicine that makes him a little drowsy, so he's just resting for a bit until the medicine –

Dad, Theo calls across the room. The woman looks over with an empty face, she doesn't really have an expression and maybe doesn't really even see Theo, it's hard to tell what she's seeing. Theo feels a hand – the bald man's saying, we have to leave him alone, let him rest and not talk, okay. You can talk to him in just a few minutes when Roger gets here. He'll be fine.

He's my dad, I want to talk to him.

Honey, he's very tired. He needs a little quiet right now: the bald man bends in front of Theo now so he can look into his eyes – and block him too, Theo thinks. You're a good son. I'd like to have a son like you. Let's give him a few minutes to himself.

That lady's here, and you're here. Does everyone have to go or just me.

Theo felt fierce looking up, mean and nervous: What's the matter with him, does he have the same thing as my mother. Does that mean I'll get it too.

The bald man, still squatting, puts his hand on Theo's head but Theo ducks away. Theo, he hasn't had a lot of rest lately, son. He's just left Australia and he hasn't slept for a couple of days. It's all just hitting him now. Mostly what he needs is time to himself, with no one pulling on him. Your father's –

You just want me out of here. Why. What's wrong with my dad.

He has a lot of work to do, and Roger's coming, and he took some medicine and he's in need of a little lie down.

Theo notices there's a bodyguard-minder guy he hasn't seen before, a large guy in black shirt and pants also here, along with the other people. Maybe that's where magic comes from – a man can appear from nowhere, if you want to believe it. Magic's just the world without science books, Theo's dad always says, and there's more to this world than meets the eye, pal, and that's why music works, it gives us a way to ride that spirit, and then he always winks. Winking's so corny but Adrian still does it. Like Gus.

Theo ducks around the bald man who's extending an arm and runs to Adrian, who's bent over still, sagging against the woman, who Theo's never seen and who has long earrings with feathers on them and short hair. She looks like an elf. She watches him out of big lemur eyes, lids slowly going up and down in a blink.

Dad, are you okay. You want to go to bed. I can help you.

His dad mumbles a little. Something that sounds like Theo. Bent over, his dad says, mokay. Little rest period, mate. Mget straight here. Loveyou.

It's like he's under a spell. Did you do something to him, Theo says to the lady. She says, no, man, the world did.

What does that mean.

One day you'll understand, when you're older.

Why does everyone always say that. I'm not a little kid.

Come on, my friend: the bald man's hand is on Theo's shoulder. Theo looks at his dad's hands, limp as empty gloves. They're bony, spidery, crabby, like a skeleton, long fingers pointing down. Theo grabs one: it's cool. Come on, Dad, let's get to bed. Theo doesn't know where he will take his father except away. The lady and the bald man both now have hands on Theo, gently but definitely there. Let him sit, Theo, he's not ready to walk.

Adrian's squeezing: Mokay. Justresting. A minute. Ready to play. Off and on.

Theo ducks away from the hands and runs for Gus: Gus. His grandfather. His dad is Gus's son. He'll want to help. Theo dodges people down the dark hall, and the entrance hall is empty now, doors closed, sun from the side windows in white bars on the tile. What is happening. Theo grabs both doors and yanks, and the heavy wood swings inward. Outside, the policemen in suits lean against the black car. Where's Gus.

A black limousine's nosing its way down the driveway and past the policemen, who bend and stare into the limo's tinted back windows as it glides, hands on belts and waists like cowboys ready to draw. Theo sees Roger driving and smiling, and two other people, a man and a woman in sunglasses sitting beside him in the front. Roger's got a beard now. He's slowing

219

the long car down until it's stopped sideways near the steps. Maybe Roger can help.

Roger opens the door and gets out, flashing his twisted smile at Theo. Roger's wearing a floppy white hat like old men at the pier wear when they fish, and he's in a blue suit with sneakers and no socks. He reaches for the rear door and opens it, and a man in a chauffeur's uniform gets out, holding a black bottle of champagne by the neck. He's wearing gloves.

The man and the lady are still sitting in the front seat. They both yawn at the same time. Roger is walking up the steps, smiling, and he bends down and gives Theo a kiss. Hey, man. Can we come in.

My dad's sick or something. But they won't let me help him.

Roger has a funny expression, his face now cloudy: he's angry. We'll sort that out, don't worry. He'll be okay. I know what he's got.

Can you help him.

Roger's stopped listening: I brought some people. Roger's mouth is funny: there's something green on one of his front teeth.

What's the matter with your tooth.

Roger smiles: It's an emerald, but people just think I've got spinach on my tooth. I'm having it taken out next week.

The man and the lady are standing behind Roger now, like ghosts, pale and dressed all in black, black suits with long sleeves. They look alike: both have yellow hair, slicked back. The police are staring.

Who are they, Roger asks.

I think they're police or something. They talked to Gus.

Roger looks at the starers and yawns again, shivering all over. Let's get inside.

The sun-heated flags of the front steps are hot under Theo's feet. The two ghosts are barefooted.

These are my friends. Paolo and Giulia. A prince and princess.

Really.

Yeah – they come from a very old family that ruled one of the Italian kingdoms before the Risorgimento.

What does that mean.

Italy was once just a collection of individual kingdoms. It only became a country in the nineteenth century.

They look alike.

They're twins. Andiamo.

The man and lady glide up the steps, sniffing. They stop and smile down at Theo.

Caro mio.

The lady's lips are very red and her skin so thin Theo sees veins in it. She sort of pats him while she looks into the house and moves up the steps.

The man's slipping off his sunglasses and looking around solemnly. He says, howdy, partner, and points a finger like a gun at Theo. Then he follows the lady and Roger.

Theo walks down the steps to the long car and shuts the doors. The police watch and smile at him, the way the kids in school smile right before they sneak up on someone to pull down his pants in front of a girl, or trip him onto asphalt. Theo runs up the steps and inside.

Roger and the Italians melt into the dark hall, swallowed in people – Roger's a sun and there are always planets circling around and around. The Italians are cats, sleepy and sleek and boneless, they move like smoke or water, they ripple. Theo's standing, staring. Someone's taking pictures. Someone's always taking pictures but especially when Roger's around.

Theo: Roger's calling back. Where's Adrian.

He's sick.

I know. Where is he. I need to talk to him.

He needs rest.

Theo hears Roger ask someone, who's here. And a voice says names. The doors are open, and green and sun are the other way, and the house looks like a cave and all those people on their way into some dark place away from light, down a slope, and Theo wants to go out, away from the cave, so he does. But he doesn't know what to do. It's afternoon. He's tired of having to talk to adults; it feels like what a job is.

Outside Theo sees the policemen at the car Roger left, their heads against the glass and hands blocking out the light: What are you looking at, Theo calls.

One turns: Nothing, just looking. The others ignore Theo.

Theo bounces down the steps, stands next to them. He notices small guns in brown holsters on two belts. One is fat and sweating a lot: Fuck off.

It's my house, Theo says, blushing.

Fuck off yourself, you bullying cunt. Colin is in the door, flanked by two minders. When did they come. People are always appearing and disappearing. Magic tricks.

You're on private property without a warrant. I could have you arrested.

What's your name, one asks smiling, pulling out a small notebook and flipping it open.

D'Artagnan. And what's your name.

Sergeant Rock.

The minders are whispering to Colin: Yeah I know, but I'm tired of being smart. It's a heavy burden. So gentlemen. Do you have a warrant.

All stared at Colin now, who stood, lean and brown and round-bellied in a towel, sunglasses on his head and a bruise on his forehead, swaying, holding a black bottle.

You certainly do not have an invitation. Ergo, you are fucking trespassing. And carrying weapons. So according to New York law and the castle doctrine concerning home invasion, if I let off a few rounds to defend myself I would be within my rights.

There's no castle doctrine in New York, asshole. That's Montana.

Colin's swigging, the minders stand blank-eyed with their sunglasses. So many people have those eyes. Theo's not breathing.

Get the fuck off my property.

Are you the lease-holder.

No, I'm the most holder: Colin undoes the towel and there's his penis, a skinny thing dangling out of a frizz of dark hair, and he's grabbing it and waggling it. So bollocks to you all – the minders are pulling him back inside.

Two of the policemen start toward the door but the other one at the car calls out – come on. Stand down. Plus, witnesses.

Fuck these rich hippies. The not-fat one stands on a step staring down at Theo, off to the side of the curving stone, mossy and cracked and green-spotted. There's a big spread of green moss like a seat on one stone block.

Let's go.

Suddenly beside Theo is one, holding out a little card. Son, would you give this to – he winks, Theo can see, the skin scrunching up under his sunglasses on the left side of his face – your dad. Tell him we're his biggest fans and we'll be back.

Theo watches them as they move away, crunching across the gravel, even their backs mad, Theo can tell from the necks and

223

the shoulders. They're scanning the house and the windows as they walk, looking around at the lawn: Theo's heart beats faster, looking too, hoping no one's doing something bad they can see. One of them slaps the top of the car before getting in, then turns to look at Theo and makes a motion across his throat with a finger: Leave the fucking kid alone, someone else says from the car.

Lots of people say they like his dad but don't really. Theo realizes his heart is pounding as he watches the police car creep down the driveway slowly, low, full of men. The house is surrounded by dangerous creatures, hidden and not, who sit and wait for someone to come out, maybe for a drink at the watering hole, and then – snap. He runs in a circle, tilting his arms and wonders if he should try again to get Gus's or Colin's attention. Or his dad. Or Mingus. Someone to do something. Maybe Gus.

Gina's suddenly in the door with two men and a lady, in bathing suits, except Gina. How many people live in his house, Theo wonders. A hundred. A million. A hotel. A hive. One man is holding a drumstick and scratching his chest with it, then twirling it, a propeller in his hand. Theo's seen drummers do it.

How do you do that, Theo calls to him. Can you show me.

The man looks at Theo and moves the stick through his fingers in a circle, his fingers rubber.

How do you do that. That's cool.

The others stand in the door but the man walks squinting down the steps, a little unsteady, and lowers himself onto the stone wall like it's a horse: C'm'ere.

Theo walks over, scratching his stomach. The man has a tattoo of a dragonfly on his shoulder and it has four green dots around it. What are the dots for, Theo asks, pointing.

My kids.

Where are they.

With their mother.

Where is she.

Either New Mexico or Portugal. Look here, little dude. Hold this for a minute: the man's holding out the drumstick, and Theo takes it. The man says, here's the spin. Lay it in your palm and hold your hand like this – his palm is up and flat.

The stick balances on Theo's palm. Now, you – the man picks it from Theo's palm, puts it on his, and then with a twitch it spins once. You start with your hand flat, and kind of flick your hand so it spins just above your hand. Then when you get that going, you do it with the hand up and down and you put enough spin on it that it doesn't fall. So you do the flat thing first: the man puts the stick back in Theo's hand. Give it a shot.

Theo twitches and the stick falls. Yeah, the man says. Gotta practice. Like playing. You got a woodshed.

What's that mean.

Gotta get out in that woodshed and practise. It's what old guys used to call practising.

Theo's trying the spinning thing and it keeps falling, clanking on the stone. Then the man leans over and plucks it up and stands – get your own stick and get to that woodshed.

That is my stick. It's from the ballroom, right.

The man looks at the stick and at Theo and flips it back. Fair enough, little man of the house. Guard your castle. Then the guy salutes.

Gina and the other man and lady have been talking on the other side of the steps: Theo, did you get something to eat – Gina's hunched over, straddling the other sidewall, looking at him from behind shades.

225

Yeah.

Okay. Good. Are you having any fun.

That word hadn't been in his mind for a while. I guess.

Do you like being tickled.

Grown-ups always act like he's a toy they want to make squeak. They do the same thing with animals. Sometimes with other grown-ups. They think it's funny.

No.

Well, then we'll take that off the list. What do you like to do.

What does anyone like to do. Talking about it is dumb, like saying, do you like to breathe. Do you like to put food in your mouth and chew it. How about taking a step. Do you like to do that. How about taking another step. Do you like that. Do you.

Theo feels like he's in the middle of something that's in the middle of something else much bigger, and every time he finds his way out of the one thing he's still stuck in something he can't see the edges of, or the end of. Sometimes in school he would be jealous of the kids with a regular mom and dad and sometimes he thought that he was the lucky one. Right now he just wants to be alone, but then he's sort of always alone. But how can you be alone in a herd of people, always milling around like cows, nosing at stuff and standing about, or taking stuff to make themselves drunk, and then they get mad or sad and want to hug you and cry over you.

I like Ike.

What. Gina's looking at him. Did you say, I like Ike.

Theo just stares at her.

Where'd you hear that.

School.

Gina laughs. How about school. Do you like school.

Some parts of it.

Like what.

I liked science. And drawing. Did you like school.

Gina's not looking anymore. One of the men has his hand on her back and she's bending away from it laughing, her chest sticking out. Theo stares. He knows what women look like underneath their clothes. He's got to find something to do and not think about the dogs or Adrian or Frieda or Gus or school or. Sometimes Theo's in the middle of an ocean and can't see the shore. He's a tiny boat and he wants to see land. The sun's in his eyes, his hair's in his eyes. The adults are rolling down the rock wall saying ow ow ow and falling off onto the gravel, and laughing. He never knows if he's talking to the real person or if it's the drug or the alcohol making them say what they say. And do what they do. It's like they're kidnapped or they're hostages. What are people like when they're not pirates. What about people who aren't ever pirates. Glue made kids in school really weird and their noses were snot faucets. They weren't hard to avoid, at least you could see it coming, their bodies signalling to the world, stay away; the way animals warn each other with stripes or a dance or a noise.

Theo is an animal, watching Gina and the other men and lady moving toward one of the big sea trees on the front lawn, the trees with bushy heads and big arms, old skin like elephants. Theo likes to be around the trees. He pats them and talks to them, and they click and sigh answers in wind.

Colin tried to grow two palm trees – our own little pleasant isle and I'm Caliban, he said. He called Gus Prospero and thought that was funny, he always laughed when he did. But Gus didn't. What's the bloody joke, Gus would say. Colin would wave his bottle and walk away.

227

Colin planted the palms, or had them planted – men came and did it, weird old guys who looked at Theo funny and one had an eye that pointed the wrong way; Theo was glad when they finished – in the front lawn's sunniest part so the palms leaned together in the grass between the legs of the driveway. The leaves hung brown and Theo wasn't sure if they were dead. They were an X. X marks the spot, Colin said about them. Here there be treasure. Yonder be monsters. He waved at the house after the planting men were gone, and the trees, still green, clacked and whispered in the air above their heads. No coconuts or anything. Just long leaves with a fringe, and circles of bark all the way up.

Will these trees be okay here.

As long as they can smell the ocean.

What about the snow.

They'll adapt. You know how the zoo has polar bears, and it gets beastly hot in the summer. They adapt.

How do you know.

That's how the world works, boyo.

The dinosaurs didn't adapt.

Theo and Colin were walking back toward the house in the late afternoon. Theo worried about the trees.

Good point. Point for the con side. Five minutes for rebuttal.

Colin bent over and made dinosaur noises and bit Theo on the arm, but not hard. Theo punched him and ran off into the grass. Colin followed, laughing and roaring. Theo ran heart pounding happy and scared of the dinosaur, zigging and zagging and turning his head to see Colin's back, him wandering away in the door's direction and looking up at the sky. Theo kept running, pretending, hearing and feeling the thumps of something heavy chasing him until he slowed and began walking, listening to his stomach growl. The trees browned up, stopped clacking, fronds got limp. Holes now where they were.

Gina and the men and the lady now sprawl in shade under the low front lawn trees, Gina waving Theo over. Theo thinks about dinosaurs tall as the trees and how fast they could run. Or pirates. If they're drunk all the time, how bad can they be. You can run away from a drunk person easily. Theo wonders if they have accidents when they sail, like drunk people in cars crashing into things. Adrian never drives anymore. Or not often. He says the label won't let him, have to protect their investment, like me hands. Insured. Theo's dad holds them up, blunt-fingered.

Colin calls the house the rogues' gallery. Theo's not sure what a rogue is. Theo's a bird and then nothing, he's empty, and then chased by lions, he's a zebra. Nobody's going to catch him. Why do adults lie so much. Outside is hot plains, lions in the shade, and inside is weird caves, the rooms: you never know what is inside one.

Theo opened a door last week looking for Gus and there were two men and two ladies, no clothes, and the ladies were lying on their backs with glistening pools of what looked like wax on their stomachs. He froze, couldn't breathe, just stood there. The men were on their backs too, their penises raw-looking and wet like sausages, not cooked. One of the ladies said, why don't you close the door. She was smiling, wide-eyed.

Theo backed out, couldn't think, his crotch throbbing, seeing everything still through the closed black door, the ladies with the pink eyes on their chests, the men with front tails, handles. Stuff flows between them and babies happen. He wants to touch one, touch things. He's seen his mother naked; when they're in Europe they go to beaches where no one wears clothes. Theo does because he has to, he's embarrassed.

Now Theo feels like he's carrying something heavy all the time and he's not strong enough, he needs to be older, bigger, for what they give him, the adults. Theo remembers India, Jamaica, Africa once: kids working, selling things, dirty, pushy. Girls with make-up. Theo on the lawn runs in a circle seeing clouds and sun and world and a plain with an antelope and people chasing, not natives but regular people, wearing regular clothes and carrying cameras and tape recorders, hundreds of them, thousands of people and they're chasing just one antelope, a small one and it's getting tired.

Theo runs back to the front door, up and in, the mouth of doors eating, swallowing him up – he's in the throat of hall, smelling the sweet smell of smoking, the Jamaica smell, and he wants a job to do, someone to tell him something that needs attention – maybe Gus. Where's Roger. Where's his dad. What happened to the dogs.

The house now a place he doesn't know, like when the snow blew in. He breathes deeply and follows the smell, a wolf. There are people in every room he slinks past, and noise, and music, and something breaking, always the sound of breaking glass. Every day something shatters.

Closed doors on the first floor. Theo grabs the long sideways handle and turns it down, like the handle on the toilet – the door swings and the room's empty – the room where Colin keeps things. More things than usual now, instruments and amps, speakers. Mike stands. Equipment loaded in.

The wolf moves to the kitchen and there's Leslie, saying to someone, I have staff coming in later.

The kitchen smells good, but Theo can't say why; it's a fat, complicated smell. Theo only smells it in restaurants. The wolf is hungry again – the food sits in shiny steel squares and Theo's spooning more and asking: Have you seen my grandfather.

What's that, honey.

Theo wonders about the dogs again, thinks about Gus. They were going to build a dog house. Where's Gus. Where is everyone.

Do you know my grandfather. Do you know where he is.

Sorry, honey, I don't know which one he is.

What time is it.

It's 4:30.

Shadows in the other big door, double-wide for servants with carts, Colin says. Roger, without a shirt, and the Italian man and lady, they all look sleepy, or underwater, moving slower than everyone around them although they're talking and laughing, and Roger's gliding toward the food – I really want white ice cream, Roger says. That's all I want.

Vanilla, Leslie is asking, her eyebrows up, smiling – I do have full-cream French vanilla with fresh vanilla bean.

White ice cream. I want a dish of white ice cream. Roger's gazing around the kitchen and his eyes land on Theo. Hello, Thee, your dad says to tell you he's fine. We're going to work later.

Roger eyes Theo without blinking. Hey listen, you want a job, we're going to need your help.

Yeah, sure. What do you want me to do.

I want you to guard the door. Your dad and I need to be left alone, and you and Mark can make sure that we get the time we need.

Okay, sure.

The Italians stare at Theo. They look grey in the kitchen light, and the lady is yawning, saying, darling, you're such a beautiful wild thing.

You mean me. Theo's not sure.

Yes, caro. You remind me of my son.

Where is he.

Sailing with his father.

Do you live together.

Sometimes.

How old is your son.

Ten. His name is Emerson.

That's not Italian.

Yes, his father's from Singapore.

The man wasn't saying anything but he smiled at someone, a slow smile that spread over his face as Theo watched, like a sheet wrinkling up. The man swam across the kitchen toward the ballroom, while the lady scratched the back of her hand slowly, her fingers white and her nails silver.

You look like a vampire.

The lady laughed. Do I, darling. What does a vampire look like.

Like you.

Well, the idea of drinking blood is distasteful to me. I'd rather have . . . ice cream.

Roger spoons up ice cream from a black bowl, his eyes on Leslie, facing away from him. He sets the bowl down and walks to Leslie and puts a hand on her back. She turns quickly, and he's whispering, and she's shaking her head and moving toward the big utensils, the big spoons and knives, picking something up.

Roger's laughing and gliding out into the ballroom, and his name's now in the air. There's a radio on, WBAI, the one Theo knows his dad likes.

That wasn't nice to call the lady a vampire. Theo says, sorry, I didn't mean to call you a vampire. Do you want to go outside.

The lady looks at him, the way everyone looks at him sooner or later, as if they're just noticing him although they may have known him for years.

Thank you, my love, let me say hello to a few people.

Okay. Theo knows what that means and moves away through the kitchen.

Where are the dogs. Theo's not seen them for a long time. Did they get out, run away. Is somebody doing something to them. Where are they. The bald man, the man from the record label, is big, and with another man carrying a leather case, and they weave through the ballroom talking to each other and occasionally waving at someone. Something weird: Theo feels pressure in his ears and a sound getting louder, rhythm, chopping, thundering, from outside. Theo runs and sees the people outside ducking and running under a waterfall of air pushing at everyone, including Theo, hair out of his eyes for the first time since the beach when the wind moved it – a helicopter.

Theo's never been this close before, and the bald man is turning to look at him and hold a hand up, a stop hand. Yeah, but Theo's not a kid, he can see, and he's too short to get chopped up and the wind feels good, strong enough that he can lean against it, and it's really loud and it's an insect with long skinny parts and the wings a blur and the big glass bulb of the head and a pilot inside who looks like a bug too, with shades on and cup earphones, and the bald record man is ducking way down and running around to the other side to climb up next to the pilot, and Theo watches while he slips earphones over his bald head and points at his watch, looking at the other man with the briefcase who holds up two fingers, and the pilot's chewing gum and he looks around for a few seconds at the people and the house and at Theo, and he gives Theo a thumbs-up signal and nods once, and Theo gives him the thumbs-up signal and the pilot grins and the bald man leans past the pilot to see Theo and wave and the pilot's looking around again and leaning forward to touch something and the noise – Theo puts his hands over his ears and understands the earphones – and the man with the briefcase is out from under the propeller, which you can't see, it's just a flat disc in the air, a saw, and what would happen, and he turns around and his dad is at one of the top windows, leaning on the ledge, and there's a long-haired head at his shoulder, and he's noticing Theo and waving, waving him back away from the helicopter, and Theo waves up and runs back and turns around and the helicopter's hovering high as the trees, just hanging, and the one lady in a dress is holding it down, it's not a dress, it's like pants, a skirt, and some are laughing and letting their clothes blow and there's underwear and one with none. The ones in bathing suits just cover their ears. Theo thinks the pilot's looking at the ladies. Then the thing flies straight up into the white sky, hazy now and hot, and tilts and flies off away from the beach over the house front. Maybe it's closer to the city that way.

Theo remembers the nightboat at someone's beach house, maybe in France, his dad grabbing him from sleep, Adrian above his bed, face gleaming and teeth flashing, up and at 'em, mate, we're gonna take a ride. Theo sleepy and his head full of glitter: Adrian carried Theo down two flights of stairs before putting him down saying, sorry, mate, you're getting too big.

They walked outside, two minders behind them, and Theo was waking up, hearing surf and they're in a car out front.

Where are we going, Theo's looking, no cars on the road, the houses black hulks, trees, too; just the wide sky dotted and at one side the low glow that was a city, an upside-down glass bowl over the world. One of the minders is driving, Chuck, maybe – Theo's trying to remember.

We're going on a boat ride, matey.

Why.

Because I have to get a package to Olympia and this is the fastest way.

What boat.

A fast one. It's called a fast boat.

Theo hears wind chimes and realizes his father has a glass with ice in it.

What are you drinking.

I'm just thirsty.

Me too. Can I have some.

It's an adult drink.

The other silhouette up front is reaching over the seat and handing Theo a bottle of water.

Mind your manners, even if you're sleepy, Adrian says.

Thanks.

Mark. It was Mark – you're welcome, in his big deep voice. Adrian tried to get him to sing on tape once, but he wouldn't.

So where's the boat: Theo's looking out.

At the marina.

Why can't you mail it, the thing.

Take too long.

What is it.

A tape, mate, songs. For Roger. It's work.

Okay.

Theo looked out at the night as they slowed and turned on gravel and drove toward white water in the moonlight, and a forest of boats. Starlight was bright white and lots of the masts were crosses. Light on the harbour rippled and glittered.

Good night for navigation, it's bright as noon out here, Adrian said, a silver case at his feet. Theo yawned and shivered; his eyes watered and everything melted. I want to go to bed.

I know, but this will be fun, my friend. And with a crew straight and true. Stalwarts all, every man jack. The car creeping now, stopping.

Mark and the other minder turn around and look at Adrian: Adrian, I should drive, Mark says.

No fuckin way, mate. This is my boat. Only I know these treacherous waters and the hazards that there be.

This really is not a good idea, Adrian. At least let one of us drive the boat, the other minder said.

Theo watched them, the dark one driving and the light one, the dark one with no hair, his head bald and smooth. Theo wanted to rub it.

Enough of this mutinous talk. I'll pretend I didn't hear that. Adrian yanked at the car door handle and grabbed at the silver case. Lots of camera people carried cases like that when they came to take pictures.

Is the tape in there, Theo asked his dad's back.

Adrian turned: The case is watertight and floats. The rest of us might go down like stones but this will survive. That'll be my legacy, the death album. The black album.

Adrian laughed, standing outside the car and slamming the

door shut. Come on, baby. Adrian crunched over the gravel, the minders turning to Theo with blank faces, and then – maybe one of us should stay here with him and the other one ride with Adrian.

No. I'm going with my dad.

Theo wanted out of the car and fumbled at the door, then was out, the door left open, and running after Adrian. Damn it, Theo heard.

Theo wore his new sneakers, stiff on his feet and no socks, he realized. Dad, wait.

Adrian ahead turned, waving his arm, come on, mate.

They wanted me to stay in the car and one of them was going to ride with you.

They're just doing what I pay them for, honey, and they're good at their jobs. It's probably easier guarding Thatcher than one of us.

One of who.

The band.

Who's Thatcher.

PM.

What.

Prime mincer. Primum mobili, head of government in a parliamentary democracy.

What.

Never mind – look at her up there. Adrian reached down for Theo's hand as they walked, and they walked that way to the dock, the long big boat at the end making the top of the T.

Wow, Theo said, the dark hulk of the boat a whale, the same shape: Is that your boat.

I just rented it. We might buy it. Quite a toy.

Dad, why do you drink so much alcohol. Theo said it

without thinking, it just came out, his father's long-fingered hand wrapped around his.

It calms me down, mate. I have to do it for my work. Otherwise I'd be crazy and I wouldn't be a good dad or good at my work.

The minders behind them, talking quietly, Theo realized, but he couldn't hear words, just the low rumble of their voices, one kind of laughing for an instant. What was funny, Theo wondered.

Isn't she yar – Adrian is clambering down into the cockpit of the boat – cockpit was a word Theo liked, the word always felt fast. Cockpit. Cockpit. Planes had them. But an old word, too.

Stinkpots can't be yar – one of the minders, teeth in the moonlight gleaming, stood beside Theo, the other bending to climb down, Adrian fumbling at the steering wheel.

I'll get us out of the marina and then you can drive – I want to relax. You got the chart, right – you know where we're going.

Yeah. I talked to harbour people. The Marseille side will be a little tricky, we may have to be met.

Just time it carefully, it'll be fine. Hell, if we get close enough I can swim it in, or ride the case like a raft. Then we can go somewhere to celebrate, somewhere on the docks with some teeth.

Aye, skip.

The minders and Theo now hunched in the boat, the big engines – two – so loud it was hard to hear, and the whole boat trembling, the sound echoing from buildings along the water street, where the confiserie was. Theo remembered sitting in the shop looking at the forest of masts and knots of seagulls. He had been on boats, but not a fast boat.

Shadow: Mark over Theo holding something, a life jacket. Gotta put this on or we can't go anywhere, Theo.

Theo looked up and took it, and slipped his arms in, while Mark bent low to cinch it up tight, stiff around his neck.

Adrian stood at the wheel with a hand on the throttle, the boat backing and rocking. The other minder stood beside him, looking backward.

Adrian spun the wheel and pushed the throttle forward and everyone staggered: it was like take-off on a plane, the hand pushing your chest. Water wings spread on either side of the boat's nose, and behind was a wide white path. They made waves and as they moved into the open water sailboats bobbed behind them, a couple with lights on in cabin windows.

Adrian laughed with his head back, bloody beautiful, what a sleek animal –

Hey, take it easy. Once we hit the channel I'm taking over.

Yeah yeah. Adrian stared forward, wind in everything, a little cool now, and Adrian's skinny chest like the bird skeletons Theo collected, Adrian grinning, the regular jarring thump of the hull on waves, hard as steel, Theo remembered from science class, water is very hard. Then how can we drink it; Theo yawned.

The minder now with a hand on the wheel, Adrian griping in words Theo couldn't hear but he knew the tone. He'd heard it through garden walls, through partitions in limos, through sailboat cabin walls, drifting up stairs and down. His dad, unhappy.

But now Adrian was grinning again, and climbing onto the side of the boat and then: gone.

The minder spun the wheel, and the other minder scrambled aft, and Theo yelled Dad without thinking, and Mark clicked

239

on a bright light and was sweeping the black and white water and the boat rocked as waves rolled under, drifting but settled, the engines reversed or slowed down, low, the minder a good driver, but – and laughing out in the water.

Mark held the light steady, and back out in the water Theo saw, barely, dark hair and white face, and splashing.

Hold on, Dad. Theo's voice squeaked.

The boat surged forward, thrumming, Mark in the bow, kneeling with a life jacket on each arm and a yellow coil of rope and then jumping off.

Bloody hell. Just wanted to wake up. Come on in, Theo, it's beautiful, baby.

No, Theo, hold on. Okay. Let me get the boat squared up to them – the other minder bubbled the boat over, and both men in the water laughed now. Theo, can you hold this for me – the spotlight like a microphone with a handle, which the other minder handed to Theo before he crawled forward to the boat's bow.

Theo waved it wildly around, then found the black water and tried to see Adrian.

Come on in, baby, it's like bath water.

Yeah, the sharks like it too, Mark called out, churning in a line.

There's not enough meat on me – just Adrian's voice in the dark, the only light the necklace from the marina and the shore behind, just pearls or stars, low and warm.

There – out there, Adrian had both life jackets, and Mark bobbed beside him, the rope floating in a line back to a cleat.

Come on, Adrian, let's pick a better spot for a swim.

No better place than here, and now is always the time. No time to waste, Bobby. Come in for a dip, Theo, and then we'll get back on the road.

Mark and Bobby were exchanging signals with their hands – Theo'd seen it before. They never told what they meant, none of the minders would tell, but Theo knew they were talking so his dad wouldn't know what they were saying. Theo'd heard Frieda and Adrian yelling about it. The minders did it with both of them. They're sheepdogs, Adrian said about minders, and even sheep don't like being herded, Adrian said. They do not want me to become angry, Frieda said.

They don't do it with me, Theo asked both of them.

They don't have to, Adrian and Frieda said.

Why, Theo asked.

Because you listen.

Theo couldn't remember when there weren't minders. Usually someone also hung around making food. Theo couldn't remember seeing his mother cook anything; Adrian did sometimes. Adrian liked fry-ups. So did Gus. In the middle of everything, early in the morning or sometimes very late, and Gus stood at the stove, watching a pan.

Fancy eating doesn't agree with me sometimes, Gus said. Sometimes after a restaurant party, with a table long as the room and Theo sleeping on a banquette while it goes on, they would return home and Gus would light up the kitchen and make toast with a fork and a frying pan. I just need some plain honest food, he said.

And Adrian did the same thing. Theo wondered, what would he do like his father.

It was chilly in the boat and Theo was iffy about swimming: What about sharks.

That's why we have Mark and Bobby. Shark distracters. No worries, my friend, come on in.

Black all around. Bobby had flicked on blinking running lights and set a lantern on the hull so warm light spilled a few feet onto the water, black and hard as a floor. Can't see anything, no telling what's in there, Theo thought. But he was going to swim.

Bobby stood at the edge of the cockpit watching: back from the boat front. Adrian and Mark splashed. Bobby yelled, we need to get out of the channel, Adrian, this is like stopping in the middle of the road.

They can drive around us. It's too bloody nice to leave.

Theo squatted on the flat side of the boat and put one leg in the water, pulled it out. It's cold, Theo yelled to his dad.

You get used to it, and then it feels like mother's arms, warm and soft. I ain't getting out.

We've got a schedule to keep. You've got work.

Roger. 10-4, copy that, baby. Adrian laughed.

Theo closed his eyes and slipped in, shocked by the water, and hung off the boat, looking up at Bobby, now just a shape between Theo and the lantern. Somewhere behind them a horn sounded, two notes.

A fourth, A and D, Adrian's voice rippled like the water.

Theo's legs dangled in the dark water and there was nothing underneath him, if he let go he could sink forever. He struggled to pull himself back into the boat, and Bobby reached down to lift.

Do I pay you, or does the label, Adrian's asking.

The agency, Mark said. We need to get moving.

Of course, the other leg of the unholy triangle. Well, my friend, let's shove off.

Out in the black there was splashing and Theo, now sitting under a blanket Bobby dug from a door in the boat's side, shivered a little but not because of being cold. Because he wasn't. Bobby put a folded orange plastic sheet next to Theo and said, if you can't warm up, son, just wrap up in this, okay.

Okay.

I'm a hopeless romantic, Adrian said, his head floating above the water between the life jackets on each arm, the rest of him paddling like a dog, Mark behind him with the rope in his teeth. Bloody world'll break your heart if you let it. Theo realized Adrian was talking at him. At least he thought so, so – okay, dad.

Adrian laughed, Bobby now helping drag him in like a caught fish, lifting his legs, with Mark pushing behind and once Adrian slipped limply over the rail Mark was up and over like an acrobat, in a single clean motion. Like a dance. Adrian shivered, his bird chest white and his pants black and soaked. Bobby had gotten things from the door – there was a room under the front of the boat, a cabin – and Bobby'd gotten more blankets and a big thermos. Theo remembered Mark and Bobby's backpacks swung off and tossed into the cabin.

Let's haul away, mateys.

Adrian'd covered his head with the blanket and was a swirl of cloth in the dark beside Mark and Bobby, like a ghost following them, not quite as tall but tall enough. The engine kicked over after its long purring and Bobby throttled up and the boat's rear dug into the water and the engines whined higher and they sliced through the black at the front and the back, the boat's nose splitting the air and the water and leaving a white scar. Adrian sang now, then he was telling them things to sing, then it was his voice, and then Mark and Bobby, they sang parts and Adrian sang parts.

Our boots and clothes are all in pawn, go down,
you blood-red roses, go down, and it's flaming
drafty round Cape Horn, go down you blood red
roses, go down, oh you pinks and posies, go down
you blood-red roses, go down.
My dear old mother said to me, my dearest son
come home from sea.

It's round Cape Horn we all must go. Round Cape Horn in the frost and snow, you've got your advance – ha, Adrian laughed – and to sea you'll go, to chase them whales through the frost and snow, it's round Cape Horn you've got to go, for that is where them whalefish blow. It's growl you may but go you must, if you growl too much your head they'll bust, *just one more pull and that will do.*

Under stars they sang, a high sound against the big engine, barely there. Theo listened to the voices of the people and the boat and the water and the night, some of the voices he couldn't understand, but all lifted on the water over the water, Theo bumping and shivering a little but holding his breath to hear.

Theo watches the copter zoom away, tail up like an angry wasp, isn't that what they do, or is that just cartoons. Theo's thinking he'd like to be a scientist and study animals, but what animals. Humans are animals too, and he sees the people scattered on the lawn and inside spilling out and he'll observe, be a scientist. Where are the dogs. He still doesn't know.

It is afternoon, and Theo's in the Hawaii shorts from yesterday and the day before and his hair's tangled and he hasn't brushed his teeth, and he can't remember what he ate, and – he's an animal. What if he had a brother or sister. A litter mate.

The horse man bounds around the house's side and Mingus sits on the horse with him, holding a bottle of that Olde English. And another lady is chasing them on the scooter, which has a rope tied to it, and there's another lady on an old tricycle, and she's standing on it bent over trying to stay on, and laughing a lot, they're all laughing, and there's another horse, another man, dressed in polo clothes, and on the back of his horse is a dog. Wait, is that a dog. It's a pile of something, like a rug, maybe, something tied down. The sun is hot.

Hello, what's your name. A lady and a man, old people, where did they come from, stand beside Theo, smiling and the lady under a floppy white hat. She's wearing a frilly dress and he's wearing a coat and a striped shirt, his hair strands greasy, and his pants are white. He has bug eyes, they both have bug eyes and their skin is wrinkly. They both hold glass glasses: Theo realizes he's staring at the bubbles, like little chains.

I have to find my dogs, Theo says, not wanting to be rude but running

Where.

Two people are rolling around on the ground, are they fighting. Can't tell. It's a man and a lady. They have bathing suits on.

Where should he run. Where are the dogs. He's being chased and needs to find his pack. There's Gina. Can he talk to her. Where's the edge of everything, there's no end to anything.

Theo's at the house front now and somebody's spray-painting the side of the house. ATAK in silver and there's a face. Two men spraying, in ripped T-shirts. Theo's past them, and the Seal is out now, on someone's shoulders, they're walking in the mouth of the front doors. Where are the dogs. There's music, and the open doors on the long RV are fins and the cable snakes out and a sound guy smokes sitting on the floor of the back. Someone's shrieking somewhere.

Theo feels cold all of a sudden and he's moving from light into shadow, into the house. He's running down the right hall, toward the phone room and the room with the microphones, and there's the Christmas tree and the presents, which two people sit among. Theo's presents. He runs in to look – what are they doing. Nothing is ever really his unless he hides it.

Those are mine, Theo says, the man and lady staring at each other and then at him, not saying anything. One of them is bleeding a little, the man, from his lip. They seem stunned.

Theo runs. Where are the dogs. He's in the ballroom and there's work going on, cables and equipment piled and pony-tailed guys – why do only the workers have ponytails – setting up instruments. Roger and Adrian. Somewhere upstairs maybe. But the sun.

Theo bolts through the French doors onto the terrace, the stone hot. Croquet and someone has a hula-hoop. A white behind. A man laying on top of a lady. They're doing it. On the grass in the sun. He's seen dogs do it too, out in the sun. Some people are cheering and beating on things, bottles and one has a small drum.

Theo's hot and instantly hard and embarrassed and he's off and away toward the trees at the lawn edge, like waiting friends. He wants to take care of something, he wants to be responsible for something, he wants a job.

In the shade he's breathing deep, underwater, a fish suddenly, breathing through gills in the gloom. He stares back at the people, on the ground, in the air, in windows. Now he's a soldier. *He's got to go back, got to get into the fortress to rescue his friends.* Where are the dogs.

Mingus lumbers out, towering over a lady. He's got Theo's BB gun, from wherever Theo left it: he can't remember. Theo lies on the ground. The enemy senses him.

Adrian's on the terrace now, people on either side of him, and Roger, and they're looking and pointing, then they're back in – were they looking for him. Theo scrambles onto his feet, his crotch rubbing against the pants. He's holding it, running. He doesn't care.

He runs past Mingus and the others, no one really noticing, and into the ballroom, where Roger and Adrian sit in a corner on two folding chairs, each holding a bottle.

Were you looking for me.

Adrian's sleepy-looking, grinning, hello, my friend. No, we weren't looking for you but I'm glad to see you.

Roger grins at him too. Keep a tight grip, man, the world will try to take everything you've got. Including that.

Theo's panting, forgetting about his hand. His face is hot: Dad Dad Dad. Can we please do something.

Like what. Adrian's taking a swig.

Like what you said.

Sure, after we rehearse. We need to set levels and get a reading on the room. Then we'll – you were going to show me something, right.

Yes. When can we do it.

Right after this.

Sad. Sad. Anxious, nervous – everybody's serious, even Adrian and Roger now with their heads together, kind of whispering.

Why are you whispering.

Just figuring out some things for my band, Roger says as he drinks from his bottle.

My band. Call me that again and I'll kick your skinny fag ass. It's Jimmy the keyboard guy, who's here now. He looks serious.

Roger stares at him and breaks into a smile. Not you, man. You're special.

Fuck you. Jimmy walks past them and out. The men fixing cables look at each other and keep doing it; the other musicians and Don say curse words and walk out onto the terrace.

Goddamn it, fucking idiot: Adrian's mad now, at Roger or at the keyboard player, Theo doesn't know. Adrian pushes Roger: The rest of humanity's not your fucking house-staff, man.

The minders begin moving toward them: Come on, now.

Roger shoves Adrian and turns on the minders: This is so fucking tedious. Let's try again when everyone's over their tantrums, shall we.

Roger moves off into the gloom of the left back hall, where Theo sees the faces of the Italian man and lady floating, along with other faces, floating.

Adrian shakes off the hands of the minders. I've put up with this for fifteen years. Having to make the bloody peace and clean up after him. This ain't working.

Dad, Dad. Theo's on him, pulling his hand.

Adrian's frowning but looking. Yeah mate. Where's your grandfather.

I don't know. You want to see my sketchpad –

Sure, mate, after I fix this mess. Tim, find out where the hell Gus is. Theo needs some attention. Where's Colin, for god's sake.

Adrian's off and Tim's saying, let's find Gus, come on. Tim's warm hand's on Theo's bare shoulder. Theo's not moving, then he feels Tim pushing, just a little. They want him to want to find Gus. Okay. Where is Gus. Where are the dogs. Somebody's playing a guitar.

Gus's shacked up. Theo's heard that before. He's heard it about his dad too. So now he figures Gus's shacked up. He was with a lady, maybe he's still with a lady. He was wearing a towel when those police came. Theo does not want to see Gus and a lady. He'll let Tim go in first. *This is a tricky mission you go first I'll cover the hall and watch your back. Aye aye skip.*

Noise, low noise rising from outside, over everything. Another helicopter – the man in the suit is back, maybe. Theo wants to watch the helicopter land, he would like to fly one, he would like to fly. Have a nest and: no, no nest. Just fly.

Theo runs away from Tim toward the light, toward the ballroom. He's through the ballroom where everyone's smoking and sprawled like dogs. Where are the dogs. He's flying over the ground, people naked but not on top of each other, some ladies lying in chairs eyes closed so he can look, so different, funny-looking, not like magazines, what if they get sunburned. And in the air a helicopter circling, just circling, it's not landing, it's tilting and the long barrel of a camera pokes out the side, shooting pictures.

Bang bang bang. Bang bang. One of the men stands holding up both hands with his middle fingers sticking up. Another one has his hands on his penis and is waggling it – is everybody supposed to be like that. Is he normal.

Can he help his dad. What should he do. This stuff happens more when Roger's around. All of it. Helicopters and fights.

Theo remembers one time he stood with his dad and Chris the regular drummer watching Roger get off a boat, and Adrian said, here comes the king. Chris said, how do you know he's the king. And Adrian said, because he ain't got shit on him, and both of them laughed. Theo didn't understand: why did you call him the king.

Adrian noticed Theo, rubbed his head. Didn't know you were there, mate. We were just quoting some lines from a movie. He ain't the king, he's just a cat I was at school with.

Try telling him that, Chris said, pulling hard on a cigarette.

Chris stomped on his cigarette with a bare foot, exhaled a cloud and crossed his arms, then lowered himself to sit as Theo followed Adrian walking down the waterside steps toward Roger, wearing a cape and a three-cornered hat. A Paul Revere hat, like the paintings in the history book. Roger grinned at Adrian and held out one of those silver suitcases they gave to each other all the time: Not bad, he said.

Damn right, Adrian said, taking the case. Theo thinks that was Venice.

Theo veers off now to find the dogs – they need somebody to take care of them. They don't like all the people, everyone wanting to pet them or feed them or dress them up or pretending to like them but not. You can't trust everybody. How do you get from safe place to safe place, who helps you. Who can help you. What if you're alone.

Sun burns, the helicopter's circling, the people mostly ignoring it now, some going inside with a flip of fingers. It's summer. Wednesday, Theo thinks. He's not sure what month it is. Maybe five o'clock.

On a desert island, shipwrecked, how to get off. He'll build a boat.

He goes to find ladders in the caretaker's cottage to make the sides of a boat: he'll put one on either side of the sliding board off at the corner of the lawn – and he'll have a boat, with a lookout. Sail away.

Theo runs for the caretaker's shed, tile roof slates raining off, a line of them outlining the shape of the cottage like drips from the eaves. Colin's been on the roof hammering at them and yelling at the sun before: Theo's seen him. The slates he's fixing break a lot and that makes him yell more.

Punching open the stiff door Theo's in the weird gloom: so much of that around here, dark in the day when the world seems bright except where he is. He listens, not wanting to see anything else. No sounds.

Theo moves toward the ladders, hung on hooks to keep them off the damp floor. They're spattered wood, and heavy: he has to strain to lift one from its hook, and then it crashes down on the hard stone floor. He hopes it's not cracked. Theo lifts it and it's heavy but he's taking it, and so starts dragging, banging his back against the door, then the door banging open and he's back in the sun, dragging and carrying, looking at the ground, hearing everything, low voices and high, laughing like flutes, the helicopter churning over everything, music from somewhere, and he's dragging, hot, toward the slide and the swing set.

Now Theo's running back to the shed, a little wet under the arms and in the middle of his chest, and he can feel wet on his scalp, sweat. Perspiration helps you cool off, dogs can't sweat so they pant, their tongues help them cool off. Theo feels sorry for animals in fur, the zoo polar bears he saw in Amsterdam and Texas and other zoos, flat as rugs, arms and legs sprawled, looking sad. Theo wondered what it would be like to be so far from home. Is this his home. Maybe Jamaica is. His dad seems happiest there.

Theo's back in the shed door and not stopping. Straight to the ladders and wrestling off another one, taller, that topples over him and he has to jump out of the way. Then he's at it, grabbing and dragging out and over the grass and the dogs have short hair but they still pant. Do they have water, Theo wonders, and thinks he will go fill their bowls when he sets up the second ladder, the other side of the ship.

Theo's leaning the ladders on the ground beside the slide for the boat sides, and then he can be inside, under the slide, like a cabin, and then he climbs the slide stairs, captain, looking over the green ocean and the people from the boat he built and then he slides down and at the bottom jumps up and runs toward the house, to give the dogs water.

Bodies are obstacles, and chairs, and he's dodging. Someone tries to trip him, smiling – adults think that's being friendly. It was Jimmy, the man who plays keyboards. Theo understands he didn't mean anything so Theo just jumps over the stretched-out skinny leg, like ivory it's so white, an elephant tusk, no shape and so white. Maybe Jimmy's sick, Theo thinks. The rest of him's pretty white too, yellowy-white. He's only wearing a pair of baggy shorts and his stomach sticks out a lot.

The dogs have water bowls outside and inside. There's yelling: Colin's standing on the ledge of a window on the third floor, next to another open window. On the lawn people are calling him names. Adrian's head pops from the other window, yelling too – get your ass inside, you bloody idiot. I'll be damned if I –

Now Colin is yelling and laughing and taking a really long step from one ledge to the next and grabbing onto the window frame and Theo can see Adrian's got an arm around Colin's legs and Colin's yelling about messing with his balance and he was doing fine until all the fucking old women started bleating – get inside, Adrian's yelling and Colin's shakily, slowly squatting until he can get both legs inside the window and now he's sitting with his back to the lawn and now he's inside and Theo can hear the yelling and he's inside the house through the ballroom and here comes Roger in a long robe with a white hat and a white cane and he's walking past the piano and he stops and sits as Theo walks toward kitchen and the indoor dog bowls and one's empty and one has a hamburger in it, bun and pickle on top. It might be from McDonald's. All the food still sits on the table, low flames under some of the pans, and the caterer is on the phone, writing on a piece of paper – and six dozen oysters, she's saying, looking up at Theo and winking.

The catering lady is talking about fish, swordfish and salmon. Sushi, she says. Theo's eaten that in Japan and he hates it.

Roger is playing piano in the other room, and he's singing. He and his dad like blues a lot. Theo doesn't like old music, but his dad plays it all the time and takes Theo to meet people who play it. They play together and Theo sleeps in a chair until it's over. Usually it's really late. It's early now, and Roger's playing in the sun and it's weird to hear this music during the day.

What day is it. Where are the dogs. Someone is taking pictures of Roger. Theo runs out through the ballroom and onto the terrace and toward the lawn and toward his ship – he can keep an eye on things from there.

Theo looks back at the windows upstairs: they're closed now. Keep the animals in. He wonders about his dad. Is he sick. Will they make a record. How long will he stay. Where's Gus. He forgot about Gus, he forgot about Tim, who's nowhere now. Maybe back with Theo's dad, minding him.

People say things at him as he passes but it's just noise like monkeys. He's a monkey. He doesn't want to think, about Adrian or the day. School. Kids like him. Theo notices the muscles in his arms as he pumps them, running, notices men with big muscles; there are a couple. Most here are skinny like his dad. So are the ladies, except for some who have big chests. The men and the ladies look kind of alike, with long hair and skinny and pale. The ladies wear short skirts and the men wear pants mostly, one man is wearing a kilt. When they wear bathing suits they dress differently. Why do women wear skirts and men wear pants – his cheeks heat as Theo thinks about how men and ladies are and he feels his crotch tingling. He runs faster to get past all the people and hopes he doesn't run into anyone coming from the beach.

He's at the sliding board, which is brand new – the play set came after they moved into the house, Colin had it delivered. Adrian and Colin thought it would be fun for Theo, but he was embarrassed they thought that. Sometimes on top of the climbing part he watches birds or clouds. But he's not a kid.

Now he's on the ladder's silver steps, perforated with holes, and climbing to the top, with curved rails and a flat place to sit, which he does, the metal hot. The slide's silver is too hot for his feet so he tucks them up, bends at the knees with his arms around his knees, but that's not right – he squats for a minute then moves back down a step and rises to stand, staring out across the ocean of lawn and people toward the country of house. An island.

The horse is walking, reins trailing on the ground, and the man who rode it is talking to some ladies, one of whom does not have a top on. The front of the man's pants stick out and one of them is touching that. Theo's instantly poking out into the slide's metal and has to adjust. The girls in school, do they know about that. What do girls know.

Theo hasn't been around girls for a while. He hasn't been around boys for a while. Standing at the top of the slide on the ocean. Are all animals like that. He knows the dogs aren't. He didn't think about mating much before but he's starting to. Theo guesses maybe that's growing up, or some of it. Does it happen to girls. It must, because from what Theo understands they have to let stuff be done to them. Do they like it. Maybe if he had a friend who was a girl.

Theo's trying to remember stuff from school and he can't. Summer makes you forget. What did he learn.

If he's a pirate as his mom says, he needs a sword, so he runs down the ladder and runs off toward – the shed or the house. His dad has real swords: he streaks for the house to ask. Again he's weaving through the grown-ups, the man from the horse gone, the horse walking with reins on the ground, eating grass. Theo stops to watch its big lips, curling to pull at the short stems. He wonders if the grass is enough – maybe there's something he could feed it in the kitchen. He sees its ribs, its skinny legs like a deer, how does it hold up the big barrel of body. Horses are scary. Theo's ridden them before with his mom, sitting in front of her and her arms around him, and it's more scary than motorcycles, which he's ridden with his mom and his dad. On the horses the ground seemed miles away, like being on a giant's shoulders. His mom told him just to relax – horses want to be told what to do. And you tell them with your hands and your knees, she said, you squeeze your legs from waist to thigh but keep them loose from knee to foot, and you also signal with the reins. Horses are happier feeling that someone's in charge. They're social animals, Frieda said: they're like us.

Someone's now rubbing the horse's neck as it crops the grass, and little patches of brown hide shiver to shake off insects. How do they do that, just move one muscle in that big country of muscle. Sometimes it would be nice to be told what to do.

Theo's focused on the door and getting inside and notices he doesn't notice as many things as he did when he was a little kid. When he was little he was constantly watching what all the people were doing around him, and wondering about what they were doing and why. Now that he's older he pays less attention – like his dad is with photographers. Someone's always taking pictures, everywhere, and Theo asked his dad once whether it bothered him. His dad said, I've had people snapping pictures of me since I was just a few years older than you. I don't even see cameras anymore, they're just part of faces, like noses.

Someone is trying to feed the horse something – Theo can't tell, but a man is laughing and squatting next to its head near the ground, holding his open hand near it, but the horse is chewing grass and moving its head away, so the man moves too, on his knees, to keep his hand near its mouth. What's in his hand. The horse puts its big nose into the hand and then yanks it out, shaking its head and snorting, and it trots a few paces away and stops, then puts its head down and snorts, and then begins cropping again. A lady is kicking the man and yelling at him in French. She's speaking fast but Theo knows it's French: Frieda yells at Adrian in French sometimes when Theo's with them.

Theo wonders what's left for him not to hear. His dad usually is quiet when she goes French. She also speaks German sometimes; sometimes in her sleep.

Theo's now beside the horse, patting its massive shoulder and it's shaking its head crazily every now and then, and snorting. Theo wonders how his mother is. Now he runs again toward the house and the swords. Theo's suddenly angry: what was in the man's hand. Mingus moves through the air now outside, in a different costume – one of his space characters, like a robot or a space knight.

Careful out there, little man, there's a lot of bastards.

What do you mean.

Watch out on that lawn. Too many white people in one place can only lead to trouble.

Is that a joke.

Sort of.

Mingus, can I –

I'm Akhnaten-K.

What.

I arrived here to shore up defences on this outpost against the Triad System.

This is an outpost.

Yeah.

I've got a ship out there that we could use to fight. If you want.

There are two ladies with Mingus who look bored: Come on, we're not babysitting.

Hold on, I have to talk to my lieutenant. Mingus puts a hand on Theo and walks him a few feet away and bends down.

Listen, man, this is just the beginning. There's a storm coming and you gotta get ready.

A storm: Theo sees nothing but the sky burning with blue. I don't see any storm – you mean today.

It's coming, man, and it'll be like a war. You gotta protect yourself. Figure out where you can hide if you have to, get your escape pod ready. Don't fool around with this stuff now, the future of the species might depend on it. Mingus looks serious, and flicks a finger off his nose at Theo as he straightens and turns to the ladies: ready for take-off, ladies. The three of them stroll onto the lawn toward the empty pool, Mingus's arms around the ladies and their arms around him, holding each other up.

Theo walks out of the sun and into the ballroom and a man and a lady are moving fast, going through the scattered clothes, pants and shirts, jackets, bending and pulling, occasionally shaking out things, jamming what they find in the black trash bag each carries. They look like they're harvesting a crop.

What are you doing, Theo asked. Is that your stuff.

Yeah, it is. They look at the hall entrances, the kitchen and the outside doors, and at Theo, and keep rummaging.

I don't think all that's yours. That's stealing.

The lady lifts someone's heavy watch, glittery before it disappears. Then she smiles sleepily and walks to him and stops, just in front of him, her eyes on him the whole time, then lifts her hand and it's on his throat, tightening a little. It's warm, squeezing, pressing a little on his Adam's apple, and he swallows. Mum's the word, she says in a low, normal voice. The man's hissing at her.

Then she's moving and harvesting again. Why didn't he yell or move, where did his brain go. He just stood like the dogs letting someone play with their ears. Is that what he'll do. But she was a lady. Ladies don't hurt.

Hey. I'm going to tell the police.

They work their way around and the man looks up and drops the pants he's holding and the two of them melt away down the back hall toward all the rooms. Theo runs into the kitchen but it's empty. The kitchen is never empty when his dad is here. Where is the catering lady. Where is his dad. The house a coral reef and people hide in all the holes.

He needs to tell someone about the robbers in the ballroom.

But he doesn't know who. There's no teacher.

There are all kinds of people, like in books Theo's read. Sometimes they fight each other and sometimes they have to work together on a quest. They try to get to a different place together or make the world grow again after a blank white winter. Sometimes they have to free somebody. Theo's quest is Adrian now. And Gus. Sometimes Theo thinks Gus is really sad. Colin, too. Theo feels it when he comes on them alone in rooms sometimes. If they're sad, Theo thinks, maybe I'm sad too and don't know it.

Theo's on the run again, now to the front and up the big stairs, rocks in a stream, he's leaping: over the fish, maybe piranhas. He mis-times one step, has to balance for long seconds and then just throw himself onto a landing to avoid falling in. He's on the bank, he made it. And this floor is where Adrian usually crashes. Noise floats, from inside and out. Theo needs a sword, and maybe he can protect the stuff in the ballroom. Stand guard with the dogs. Where are the dogs.

Theo's creeping down the shadowed hall, one of the tunnels here; everywhere's a tunnel unless it's outside. The house in Jamaica is so light. Theo has a sword in his hand, going from door to door, looking for the monster – it's here in one of these caves. It might be asleep if he's lucky. Bells. Chimes. The big clock on the first floor that's stopped at two minutes to twelve is ringing. Colin winds it every week with a key. The time never changes but it chimes. It's alive, singing every now and then. Theo puts his ear against the case because he can feel the chimes all over. Colin calls Theo a headbanger because of that. You're one of us, Colin says. What does that mean – Colin just says, god's mercy on you. Theo hates when adults say things like that.

You'll understand later; it's like poetry, Colin says. Theo wants to know now.

Who could he tell about the stealing. Theo's guessing at doors. There's Arabic music behind one, the light from the window at the hall's end stopping right at that door, a sundial or a signal. Theo takes the handle and opens.

It's one of the rooms with some old furniture but it smells sweet. Roger and his dad are there on a dim red shiny sofa with a fringe and no legs. Adrian has one of his big acoustic guitars in his hands, Theo knows it's called a dreadnought.

Adrian leans back. Roger holds a bottle in his hand. The couch sags, its guts a yellow-white cloud, and a minder's bending next to the door, and ladies. One lady is asleep on a pile of cushions without any clothes on. Adrian's briefcase is beside him on a low table. A lady is leaning and in the middle of tying a piece of colourful cloth around Adrian's arm, one of the things his dad brought from Morocco. Everyone's looking at Theo, except the sleeping lady. But no one's moving or saying anything: a room full of animals watching from deep in their heads, or inside something else. What's it like in there. Adrian says, you're fired, to the straightening minder, Billy or Bobby, who's apparently grabbing up something from under his pants at the calf.

Dad, a man and lady are stealing stuff in the ballroom. They're taking things that aren't theirs.

Sound equipment.

No, they were picking up other people's stuff and going through it.

Bloody Hamptons.

Ratty cushions everywhere, and another low round table, and two mattresses, and the other old amputated sofa, and flowers. Vases of flowers – Leslie's flowers or someone else's – and on dark wood wall a man is spray-painting something inside a long rectangle he's already painted. He's painting a sun. It's a window.

Go tell Colin.

I can't find him. I don't know where he is. Or Gus.

Okay. It's okay, darling. It's a lesson in non-attachment. We'll make the place an ashram. Adrian and Roger both laughed. Sexy Sadie, Roger said to Adrian. No, that's your job, Adrian growled, sniffing.

What should I do. Theo felt awkward, everyone strange; strangers.

Nothing, love. It's a charitable donation, it's baraka. Go have some fun.

Can I stay with you.

Rustling among the others, shifting, some slumping lower. Roger exhales cigarette smoke toward the ceiling. The lady finishes tying the scarf thing on Adrian's arm, tightly. She tugs on it.

No, love, we're doing business right now. Go have a good life.

What do I do.

Adrian stares at Theo, and laughs.

Escape from me, mate – get out and get some sun.

I've been in the sun all day. Why don't you come with me. You and Roger could talk outside.

Theo's impatient and filling with wild, he wants to kick something, bite. Adrian seems fine as far as Theo can see. So what happened before.

Nah, my friend, we need some quiet to work. There're too many people around, too many settlers movin' in, pardner. Too many thieves. We have to work. We're going to record

261

here, remember, and that takes a lot of work, a lot of planning. You're going to help, yeah.

Theo's tapping his legs. Dad.

Adrian's face droops slightly. Aw, love, I'm sorry. I can't right now.

Why don't you get a normal job.

Ah, mate. I ain't normal, I'm afraid. You and I, we're carnies. We got the sawdust in our blood. Sometimes that's hard.

Why is it hard.

You're making my head hurt. Adrian's smiling with half his mouth. Your mind's always on turbocharge. You'll make a good scientist, or a lawyer, god forbid. You'll make a good whatever you fucking want to be, my friend. You can escape. Me – Adrian laughs hard, and his eyes slowly close, then open. The show must go on. And right now, mate – Theo feels a hand on his shoulder and Billy looms, a darker thing in the dark but the hand was kind, just there – you gotta let me get on with the act.

I want to go back to school. Theo doesn't know what else to say, swallowing.

The hand's just there, waiting, warm on Theo's bare shoulder, the hand big.

I know, I know. Go back to the world, mate, I'll be there in a while.

I want to live somewhere else. Theo's heart kicked.

The spray-painted window is finished – there's a sun and a palm tree and a naked woman's outline and a little plane towing a banner in the sky that says 'Lies'.

Later, mate. We'll figure it all out.

The hand. Answers. Theo's wondering. Where. Where do they come from. You make the answers up or there aren't any.

262

Billy moves him, Theo realizes, before he's realized it. Adrian's hands are on the guitar and his eyes are closed. Everyone else seems to be waiting for something: Theo to leave, he figures.

The man spray-paints a mark on the wall like Theo's seen around his school in Manhattan. A tag.

What does he do now – Theo doesn't know. Theo looks at Roger: Roger's head is tilted back, watching him. Theo thinks about Diana, Roger's daughter. Roger's winking and nodding at Theo: It's okay, he might be saying, but Theo's not sure. It's hard to tell, adults want you to agree with them: just say okay.

Okay, Theo says, to the air, and the hand.

The door closes and clicks behind him, and Theo's off running, down the tunnel, away from the army, dark people in black uniforms, down the stairs, jumping. Now he's in the curving part of the back hall and he hears laughing and ahead sees a slick of something on the tiles, water maybe, and ladies and men at the other end in wet shirts and bare skin – no way for Theo to get past without being seen, and so he stops where it's a little darker and sees the first lady start running in the hall in a kind of crouch and then sprawl onto the floor and slide on her stomach toward Theo and everyone's hair wet-looking and hers long and her laughing and one of the men has one of the big tins of oil from the pantry and he's pouring it onto the floor and – gunshots.

Or fireworks. Theo's not sure. So Theo goes back away from the sliders, he backtracks toward the enemy, out another way. Sound from rooms and Theo's past it, taking the other way toward the front hall, and he's in it, full of junk, and new things hanging from the chandelier, including a garden hose now, and sneakers, pink, and he's outside.

The butterflies – he wonders about them. His dad should see. His dad's not the same with other people around. Maybe he wouldn't do it if they weren't around. Theo feels like maybe if he could get his dad to do stuff with him it would be better for his dad. People are always offering Adrian things to swallow or drink. He never says no. He's so polite, Theo thinks. Maybe if he could be with his dad he could help him, he could be the person to say no. If he could just get his dad's attention. He needs to be more interesting: his dad might pay more attention. His mom too. Maybe. So he needs to learn something.

He's sort of good at sports, but not great. He can add up numbers really fast. He learned how to play Not Fade Away on the drums. If he played music, his dad would notice. Maybe he can go to a music school or take lessons. Maybe he could ask his dad to teach him to play guitar. He likes to hear music. He likes to fish and throw things. Theo runs through the driveway gravel, hard on his feet, and onto the grass and around the end of the house toward the rear lawn and his ship, which he forgot about. Then he sees the dogs under the hedge on the left, three of them, all lying on their sides with their tongues out. Not panting, just. Eyes big and open. His heart swells open and he runs.

Paz's eye doesn't move when Theo kneels and reaches under the stiff green bushes with the waxy leaves that Theo can't remember the name of. He pulls on Paz, who's limp and heavy, and pats her head, talks to her, dogs can't understand or maybe they can, so he's saying, what's the matter, what's happened to you, and Paz stares now ahead, tongue hanging out like meat half-swallowed, and her mouth's frothy, foamy. Theo lifts a paw and it just drops. Her eye rolls slowly up at Theo. The skin over it that looks sort of like an eyebrow is droopy. Theo thinks of a whale's eye looking at Paz, looking back at him; but she doesn't really seem there, the eye's just open.

What did they eat. Theo remembers the man with his hand under the horse's mouth and. What should he do. They need help but who. Maybe some water. What do you do – adults are supposed to know. Gus's an adult – where's Gus.

Alex and Baron not moving – Theo puts his hands on their sides. Hearts beating hard and fast, like Theo's. They're all together. He feels Paz – her heart is pounding. What did they eat.

Theo's angry. He looks for the man. But what if it's someone else. He's mad. Maybe it's the man and lady stealing. Theo's been good all day all year a million years: he's listened and done what he was told to do. He can't think but he sees clearly. Everyone. Everywhere.

Theo hates them all, hates the stupid house. Maybe the catering lady can help. He runs.

No one pays attention. Sometimes he knows people but not today. He's an orphan. He has a grandfather but not here. The ballroom's full of equipment and people smoking, waiting. Theo pounds toward the big kitchen and the catering lady and now an assistant maybe – another lady, younger than the main lady, wearing the same T-shirt and apron and both of them look very serious.

The dogs are really sick. Something happened. We have to help them. Theo's panting at the catering lady – he can't remember her name. She looks down at him, a little annoyed.

What's wrong. What do you mean.

I think somebody gave them something that made them sick.

The lady's frowning and making a face, then she looks at the big watch on her wrist. You should tell your father.

I can't – he's busy.

How about, um, Colin.

I don't know where he is.

Are you sure they're not just tired or. How do you know.

They have foam. On their mouths. And they're just lying there. Like when they're sick, they try to hide, or they did something bad, they're under the hedge. What if they die.

Still frowning, she's looking at him with her mouth funny: Annette, can you keep things going for a minute. Watch the pasta. I'll be back. She sounds Australian, why didn't he hear before.

Are you from another country.

She's wiping her hands and saying, yes, honey, I'm from New Zealand. Okay, let's take a look.

Do you miss it.

You're a little gooney bird: she's smiling as they walk fast, Theo's in front of her like one of the dogs, hopping and anxious. Sometimes I do, yes. But I get back there twice a year at least, so I do see it enough to stave off the homesickness.

Where does your son go to school.

In New York.

Where.

Why do you want to know.

Do you like cooking here.

Yes I do. It's my job to like it.

But do you always. Lots of people don't like their jobs. At least sometimes. My dad.

What your dad does is not a job.

He says it is. He says no one understands how hard it is.

That could be. But you don't want to tell the guy who's out digging up a street that your job is tough, if your job is being a star.

He says it's like building a castle in a swamp.

Hmm. People who build real houses might argue with him on what's harder.

Come on, we need to run.

They're weaving through people on the lawn. Someone's building something on the grass at the house's other side: is it Mingus again. Maybe a spaceship. Theo points at the dogs, brown and black shapes under the dusty green leaves. No one else pays attention to Theo and the lady or to the dogs.

Mingus is beside him suddenly, in his cape: where did he come from. The lady jumps. She doesn't know Mingus. Mingus has on a knit hat with ear flaps and his lime wraparound sunglasses. Mingus is holding a spray can and one of the pitchforks from the gardener's shed. There are other men behind him holding pitchforks and hoes and shovels. A couple are wrapped in towels. Mingus leans down to Theo and whispers: *Battle stations.*

What.

Mingus, already gone, yells out, *from the microcosm to the macrocosm, motherfucker*, and lumbers forward with the pitchfork stuck out while the others start clanging their tools against each other, sort of fighting, except most of them are really just hitting their tools together and not really fighting. Mingus runs at one of the men holding a shovel and the man swings the shovel at the pitchfork. There's a lot of clanging and they scatter like atoms, banging around between Theo and the hedge.

Somebody's going to get hurt. The lady is frowning. Theo's

267

just trying to run around them to the hedge, with the lady beside him.

Maybe we should have brought some water.

I got the equation, motherfucker, Mingus yells, running at two men half-heartedly banging rusty snow shovels who Theo dodges around.

Now Theo's skidding on his knees and he's beside the dogs. Theo's frantic, his mind everywhere. Why is he so helpless. Is being an adult just being old. Aren't they supposed to be smart. The lady might help. The dogs look the same. Their eyes are open.

The lady is on her knees too, pushing her pink hair out of her eyes as she leans over, petting. She lifts a paw and lets it drop, lifts a head.

All three of them at the same time, and they were okay earlier, no sign of anything wrong.

No, they were fine.

Well, it looks like they ate something bad.

Like poison.

Or it could be something that's not really poison but just bad for animals.

Like what. What do you mean.

Maybe they found something they shouldn't eat. There are a lot of people around here. Do you know all of them.

I think my dad might.

Theo thought of the robbers and the man trying to feed the horse. Did his dad know them. What about the stuff others were doing. The only safe place was in his room. He should take the dogs to his room. How. Take them to the doctor. The vet. Where is a vet. He's too young, how is he supposed to know.

This one's not doing too well, sweetie.

Paz is shaking now – the littlest one. She's just shaking. The lady has a hand on Paz, but then Paz tilts her head up, makes a noise. A moan, not like a dog. Her eyes are wild, wide. Then her head falls. The dirt gets dark under her, a spreading stain. The others pant. Eyes closed but breathing.

Is she okay. What's the matter.

Oh, honey. I think she's gone.

You mean dead. Why don't you just say it. I'm not a baby.

I'm sorry. I know.

Theo angry, angry at everyone, at everyone. Not the lady. But grown-ups – somebody did this to the dogs. He never made it back to his ship, or got a sword, or anything. Theo's going to find the man who tried to feed the horse.

The lady strokes Paz, her apron dragging in the grass and dirt, her on her knees now leaning in, the other dogs, people voices, a seagull, splinters of light, Theo's crying a little, his eyes are wet. She didn't do anything to anybody and she's dead. Petting.

Laughing. Theo jumps and runs toward the laughers – shutup shutup shutup. They stare, making weird faces. He runs, where is the man who tried to do that to the horse. It was him: maybe he thought it would be funny. Theo thinks maybe adults forget, because that makes a lot of stuff they do easier, and what they see just becomes like images on a TV screen or movie screen, not people or animals or trees but things, like when you're in a car – Theo's dad said nothing outside is real, and so it's easy to be mean in cars or dumb in cars. People forget the laws of physics, nothing's real out there, it's just another movie. Or like one of those mecha suits, Adrian said: like war of the worlds, feeble creatures in armour, that's what we are.

They were in the back of a car in Los Angeles in the biggest

269

car sea Theo had seen, lane after lane of cars in long shimmering snakes of metal, slowing and stopping then wriggling forward, with twitches rippling from stops ahead, the red lights like flaring eyes. The weird green puffs of palm trees like frozen explosions above the beat-up concrete barriers along the highway, dry brown hills and dipping machines like dinosaurs drinking – his father said they were pumping oil – and motorcycles riding between the cars, going even faster – just crack your door and they're dead, Adrian said as a motorcycle blurred past – or if your arm's out of the window it's on the pavement like meat off a truck. Adrian's drinking a beer, slouched against the door, holding his stomach.

Shivering. His dad was sick. They were going to get medicine. Except it wasn't a regular drugstore – his dad sometimes called them chemists, that's what they were in England. They went to a building of apartments with big black trash bags out front leaking stuff dogs were licking. There was a couch and men sitting on it, their knees as high as their heads, staring. The driver and the minder got out, unbuttoning their coats. His dad's eyes were closed: Sorry, mate. Not a very pretty sight, am I. There were the big puffs of palm trees, and graffiti on everything. Pink and green and blue houses, iron bars. Cars without wheels.

It's okay. Everybody gets sick sometimes.

Yeah. His dad started crying.

Maybe we should go to the doctor. Theo's heart beat faster – was there something in the car that could help: Do you want a pillow or something, Dad.

Don't you worry. I never want you to worry about me, okay. I will never.

Never what.

Nothing, love. Let me just rest, eh.

Where is the doctor. Is this his house.

Doctors can be ladies too.

Is this her house.

Yes. No more questions.

Theo's father was very white. Theo wondered if people got whiter before they died. Maybe the blood goes back inside to help. His heart beat like the birds he held in his hands sometimes.

Where's my mother.

Don't know.

Why.

His father just held up a hand, his face in the dark car glowing around the sunglasses because of the white and the sweat. The car was running and the air conditioning was on. Maybe Theo could make it colder.

Do you want me to make the AC colder.

Theo's father shook his head. Where the fuck are they.

I don't know.

Theo's father gritted his teeth. I know. Just talking out loud.

I thought talking hurt.

It does.

Theo patted his father's thin leg because he'd seen his mother do it. He didn't know what else to do.

She was the littlest one. She liked it if you just rubbed her ears. She would close her eyes if you scratched her throat. She was scared of seagulls. When she was really excited her lips would lift from her teeth like she was snarling, but it was just happiness, like when she saw Theo again after he'd been gone awhile. She waited outside his door every morning.

Theo runs now, angry and angrier, like running built up a charge. The more he remembers her, the madder he becomes. Anger, red and yellow, everywhere, and in the stupid faces looking at him. Dumb and mean and rude. Hurt someone. Make someone pay attention to her. She's not invisible.

The cooking lady yells something at his back. What about the other dogs, Theo thinks suddenly, he shouldn't leave them, but he can't stop. He zags to the house through people, ladies without shirts on and people dancing now around a tape player, and some people hold sparklers although it's sunny and yellow, that's stupid, he's swooping like a bird into the house through the big glass doors smeary and dirty, flaking paint on the terrace like fake snow in a movie, it's all fake, these people aren't friends, he has no family, only minders, even Dad and Mom just mind him and then go away and leave him with other minders, do other kids think this. Theo doesn't want to think at all.

Blurs, walls, halls, stairs, he's slamming open doors unless they're locked, looking. He must tell his dad but he's not in the room, neither is Roger, just people falling all over the furniture and smoke and music, a cave of sleepers waiting for something. What. His dad probably. Everyone woke up when Adrian was around. And Roger. Don't people have things to do. Where is the man who fed the horse. Theo's going to find him. Then what.

A gun. On the table. It's candy. Made of chocolate. Breaks under his hand, brown. Did he just imagine it. Where's the gun now. It's dark. The table's dark. It's a stale soft pretzel. It's too dark to see. Is he crazy. Theo keeps running, out of the mostly empty room. A lot of empty rooms, or ones he and Gus and Colin once used or stayed in and moved from. Colin calls it the frontier effect, just keep moving West, it's the American way, or used to be: got problems, just pick up and go till you come to where nobody knows you and start over. That's what made America so crazy, Colin says, running out of places to escape. People had to stay put and they got cranky about it.

Is that true.

Theo and Colin one cold night, reading by a camping lantern and some candles stuck in a chandelier using the big A of a wooden stepladder: Gus was in his room that night, wrapped in blankets in a chair, watching his television. It was Wheel of Fortune time and nothing interrupted that.

Read the history. When the frontier closed at the end of the nineteenth century, when everybody got to the water's edge and said, nowhere else to go, pardner, America started taking over other places: the Sandwich Islands, the Philippines, Cuba.

Theo looked up – Colin wore two coats and on his head a towel with a headband, and long black ladies gloves and a kilt with pants underneath: Christ, I'm glad no Scotsman's here to see this desecration.

I never heard of that. What are the Sandwich Islands.

That's Hawaii now. Back then it was a kingdom, ruled by a queen. American businessmen and the government staged a coup and got rid of her, and parked their dimpled rumps on the throne.

How do you know all this.

My son – Colin touched his nose – I am wise in all manner of ways. I got A-levels in everything at school. Almost was an Old Boy.

What does that mean.

Just means I missed out on the chance to be a contender, instead of what I am now, which is, let us face it, a bum. You're my brother, you should have looked out for me.

273

Theo'd learned a long time ago when to just skip things, but sometimes he still asked when he sort of forgot not to.

My dad doesn't think you're nobody.

Well, I've got everyone fooled. *Voilà – c'est un coup de maître.*

Colin stood up from the thing he was working on, which was supposed to be a table, made of thick slabs of heavy dark wood planks that he'd found in the basement along with stacks of heavy brown doors; the table covered with a layer of nails he'd hammered into it like tiny silver toadstools, the little round heads, many bent, or like silver worms crawling from the brown ground.

Theo shivered: It's cold.

Let's make a fire.

Okay.

You start.

Okay.

Theo crawled to the pile of broken furniture in the corner of the room, across the frozen tundra, in the dark with bears out there, have to get the fire going, the parquet hard on his elbows and knees even through layers of pants and coat. He reached the pile: chunks of slag Colin called it, culled from around the house and stacked on a rusted red-brown Radio Flyer wagon, from the basement also, so it could be rolled from room to room. Theo banged down a few sticks, still with metal on their feet, table and chair legs with curly wood parts and insides white as bread. He pushed the sticks in front of him as he crawled back to the firepit while Colin sang a song about Cape Cod girls, something something don't use no combs, they comb their hair with the codfish bones.

Why didn't you just roll the slag wag over here.

I was playing.

Okay then, soldier, let's bivouac and reconnoitre.

Theo stacked the pieces in an X in the firepit, a ring of bricks filled with sand. Overhead hung a beach umbrella minus its pole and covered with aluminum foil, with a Chinese dragon costume meant for a parade, with its mouth stretched from the umbrella hole made with garden shears and a box cutter to a closed window above which the dragon's tail dangled. Colin and Theo had spent a fall day putting this together – you know the story of the ant and the grasshopper, right, Colin said then. We'll be prepared, while the grasshopper who's living on brandy and screenplays right now will be out in the cold. Colin thought it was funny that the dragon would inhale fire instead of breathing it out.

Colin now up and moving threw open the window and hung the dragon's tail in the opening so the sparks and ash would have an escape route. There was a big black star of smoke on the ceiling even though they'd only used the firepit a couple of times before. Theo figured the dragon would catch on fire but Colin just said, o ye of little faith. We just want to filter the ash and if it does spark up, we can douse it fast enough. A grey five-gallon paint can full of cloudy water sat near the window, too heavy for Theo to lift. There'd been a fire extinguisher but its insides were all out, powder in a room corner. Colin used the canister for bowling.

Colin rubbed his hands together and moved toward the pit, taking one of the books piled as kindling and opening it to rip pages and stuff them among the furniture limbs.

We're in a bloody Dickens novel.

It's like camping.

Theo scooted close to the bricks, watching Colin hold a

lighter under the paper. The paint and shiny parts on the wood smoked first, and Theo coughed: you could see bubbles, watch the skin peel on the wood before it flamed blue then orange.

Colin, do you think there are aliens.

Colin looked up, his face shadowy and grinning. You mean like ETs.

Yeah.

I do. In fact, I think you might be one. I mean, how do I know, how could I tell.

Do you think there's a god.

Hmm. That's a tougher one.

My dad says he thinks I shouldn't fall for the lies. He says we're on our own down here.

That's a wee bit harsh, I'd say.

Colin stared: come on, babies, dance, dance for me, you wee fairies. Theo, watching the orange, rested his chin on a brick, his eyes beginning to water.

Colin yawned: So I'd say, if we're on our own, we need to take care of each other. Right, mate. That's what we do.

Theo didn't say anything, everything now blurry, his lungs beginning to sting. He coughed.

Better back up, eh. Keep those lungs nice and fresh. Speaking of which.

Colin fingered a cigarette out of a pack on the floor, him sitting cross-legged, and held it over a small flame that licked it, and it started to smoke. Colin moved it up and inhaled, the orange tip flaring in a crescent – not all the way lit. He took it out of his mouth and looked at the end, then blew on it and pretended to screw it in, making a twisting motion with his fist. Ahh, he said, exhaling toward the umbrella, we're blessed, my friend. We've got heat and light on a black night. All we need is some grub. How about it – should I open a few tins.

Okay.

It's the room with the pit and the black star, windows wide, the dragon fluttering. No one's here, so Theo moves on, his mind running too.

Not as mad now, Theo's wondering: go back and help the other dogs. Or bury her. He left the lady outside. Maybe he should run away. It's hard to stay mad, you have to try, keep reminding yourself why. He's just sad, but it's so sunny.

Theo hears agitated voices from an open pair of pocket doors ahead, the billiard room, it used to be, and he's running but now he doesn't know where, he's just running and he's looking inside, and on the cushions that Italian lady who's Roger's friend. People shake her, she's asleep but she's not waking up, she's limp. Someone's standing her up, or trying. Theo stops to watch – maybe he should help. What can he do.

The lady's clothes are messed up and twisted, and her so white, her yellow hair. What are they doing to her: they're dragging her around, trying to make her walk but she's not even awake. Where is his father. Someone's pinching her. People look scared. They notice Theo, someone says, not now, go away, but then forget him, he's just there, and the Italian lady can't wake up. What happened to her. Maybe it's the same man who hurt Paz.

What's wrong, Theo asks, but no one says anything. He knows no one in this room; well, he knows the lady. Two men are dragging her around but nothing, she's just clothes.

Where's the phone, man. Where's the fucking phone.

Someone says that, and Theo says, I know, it's this way, and out of the clot of people standing – there are a couple of others who are half-asleep on cushions, just watching with their eyes almost shut. A short man runs at Theo – come on, let's go.

They weave down the back hall to the little phone room, where the real phone is, near the main entrance hall, a little room like a phone booth. Colin says the man who built the house didn't want to hear the phone so he put it in a little room by itself. Theo wondered if that man was among the voices you could hear around the gazebo some nights, the sounds of a party, a lot of voices, even some laughing. Right now nobody is laughing – one of the first times today, no laughing. Nothing funny.

Here, Theo says as they come to the little room. Its stained glass door, with birds and deer, leans up against the wall in one of the other rooms. I'm going to find my dad.

Theo runs up the curving stairs two at a time, his dad and Roger when they're together harder to find now. Roger's coming out of a room on this hall with his arms around two ladies and a cigarette in each hand: he's got a New York Yankees hat jammed down backward over his hair. His ribs poke out; a skeleton with some skin on it.

Theo the magnificent, what news do you bring us.

Your friend is sick. The one you came from the car with, she's not waking up.

Shit.

Where's my dad.

Roger unloops an arm to breathe from one of the cigarettes. Then he unhooks the other arm and begins kicking and pounding at a wooden door, fast, and saying, goddamnit, goddamnit. The ladies stare, one tries to rub his back. He stops, stares at Theo: Bitch.

278

The lady stops rubbing. Is Roger talking to the lady, or to Theo, or to the sick lady.

Is anyone handling it. Where the fuck are Billy and Del – Roger's talking to Theo.

There's a man making a phone call.

Who.

The man you mean. I don't know his name. He's short.

Who did he call.

I don't know. I came to find my dad.

Okay, mate.

Roger digs into his jeans pocket – those weren't the pants he was wearing earlier, they're too big for him, they might be a lady's pants, they have pictures sewn onto them, and some words, 'Unwashed and Happily Slightly Dazed', on one of the legs near the bottom – and Roger's punching at a little black box with a finger. His dad has one too. It's for talking to minders. Adrian showed him – you touch buttons with numbers and you can send a message.

I guess we will need to make sure the lawyers are awake. I'll talk to your dad. Wait here a minute.

I want to talk to my dad.

Not now, son, he's busy.

What is he doing. I want to talk to him.

Roger turns and walks back to Theo and kneels, his face inches from Theo's and puts a big cool spidery hand on Theo's hot shoulder.

I need you to help me. Can you do that. Me and your dad's depending on you.

Sure. Theo stares at Roger's eyes, the ladies behind with arms around each other. What do you want me to do.

Find Colin and get him up here right now. Fast as you can,

okay. It's really important. It's really important for your dad, okay.

Okay.

Theo hurls himself down the hall and the stairs. Theo wondered if this was about the police, or why the sick lady might be sick. Is that his mom's kind of sick. Or is it about something else. So much was covered up, like clouds always over the sun. Plenty of light but nobody wants it.

Theo's pelting down the stairs, his heels hurting on the old dark wood where the carpet had been, down down down, a race. He needs to help. He doesn't want anything else to happen today. The house is untied, slowly drifting from shore, and no one to crew or steer or paddle except him, and he's not big enough.

This ship fills with smells and noise, music and voices, food and sweet smoke and harsh smoke. Theo's down and pounding, darting, looking and listening – he usually finds Colin by voice. Outside now, and Gus: there's Gus, brown and smoking a pipe, making a sweet smell, with a glass of something brown – either rum or the thick beer he likes. Theo sometimes brings him the bottles in his room. Gus's talking to a lady, two ladies, one wearing a bathing suit and one in overalls and no shirt, and the three of them on the terrace edge, on the wall, leaning back on arms. The ladies smoke cigarettes.

Gus – Dad needs help. Roger says to get Colin.

Why. What's wrong.

I don't know. A lady is very sick inside, Roger's friend is very sick.

Sick. What do you mean.

She won't wake up.

Theo sees Gus's eyes are droopy, and the ladies' eyes too.

Too many of the wrong kind of people here. I've talked to him about it, but doesn't make any difference. Not a proper place for a boy.

Where's Colin. We have to help.

Okay – bang on, then. Let's find Colin. Don't know what Colin can do except hold the bag.

What.

Let's find Colin, indeed, boy.

Gus stands up but he's wobbly, and Theo's running around the yard, looking. Colin could be inside. He could be in a room.

Have you seen Colin. Theo's saying it to the nearest people, but he's saying it to everybody. He doesn't know who he's saying it to.

People are pointing – Theo veers left toward the gazebo, sees at the lawn's end his boat, sitting, waiting. What bag. Why does Colin need to hold it.

A few people sprawl around the gazebo, and there's a tape player in there, and music. Old-time music. And there's Colin. And the Seal, and Gina, and Mingus.

Colin. Dad needs help.

Theo's panting up the steps and Colin's cross-legged staring at him from behind sunglasses. What's the situation.

Roger says to hurry, it's important. They're on the third floor. And Roger's friend is really sick, she won't wake up.

Colin smiles. Why. What's funny: Theo's confused.

Colin stands and salutes, says, bury me under the old oak tree, and jogs off with a cigarette in his mouth and his head down, toward the French doors and in. Take care of Theo, he turns to yell back.

What. Theo's spinning.

What's happened, son. Mingus is asking, from behind his yellow space glasses.

I don't know, Theo answers, but thinks: everything. He remembers Paz, and sits on the gazebo step, picks at flaking faint red paint, other chips littering the grass around the gazebo. Theo gets up and walks scuffling through the grass to where he can see the hedge and the dogs. The catering lady is there with her helper and they seem to be trying to get water into the dogs. Theo can't see Paz, he just sees the lady holding a head while the helper pours water from a cup into a mouth. Theo feels really sad, and mad, and his chest hurts.

The horse crops at grass near the dunes, reins hanging down on the ground. People drink and smoke, some eat. Music bleeds from everywhere. Some people sleep, or at least don't move or talk. Maybe they're dead too.

Theo feels like he's bad, leaving the lady with the dogs, and he left his dad with Roger, and he let his mom go, and he left Gus. Colin he gave bad news to, he thinks – he didn't think Colin liked going inside. What's left for Theo to run away from. He ran away from school too, but his mom helped, and his dad didn't disagree. He needs to run toward something. His ship. Sail away to some place. Was it school or the kids. Or Manhattan. Scary winos. What's different here.

Did Theo let everyone down, the dogs, his parents, himself. He can't help anyone, he's just a kid, how can he help adults. Why don't they know more.

Theo runs back to Mingus and the gazebo. He has a lot of questions. Always questions – how does he get answers. Himself. He is the answerer. He can't wait.

Theo's at the gazebo, his hair and the sun in his eyes. What's the answer now.

He turns and runs back toward the two ladies kneeling. He's going to bury Paz. He'll take her to the dunes. Would anyone notice if he just kept walking away down the beach. Are the police coming. What's going to happen to his dad. What did Roger mean. He turns and runs toward the house's dark bulk.

Theo's streaking now through the French doors and two men in the ballroom are curling up cords and moving speakers into touring cases. And there's Roger, with a clump of people, the soundmen, the band, they're talking.

Here's the beast, Roger says, looking down at Theo from his eyes. His head's a tower with someone in it who's just watching, always watching.

I'm not a beast.

Sorry, I know you're not.

Where's my dad.

He's on the phone.

Who is he talking to.

Lawyers.

About what.

Police.

Why.

Because the police will be here soon.

Why.

Because they don't like us, and they don't like people like us.

Why.

For Chrissake, Theo. Pick another letter. How about double-yew or ex.

Why are they packing.

The men have moved away from Roger and move around the room doing things to equipment.

Change of plan.

Wait. You mean my dad's not going to record here.

No, we're not.

Why.

Roger's cigarette fumes up around his face and gathers at the ceiling. Roger's squinting at Theo and then something else, maybe what's out the window.

Everything's wrong.

What do you mean.

It just didn't work. We thought it would but it's not happening here. The sound's bad. We're going to France.

France. Why. Can I come.

Sure you can come. Ask your dad.

I can't ever get to talk to him.

Roger inhales, exhales, a dragon. He laughs and rubs the top of Theo's head, then he scratches his ribs, leaving red stripes. His fingers are claws

You know, your father has a really important job. This band is tough on everybody. It's tough on me, it's tough on your dad, and it's really tough on the people close to us. Some things have to suffer for the sake of this big responsibility.

What about other responsibilities.

Yeah, well, sometimes you have to choose. You have to decide what's more important than what. That's part of being a grown-up.

Kids have to do that too.

Yeah, they do. That's part of growing up, when you get to that point. I think. You have to decide what you can let go and what you can't. What you can live with and what you can't live without. You find out things that used to be true aren't anymore. And you have to figure out how to adapt and, you know, keep moving. Keep swimming.

Sometimes I feel like an orphan.

Roger laughs: Yeah. Me too.

Theo's angry: It's not funny.

Roger makes a fake serious face, exhales smoke, tries to rub Theo's head again but Theo ducks away: I'm not a dog.

Yeah, baby, I know.

Somebody poisoned my dog. She's dead.

Roger moves his eyes down to look hard at Theo. When did this happen.

Just now. Today.

How do you know it's poison.

All the dogs are sick and can't move and they're foamy. And Paz is littlest and she died. Theo's crying but angry. Tears he's wiping away.

I'm sorry. Somebody here now did it.

Yeah. I know who did it. It was a man. I'm going to bury her.

How do you know.

I just do. I saw him try to make the horse eat something.

Fuck. Roger looks around then shakes ash onto the floor. Idiots.

Is your friend going to die.

Roger looks at Theo hard: I hope not.

Is she poisoned too.

No, she's just unlucky.

How.

Never mind, mate. She's a victim of purity.

What.

Nothing. There's an ambulance coming, and there'll be police. Maybe reporters, for fuck's sake.

Are they going to arrest somebody.

They'll try.

Is my dad in trouble.

It's his house. And he's not unknown to them. They'll make it his fault.

How.

He let it happen.

Can we save him.

That's what Colin's doing.

How.

He's going to take one for the team.

What.

I told you, man, it's hard on everybody. Colin's doing a job.

Does that mean like getting arrested, Theo asks.

If necessary, he'll say it's his fault.

But he didn't do anything.

We can't have your dad in more trouble. He won't be able to live here anymore, and you don't want that, right.

How come you're not in trouble.

Roger smiled. I'm always in trouble, just not this time. I'm a guest.

She's your friend.

Yeah, but I can't control what she does. Our car's clean.

I don't understand.

It's okay, son. It's okay. It's being handled. That's why your dad's talking to the lawyers.

My dad's making Colin get arrested even though he didn't do anything.

Roger stares out into the light. It's part of Colin's job.

What kind of job is that.

The kind people like Colin do for people like us, because that's his job.

Theo thinks but doesn't know what to say, he's full of sadness and sharp edges, together, he feels like he'll cut someone if he touches them.

Theo thinks about what Roger said before and feels something important has stopped being true. Theo thinks about his dad talking to lawyers, Colin waiting for the police to take him instead of – who. His dad. Roger. Who.

Whatever the new truth will be, it's coming quickly. And right now he wants to get out of that room and the smoke and the smelly guys in T-shirts with wet moons from the heat. Roger's lighting another cigarette and looking at Theo.

Figure out what you can't live without, son, and let the rest go. Roger's saying this to Theo, leaning over to say it.

You're not my dad.

No. But I've known you your whole life. I was in Tunisia with Frieda and your dad when she got pregnant. Your dad wrote a song about you before you were born.

I'm not like you.

Yeah, maybe not. Roger laughs: I sure hope not, for your sake.

You don't want people to be like you. What does that make you.

Maybe when you're older you'll get it. If you even remember. Roger laughed again.

You're always laughing. I don't see what's so funny.

Theo, man, I'm not the enemy. I'm a friend. I just want to help.

That's what everybody says. Because my dad's famous.

Roger's looking at Theo the way adults look at things from an oven to figure out whether they're cooked or not. Roger's assessing whether Theo's ready for something. More advice they think he's too young to understand.

287

Your dad's trying, mate. He loves you very much, but you're going to have to figure out a lot of things yourself. He's hopeless. Roger laughs.

I don't need any more advice.

No more advice, my friend. But maybe some news.

News. Are the police here.

No, that's not the news. But we'll handle them, no worries.

His dad's slinking into the ballroom now; Adrian's blinking at the bright light and someone's handing him sunglasses and Theo's running to him.

Why is Colin going to jail.

Whoa, hold on, mate. Colin's not going to jail. Jesus, it's like a bloody office in here. I gotta take it slow or I'll get the bends.

Why would you make Colin get arrested.

Adrian stares at Theo a long time, then at Roger, who inhales from his cigarette. Adrian looks around the ballroom, at the men boxing equipment and thumbing hair out of their eyes, the people looking in from the halls, someone ducking out of the sun to collapse and sprawl on pillows, everyone really looking at Roger and Adrian, even if they aren't, even if they smoke and talk and look out at the light through the smeared glass doors. Everything was a lie.

Look. I'm a crap dad. I love you so hard there aren't words for it, but I'm a selfish, weak bastard. I'm too much of a child to be a good parent. But I'm trying my damndest. And I have to play. I'd slit my mother's throat for a good song. Adrian tilted his head to look down at Theo and frowned. Come on, mate, let's get some peace.

Theo sees Gus's wife, Roe, alone in England, her face. His grandmother. The most normal person he knows. Theo's head swims in light and heat and feelings and even the air's agitated and unhappy.

In the sun Theo notices lines on his dad's face, outside the shades, and on his cheeks and elsewhere, fine lines like old people have. Lines in all kinds of directions, like a map, with all the lines leading to the eyes and mouth, the eyes covered but the mouth there like a volcano or a mountain. Roads across a white desert. They walked, toward open space among the others, all the people.

See, here's the deal. Remember the trial, when we stayed in the hotel. I'm on probation and if I get popped again right now I could lose my visa and we couldn't work in the US again. And I could go to jail. One of a bodyguard's jobs is take a bullet to save the person he's guarding. That's what Colin's doing.

Isn't Colin your friend.

He is. And that's what friends do for each other. He won't really have much happen, except endure some rudeness, I'm sure. Beastly treatment from beasts, what can you expect. You lie down with dogs and you get up smelling like rotten meat.

What do you do for him.

I pay him good money.

Adrian and Theo weave over the grass in a sea of sound. Theo tries hard to pay attention, but things are so slippery. Ideas and people.

Roger said you're hopeless.

Adrian snorts: I suppose I am. I'm also hopeful, however, mate. Our ship will keep sailing, and we'll pass through this little squall. You know, in New Guinea kids your age are allowed complete freedom to come and go. Their parents just assume they're smart enough to make decisions for themselves. And everybody has a hand in helping get them to that point, the whole village. That's the way I feel mate, I want you to be free.

Theo squints in the late sun, lower now. His hair's in his eyes, white salt on his skin, which is dry and tight, like it's too small. Maybe it'll crack open and he'll slip out and leave something that looks like a boy behind. But what will he be.

There's a siren from the front side of the house where the road is, quiet but getting louder. Christ: Adrian turns and goes back toward the house, where Roger is gesturing at him, flapping his arm, saying, come here. Roger puts an arm around Adrian's neck and talks into his ear, and they sink into the dark.

Theo runs around the side of the house, past the sunken pool with music floating up, and around the house's side and there's an ambulance and a police car, and a black car with a long antenna curling from the front up over the top to the back, like a grasshopper. Two men in light blue shirts and dark blue trousers and heavy black shoes, with sleeves rolled up, are hopping up the steps. One carries a red box like a fishing tackle box or a toolbox. His arms are dark with hair. Two ODs, someone is saying, one of them or someone inside the open front doors who Theo can't see.

The black car sits, while one of the soundmen carries equipment from the house toward the mobile recording unit, the RV, cables gone: untied, ready to cast off.

Theo's seen someone revived before, in Jamaica. He doesn't want to see it now. He wants to bury Paz and go back to the water. He wants to be as far from the house as he can get without getting in trouble. But – who would notice. No one in this village.

Theo feels the world, huge around him, but he's inside

something, another world, both slowly circling, and maybe there are openings between, but only when things line up and you have to jump, run, to make it through, to get to the new place. And maybe there's another world outside of that one, but you can't know until you get there. Cocoons.

The black car's wings open, and men bend and get out, in suits. Theo's father has suits, closets of them, made by a man who comes and measures his father, a man who always carries a cigarette behind his ear and wears a tie and vest with rolled-up shirt sleeves, a British man from Manhattan. Adrian only wears the suits when he goes to court – another world, and his father eels through and back out by camouflaging himself, he says. Colin says it's like getting washed into the sewers, you just hold your breath and ride the flow and hope the cleaners can get the smell out of your posh togs.

The men gesture at Theo. Come here, they say with their hands. It's the police from earlier. One calls over: Come here, son.

Why.

We want to talk to you. Make sure you're okay.

I'm fine.

Well. We'll let Child Protective Services see if that's true.

I'm not a child.

Theo sees teeth – they're laughing.

Theo closes his eyes and runs, opening his eyes when he's facing away and back around the big grey mountain of a house's side. Theo thinks of his butterflies at the top, fluttering at the summit, like snow, or flower petals.

He remembers in Jamaica one night he woke to Adrian and

Frieda screaming at each other and Frieda throwing things at Adrian, and Adrian calling her a daft cunt and Frieda waving a knife at Adrian, and people running between them, and Theo in a hammock on the sleeping porch slipped down and out through the wooden door, which he liked the feel of, that door solid and warm, carved with leaves, someone on the island had made it as gift, and Theo rubbed his hand on it walking out into the stars and the wind – there's always wind around, which he likes, something alive that shows up everywhere – and Theo laid himself out on the ground, the sandy bit of the garden between the big floppy cactuses and paddle-leafed green plants he didn't know, just big and thick as hands, and he cried a little, he wasn't sure why because it wasn't like he hadn't heard Adrian and Frieda do that before, in fact he'd heard them doing about everything they could do together, but tonight he just felt small and he lay there, and over him two tall palms leaned together and swayed slowly in the wind, just a little because they were big trees, but like placid animals, creatures tall and looking down and up and around, at the humans and everything, and clacking together, making small noises as they touched, soft wooden sounds almost musical, but not chatty, just sounds every now and then, and the wind lifted their long leaves – fronds, Theo knew they were called – and let them drop, like wind was curious and just wanted to feel, and then gently let the fronds fall back so they clicked a little too, every now and then. And he just lay there, looking up at the tall dark beings above him, and he heard a voice, or voices, in his head. *Okay. It's okay, everything will be okay.*

Then the screen door slammed and he heard Frieda shuffling out, calling his name – Theo, baby – and she was crying. Weaving in the air, the trees looked down as she bent over Theo and said, I'm sorry, baby. We're just terrible for each other, aren't we, my love.

It's okay, Theo said.

Theo's running for a shovel in the gardener's shed, and he's running past everything and pushing and straining at the door, and in the fanned light he sees an old wood and iron shovel, which he grabs and it's heavy and he runs back out the open door and he's light-headed and a little nauseous, which happens from not eating but also other times.

Paz lies under the bushes, and the catering lady's not there but her assistant is, doing something on her knees. Theo's running with the shovel and sees him, sees the man who fed the horse, and Theo feels hotter and he's running toward the man, who's turning to sit down on a bedspread, a pink spread with little pompoms on it, or knobs, or little bulbs, Theo doesn't know what they'd be called, and the man is facing a group of people who are passing around a wine bottle and taking off shirts and Theo's behind the man now and swinging the shovel and Theo sees faces across from him, and words coming out of them and the man leaning back on an arm and turning with a half-smile to strain and look and Theo's swinging the shovel and the flat of it hits the man on the back of the head and he's face first into the grass and there's yelling and jumping and the wine turned over and spilling on the spread, and it's red wine, and Theo lifts the shovel again and is yelling and he's holding the shovel like a sword, the blade down and he's going to stab down and end the story and he can't see and then he can and he yells sound because there aren't any words and in the white is a small brown bird, on the lawn, watching, staring at him with its round cocked head, watching, and somebody else yells too and he drops the shovel and runs and he's running across the lawn fast, and he's over the dazzling terrace and the sparkle and heat and into the thick gloom of the ballroom like underwater, where it gets dark fast, except in places like Jamaica where Theo's been swimming and the sand is so white it's light and even hurts your eyes, but here the ocean's dark as the house, it's all dark, and Theo's in and not thinking or thinking but trying not to – what's wrong is everything, this place, he can't breathe anymore, he's in trouble, he doesn't know, he's running around and past people and up the back stairs that the servants used, the way narrower and plainer, and harder, no carpet, just yellow and brown wood and walls of yellow and he's running up and up and his stomach hurts and he can't breathe but he's at the top of the house, the level below the attic, and he runs the steps toward the last stairs up to his room and he opens the door and slams it and he's in butterflies, the room's blurry with them.

It's hot and he's so dizzy he sits, in the middle of the floor, or he collapses, wondering if the police will come for him now. He'll be by himself, because his dad has Colin and Theo's got nobody between him and the world, just like a car with no brakes, he can't stop. He can't stop and he's crying a little, listening to how quiet even an attic full of butterflies is, their wings barely there, and he breathes. He breathes. He hears whispers. It's wings.

Air flickers here, the room bright from both ends, windows closed at the house's front but open at the far end from the room door, through which Theo has burst and stopped and torn cocoons hang from branches – pupa cases, plastic-looking, peeled and curled back, mostly, still a few like fruit, waiting to open. But Theo sits in the air, watching and thinking about where he can go. He can't go any higher.

How is Theo going to take care of Paz. He can't go back now, they'll be mad or arrest him. Or send him away. Where would he go. Maybe he could be in jail with Colin. Do police let you have a roommate. He sees white – it's the page of a book in sun, he remembers from a school window – reading, reading about the world, in the quiet. His teacher laughing, like music. He needs to know about the worlds, one within another like an egg in a nest, or in hands. He wants to learn more. That's the doors, between the worlds.

Theo stands weird and sad, the air alive as if bright leaves fell up instead of down in fall, came alive and flew away. He's walking now, and there's a small one on the slanting wall. He reaches out to touch it and it flickers away: he sees on his finger dust, butterfly yellow dust. He licks it: a taste like nothing.

They need to fly out: Theo tries to herd them out the rear window, over the back lawn, holding his hands in the air and shooing or trying to, but they curl and spin back and sideways and not forward, looping through the air or fluttering up and down. Some go out, some just keep stirring up the attic air. Theo wonders what they see, if they feel scared.

Open the other window, windows: at the front, over the front door. But maybe they'll see him. He doesn't care. He moves over the smooth boards, from carpet to wood, and grabs the iron handles and cranks them, flapping open the windows but slowly: maybe no one will notice.

Slowly he goes to the window ledge, one of the side panes, a triangle, a sail, and sits cross-legged, eyes just higher than the edge. Cars scattered all over, and the ambulance and police car sit close, ambulance doors open: Theo hears laughing. Shaking his head, one of the attendants peels off gloves and one falls, a blue patch on the brown pea gravel. Theo moves closer, sees heads on the steps below. They look back into the house, and more heads come out – Colin with men in suits, Colin in a shirt and shoes. The men in suits laugh, too, pointing back into the house.

What's funny. Theo never knows.

Birds look down on people. Theo's above things. Everyone is just a head, carried around on feet and with hands to put things in its mouth. Everything is inside that head. Kids have less to carry around. But everyone wears that skull, everything cooped up in there. And how do you connect to someone else if everything's inside there. Are words the only way.

He's above, watching. Things are smaller. The cars and people. Trees still big, but just standing, swaying a little. Theo wonders if he killed the man. The police were laughing. But they haven't left yet: one stands outside the flapped-open rear of the car talking to Colin. Theo can't hear words, only the talking, rising and falling. Butterflies drift around him like ash from fire, some flitting out the window. Theo decides to go down. There's nowhere else to go.

four.

and hand in hand,
on the edge of the sand,
they danced
by the light of the moon.
                              – Edward Lear

Theo's thumping down the stairs, and he's left his door open so butterflies can ride everywhere – more ways to escape. He wants to help. Something's wrong with him and he doesn't know what it is. He floats on a big ocean, watching ships go by. No shore.

Down the back stairs and toward Paz, out the ballroom, people staring at him. The guy he hit is in a chair, with a sweaty plastic bag of ice held to his head, in a circle of others. Now he's frowning at Theo.

What the hell, little man. You're lucky you're Adrian's kid. Must be nice. I feel a lawsuit coming on, maybe.

You killed my dog.

What are you talking about.

My dog died because you poisoned her like you tried to poison that horse.

Look, I didn't do anything to your dog. But there's so much shit lying around here. It's a good thing there aren't any toddlers around. It sounds like your dog ate something it shouldn't have. Tough titty in the city. Sorry, but you shouldn't go around swinging shovels at people, unless they want you to, of course. That could be a cure for something: the guy laughed. Except for the headache and the haematoma, I think, like, that cleared up a lot of static for me. Like I'm tuned in better.

I hate this place, Theo said.

Nothing's ever wrong, or bad. Blue skies forever, mate. Lawyers and money: Theo remembers Adrian's voice. Pay 'em off, just pay 'em off and keep moving.

He's Adrian's kid. He can do whatever the fuck he wants. Get away with anything. What happens when you don't have a fence of lawyers or money, or a portable phone like the boys on the beach. Was he like them.

Escape or die: the story. Not die die, but become somebody else. Maybe growing up is kind of dying. The old you, then different yous. Which one's the one. A million yous, a new one every second. Pick one. Or no you. *The story doesn't die.*

What if the old you's poisoned. What has he already swallowed. Theo's face reddens.

Theo walks toward the hedge angry and on the way picks up the shovel he dropped, still where he swung it. Theo hits his head with the heel of his other hand as he walks. It feels good and he keeps doing it. Hard, he does it hard, and now he's talking, low, saying shit shit shit then fuck fuck fuck. Fuck. Then Paz. And he stops talking and hitting and he's dizzy and he spins to get dizzier, dropping the shovel and whirling. Air and voices and something else – maybe ocean, maybe the roaring's in Theo. His name means god, people tell him.

What can he live without. What can he not live without. What to give up, if he has to. Does he know any of that. Everything's free, everything's floating and spinning, maybe Paz even, he's trying to stand still and he can't, he's falling over, tripping on the shovel and banging a shin and the pain is light, he can see it. He's sprawling on the bristly grass, pony fur, horse hair, wiry and stiff. The big world shifts under him, still sliding even with his eyes closed, the spin continues. For a while he goes away, he's just a feeling and everything's bigger and brighter, and then it slows and slows and then locks. Theo can hear the click. He opens his eyes on his back. Way up high, gulls, almost too far to see.

Voices and music. Nothing changes. Nobody knows about Colin or the lady, or maybe they do. The show must go on, Adrian says, all the time. The show must go on, baby, that's all there is. There's the show, and everything else is just waiting for the show.

This is his show, Theo thinks, on his back, and he needs to get up and go.

He crawls onto his hands and knees, and stands, and walks to the place where Paz is, and the other dogs, still there, but lifting heads a little, he can see. The assistant is there, sitting with a bowl of water.

Thanks, Theo says, for helping them.

The lady's a teenager, Theo thinks. He'll be a teenager in three years. She looks up at him – she's wearing a baseball hat and smiling, and an apron, and she has shorts on, and a watch. It's six. She's kind of pretty. He can't help looking at where the apron swells.

Hey – Leslie said to stay here with them until she could figure out what to do. She's working right now, but was going to try to talk to your dad, about what to do with the. With the one who's gone. The other ones are a little better I think. They're drinking a lot more.

Theo knelt to pet them, and their eyes followed him while he did. They seemed more tired now than anything else, the foam like toothpaste around their mouths, dried. Theo wondered what they ate: search the house and protect them, look for bad stuff at dog level and put it away. Maybe tell grown-ups, make a rule. Some rules he could ask his dad about. Some rules.

Tail, wag. A beat. On the ground. Thump thump thump. Then resting. Just like when they don't want to go outside for a walk when it's cold or snowy.

Theo says, thanks. I'm going to bury her now.

Where. She's pushing hair out of her eyes, and Theo does too, reminded that his hair's in the way.

In the trees over there, I guess. I don't know where my dad is.

Theo didn't want to do it alone, he didn't know what should happen. He didn't want to just dump her in a hole.

Um. Can you carry the shovel for me.

The lady looks around and back at the house, her face a little funny. She doesn't want to. Please.

Yeah, okay. But I have to get back to work.

Okay. Okay, let's go.

The lady rises off her knees, then leans to brush them off – her brown knees. She's tanned. Then Theo hands her the shovel, and he drops and scoots and reaches. He feels bad – he has to drag Paz, past the others, her stomach rubs against their noses and they just stare at him. Theo has her out in the sun now and squats to put arms under her – she's limp. How long does it take to stiffen, he wonders. He wishes really hard that it doesn't happen until he's not touching her. She's still warm. Some people are looking, but not the poison guy. He's on his back staring straight up. Theo feels a rush of warmth. He walks fast toward the trees, the lady turning with him. Birds scream.

Theo just walks, he's not sure where, just in, where no one can see. He doesn't want anyone to see her. She was shy. The lady's not saying anything.

The lady's looking around. How about over there. She's pointing.

No, over there – Theo's walking to the left and stopping under a spreading tree with a forked trunk, Theo's tree, a twisted Y, a million years old, wrinkled and swirling. It looks like rock that flowed and froze, or like it's raising arms. Here.

The ground and trees are dappled with light and dark. 'Dapple' was a vocabulary word, when they studied elaboration in school. School. Theo sees desks and kids bent over paper, and playground sounds outside, the younger kids at recess earlier. The lady's handing him the shovel: I need to be getting back, okay.

Can you wait a minute. Please. Theo doesn't want to do this alone.

I'm sorry, but I have to get back to work. Sorry. She was a good dog, I bet.

Yeah. Um, thanks.

The lady waves her hand and walks away, fast. She's wearing sneakers.

Theo's digging, the soil sandy, with brown mixed in the white. The hole keeps filling back up. He thinks if he does it really fast and gets her in it will work, so he shovels crazily, manically, which makes him laugh, but he feels funny laughing when she's lying there. He digs on, flinging shovels of chocolate and sugar into the shade. Sound echoes out from the house, laughing. Theo wants them to be quiet.

Theo's arms turning limp with exertion. The sand creeps back into the hole, which isn't a hole, more like a cone. He kneels and lays her in the hole, and has to fold her and her back legs rise above the ground. He shivers, pushing hard on her once, and then he digs a couple of feet away and scoops sand over her. Grains not really covering her, just sliding off. He keeps at it, watching the dirt rise around her like water until it begins to lap at her sides and then slowly covers her more and more. Her eyes are half-open. He leaves that for last.

Theo stops to rest, breathing hard. The shovel's tall, so he has to choke up on it, like in baseball the times he's been able to play. He remembers hearing Adrian say to the bass player, man, you're holding that thing like you're choking a woman. Theo's wearing gloves made of sand, his hands are sticky and the soil's adhering, and to patches on his legs and stomach. She's lying there. Her eyes.

Keep shovelling – Theo's mad to finish, just throws soil at the place until he can make himself look – she's just an outline now, all of her covered, so he slows a little but keeps shovelling until there's just a pile. Then he looks around, looking for limbs or rocks to put on top and hide her. He doesn't know what might come looking, but he doesn't want her dug up. He wonders if the others found her, would they. What would keep them from it. Nothing. She's just food now. What keeps people off each other. Sometimes nothing. People have canine teeth. Theo's washed with sadness. He can feel it moving over and through him. He wants to get out.

Theo lays grey driftwood on the pile, but there aren't rocks here. There is, he sees, a small stack of bricks a little further in. They look old, he sees, taking one in each hand. Maybe from building the house, and they've sat since then. Or Colin decided to make something and then forgot. He lays the bricks on top, then piles on more, so she won't float up. She's asleep.

No flowers around. He sits cross-legged beside her, not knowing what to do, and a song from school comes into his head. He sings, quietly, you are my sunshine. My only sunshine.

When he's finished, he gets up to find something to mark her. He combs through the trees, coming out at the dunes, finding nothing. Beer cans, and an old flip-flop. He'll go back to the house and find something. Bring it later. Bring her some water. He weaves scuffing through the dry sand, squeaking, kicking clouds, kicking harder and harder, around the trees and down the path between the dunes toward the house, the heavy wood trestles of the walkway appearing like signs reminding him. This way to the world. Which world.

Walking, Theo kicks at grass. Frieda and Adrian think they treat him like an adult, and he's around adults all the time. Frieda and Adrian let him call them by their names and say when he goes to bed and what he eats and what he wears and where he sleeps and curse around him and talk about sex but that's not treating him like an adult, that's just doing what kids think being an adult is. He's on the water, and it's deep and black and he doesn't know what's in it, but things flash, he sees silver and eyes and swirls and there's huge life down there but he's floating over it – what else is there. When does he get to see it. Maybe he's seeing now and doesn't know it, because he's a kid. Maybe all you ever see is just the flash.

Theo moves over the lawn, among people scattered further apart now, fewer outside, the late afternoon sun hotter, or maybe people have left. He hopes so. Theo's thinking of what to put on Paz's grave. Mingus and the Seal and Gina and some other adults have brought chairs into the gazebo, and coolers, and Theo's sliding up the flaking wood steps: maybe he'll ask here.

Mingus looms in his costume, sweat pouring down around his helmet and wraparound shades.

You know, you can moan about how this's ugly and you need

that and you need to be someplace else with other people, but you know, it's like every day I'm kicking down Avenue A and stepping over the dog shit and garbage and worn-out shit and glue sniffers and toothless fucking winos and crack whores and syringes and ugly this and that and I'm just, you have to find the magic, find the magic, it's there, it's everywhere, just find the magic, there's something shiny, you just never know where it's going to come from, that's the magic. I mean there's no escaping the yin and yang, like if you're Elizabeth the Second and you never even touch the ground your life is so exalted and everything you touch is beautiful, you still have streaks in your silk knickers, you dig. And of course there's the oldest story of all, the only one, man, decline and fall, attachment and loss, like every life is a little civilization that has some sun and then is overrun by the Visigoths, you know, sickness and old age and the old rags. Yeah, I'm high, but that doesn't mean it's not true, and the sooner we all just get over it – like, the most broke-ass sidewalks in Manhattan glitter in the sun, if you look close. Just look at the street and it sparkles, and the rainbows in the oil, man, it's beautiful, even a slab of asphalt. It doesn't get any more basic. That's what I see. Just pay attention, just wake up and pay attention. The world is talking to you. And I am awake. Can I get another bump.

Do you plan to shut up this year, one of the men says.

Pearls before swine as usual.

Above on the gazebo ceiling mildew spots on the white, constellations, black stars in a white sky. Backward. Even outside here like an inside, something backward. It's not right.

Theo stands and walks away, no one seeming to notice. He'll look in the house for something, and he runs now, to the side of the house and peeks around the corner, then runs to the

308

front door, open wide, and in, over the black and white tiles and the disarrayed collection of Colin's toppled chesspieces. He looks, but nothing seems right for Paz, and he runs down the right hall, and there's Billy the minder at a door.

Is my dad in there.

Yeah, but we have to leave him alone right now.

I need to see him, Theo knocking and saying, Dad.

Adrian from inside says, it's okay, Billy.

Theo and Adrian sit cross-legged facing each other, under a window. The late sun lights up the room, and Theo watches the dust, up and down. An acoustic guitar lies on the floor beside Adrian – Theo can't tell them apart; his dad buys seats for them on planes. Once he and Adrian and some people flew on a small plane between two islands and Adrian kept his hand on the white guitar case the whole flight. Adrian leans against velvet cushions and a cloth beanbag chair the colour of wine. A couple of tape players, too. It feels weird, then Theo realizes it's because they're alone.

What happened to everyone.

Yeah, that's always the question, isn't it. Adrian laughs, coughs.

Why did you make Colin go to jail.

Adrian breathes deeply, purses his mouth, grins with half his mouth. You know what I am aside from being your dad.

Theo's puzzled – is this like a riddle.

Adrian halfsmiles again. I'm a person. I'm inordinately fond of myself, lazy, selfish, weak, arrogant – ask your mother, who could give you a list of things I'm not. And of course, she's a person too, aside from being your mother. And I'm a coward. I make friends take falls for me.

You mean Colin.

Adrian nods, exhaling smoke.

So when I was your age and I learned stuff I didn't like about people I loved – your grandfather was a right bastard, I thought – I built my own perfect human, out of parts, an arm, a leg, left eye – I cut up pictures of people I liked and made one person out of them and taped it to the wall. It was ugly but it was paper so you couldn't break it. Every now and then I'd stick somebody new in there, swap out somebody, so it was like it was alive in a way. Does that make any sense to you. Do you understand what I mean.

I guess.

Or, instead of building an idol, you could, you know, put up a mirror.

So you can look at yourself.

Well, like maybe you don't need an idol. Maybe it's just in the way. You know.

I guess. Is this like church.

Ha. No.

Do you think there's a god.

Hmm. Me. I do.

Adrian pointed with his big hand at Theo's head, and at his own head. I think god's in here. A little piece. And all the pieces together equal god.

But that's just us.

Yep.

Theo's dad squints through the smoke, the hand-rolled cigarette wrinkled and bent and wider at the burning end than the mouth end, then grins around the cigarette, at the corner of his mouth. We've all got a little of the fire in us, a little piece.

Even bad people.

You know, Adrian says, rubbing his nose, I'm not sure they're bad as much as they're just confused.

Some people like doing bad things. They think that's good.

You know, mate, sometimes people can be damaged or sick. They might have had bad things done to them that broke them. But humans are pretty amazing. Sometimes even the brokest toy can be fixed, even if it's just for a little bit. But sometimes fixing makes it worse, because then they see what they've been before. Did she put on his knowledge with his power, before the indifferent beak could let her drop.

What.

Old poem I learned in school. About a lady and a swan. Adrian took a deep drag on the cigarette. I'm sorry, mate.

For what.

Pretty much everything. I'm trying. I want to be a good father to you.

You are. The best.

What else are you gonna say. You're a peacemaker, that's your nature, especially after growing up in so much war. Later you'll go grumbling about what a full cock-up your dad was, tell your wife about it.

Adrian reaches for the guitar and slides it into his lap, the way he pulls Theo into it, or used to. Theo is too old for that now. Adrian looks at Theo and starts playing: Theo knows it's the blues.

It's okay, Dad. I won't say that.

Adrian's eyes are closed and Theo isn't sure if he hears. The dust in the air is like snow.

Adrian says, you know, there's somebody you need to meet. You should have met her by now. It's time for you to meet her, I think.

Theo hears, and remembers Roger saying there's news, then remembers a wintertime with Colin and Gus, and pushing through the first-floor snow, with flashlights, and the only world was what was in the flashlights. Nothing else, just black. Or was this a dream. Them walking, the snow whispering, dry as sand, Gus muttering something. Theo said, I wonder if there are people somewhere doing the same thing right now, or are we the only ones in the whole world doing this.

Colin laughed: I hope we're the only ones fighting Siberia inside their own house just to get to the icebox. There's a bloody irony. But, you know, I take it this way. I think nobody's alone. I mean, you have your family, but sometimes it's like monsters, or jail, something you have to escape. But your tribe's out there, maybe scattered all over fuckall – come on, language, Gus said – right, sorry, but they're there and maybe they're even looking for you and eventually you're all together lying on the beach, grinning at each other, getting matching tans.

Theo says, who is she.

Adrian tilts his head back and shakes it. Her mother was mad at me. And she's not anymore.

Why was she mad.

Christ, Theo. There's a list. Just check stuff off and whatever it is, it's there. Look, mate, I've never had a job except being in this band, and it's the only thing I know how to do. I'm still learning about everything else. Maybe I'll get it right eventually.

When can I meet her.

Soon.

How soon.

We're figuring it out, okay. It has to be neutral territory. And the recording's off here. The vibe's not right, the house's dead.

So you're leaving again.

Not immediately, love.

I want to go to a school. And I'm getting out of here.

Out of here. This house.

Yes.

How do you plan on that.

I don't know yet.

Making your break, eh. Okay. I hear you. I hear you.

Theo thinks about what he can't live without, and what he can let go, let sink into the dark underneath ocean, even if something has to drown, die. But that's too hard, he doesn't know how to think about it. What does he live with: he's not sure. Maybe he doesn't want to stop being a kid. Everything else is blank and big and. And.

I need to find something for Paz's grave.

Theo waits, but Adrian says nothing. He's staring at Theo, and just takes a deep breath from his cigarette, looking like he is deciding something. Ah. Let's give her a good send-off. Come on.

You mean you want to see it.

Yeah.

Adrian stands straight up from his crossed-leg position, leaning on the guitar for an instant and shaking his head. Then he sinks again, to crouch between his spread legs, squatting.

What are you doing.

Getting my bearings. All right, let's go. We'll bring an offering, a libation.

Theo doesn't know what that is: I don't want any other people. Just you.

Okay, that's cool.

Not even Billy.

Got it.

A libation's like an offering, something to help the dead cross over.

Cross over what.

Adrian's opening the door: From here to there. Billy, take five. I'm going out with Theo.

You sure.

Yeah.

They move down the hall, dark wood and gold light.

You mean being dead.

Crossing over is just an expression. Humans have a million views of death and ways of describing it. The ancient Greeks believed when you died you crossed a river, and you were ferried across the river to the land of the dead by Charon, the boatman, and they buried you with coins so you could pay Charon to take you across.

What happened if you didn't have a coin.

You were doomed to wander the shore, not able to rest yet.

The dark hall flows and leads to the delta of ballroom and then the wide lawn ocean, and Theo and Adrian are crossing the terrace, and everyone outside has found shade. Theo notices how pale Adrian looks, how white. Theo looks at a man, white as his dad, limp in a brown wooden chair with arms splayed wide like he's been shot, head turned, mouth open. All these people, so pale. Adrian turns back to the doors and says, come on. We'll get some wine and some oil, make it a proper homage to Paz.

What's wine and oil for.

We'll pour them on her grave, it's an offering. To her spirit, and to the spirits she'll be joining. Is that okay, do you think.

I guess. She didn't drink wine.

All the better for her. But it's more a gift for the spirits, to show respect, something to honour her by pleasing those she'll be joining. Let's check out the kitchen.

People drinking Cokes, people with coffee, food on dirty plates, someone pouring something on a woman's stomach and licking it off. Conversation about galleries, fuckers, projects, the jets, Tribeca, shit, copper wire is a warmer sound, product. People talking at Adrian, Adrian talking back, Theo drifting through, drifting. Leslie the caterer and her assistant huddle over a pad of paper in two chairs. Food steams in silver.

Roger enters from the dark back, with people, everyone serious. Hey: Roger's calling at Adrian. We got another problem. Adrian slowly turns from two ladies, says, so handle it, over the other noise. Nah, Roger says, we have to talk lawyers.

Christ.

Adrian walks over to Theo leaning in the door opening, watching – here, pour some of this on Paz's grave and get some oil from Leslie there – Adrian points at her – and I'll catch up with you. Promise. He rubs his face with his hand.

Kay.

Theo takes the dusty bottle and walks fast, but he doesn't think Paz would like wine and passes through the French doors and over the warm tiles of the terrace and onto the grass and turns the bottle over, pouring as he walks in a big curve away from the trees then back toward them, and some people look at him, and the bottle's empty and he drops it; it's libation for everything. Everybody.

Theo walks toward the trees, and white feathers on the ground in a patch of grey-green grass, small feathers and bigger feathers, white and grey and brown, and it could be a pigeon or a gull maybe, or a tern. There's nothing but feathers, so maybe it wasn't an attack, and he picks up a couple of the long ones, and walks now toward the trees. Voices, music, and his head is light, floating over his body, and he walks.

Through the trees to Paz. He's crossing to her land and he finds her pile, the wood, and he sticks the feathers in the dirt and stands for a minute looking. He wants to put something shiny there, but there's nothing, and he says, good dog.

His pants have a pocket on the back, he remembers, and he jams his hand in it – nothing. Wait – a quarter. Theo's not sure where it should go, so he just places it flat near the end where her head is. Now she can pay the boatman. Then he weaves out, thinking maybe he should carry coins with him all the time, just in case.

What now. He moves out of the trees, from under the trees, onto the lawn.

Someone's shooting balls of fire from a cardboard tube at other running people, one of whom is arching and yelling and slapping at his back. Somebody else has the hose out, showering some other people. The man is back on the horse, and a lady in a bathing suit sits behind him, holding onto the saddle, not him, while the horse walks backward, stiffly. A chair is stuck in a third-floor window. A couple of people sleep. In the gazebo, Mingus stares out at Theo or in his direction. Mingus is holding his bow with an arrow notched on the string. People behind him flicker in the shadow there: Theo can't tell what they're doing. The sun's definitely on its way down.

Just below the roof peaks, mountains jutting up and down the line of the roof. From his open windows he sees flakes of colour flutter, out and away, up and down on the air like it's

316

waves they ride. The Italian lady might die, maybe, and Colin's with the police – his dad's sad. And there's Gus, back in his chair under the umbrella, alone, smoking his pipe.

And there's the Seal, coming his way, toward the ocean.

Theo says, where are you going.

Going for a swim.

You can swim.

Yes, I can.

Theo notices the stumps of his arms have tiny nubs, like baby toes.

I can also fly.

You can fly.

Yes.

How.

Like this: the Seal stands, spreads his stumpy arms like a penguin and closes his eyes. There's another planet that I think I'll check out. I'll bring you back a souvenir.

Thanks. Bye.

Theo walks, not scared of Seal, and Theo's closing eyes now, wondering how far he can go without seeing.

Theo's blind, hearing everything and feeling things up through his feet, the feelings growing up, dry grass and gritty sand, he knows the lawn's table-flat, still wants to peek, but doesn't. Theo walks listening to his breathing, and his heart, which he can imagine but, he realizes, he can't hear. Last sun on his back.

For a while, just breathing, the sound like under water, and walking in flaming dark behind his eyes. Then what happens tomorrow, he starts thinking. What about next week. Two months. Who will be here. He opens his eyes on the bright back lawn: where is this, what place. Nothing fits, and then it does. But he doesn't know what to call it. He is not going to live here anymore.

He steers toward Gus, brown as an American football, his big stomach peaceful and safe, him anchored now in his place, smoking his pipe. He sees Theo and yells: Cheers.

Theo walks over and plops next to Gus. Hi, Gus.

You look a little stormy, what's on your mind.

Theo's not sure what to say, because he's not sure what's on his mind. I don't know. Dad's leaving. Colin's gone. Is it just me and you now.

Gus nods, reaches for a painted glass full of, Theo knows, rum. He can smell it in the air, see tiny sparkles of it.

Just for a few hours, I reckon, till he makes bail, then that'll go away and Colin'll be back. Tempest in a teapot.

And it'll be like it was.

Sure.

Theo poked at the ground with a finger, hoping it would wake up and shake, maybe roar, thinking about the way it was. Is. There's only is. Maybe what he has to give up is the was. But he's just a kid, how is he supposed to know this stuff.

What's that, Gus asks, puffing on his weird curving pipe, then looking at the pipe. Smoking is such a weird thing to do; who thought of it first.

Nothing. I didn't say anything, Theo says. Grown-ups get to make messes but they don't have to clean them up, Theo thinks. Then, maybe he just doesn't see the cleaning up.

Hmm, Gus makes a noise. You say a lot even when you're not saying anything. You're upset about – oh, everything. Dad and Mum and these weird people and Colin and Johnny Law here after Colin, and the rest of us too if we're not careful. Something like that.

318

Gus looks at Theo. You're a thinker. Your dad was like you when he was your age. Kept a lot inside, worried a lot.

I need to go back to school. Somewhere else. I want to.

School, eh. Gus, Theo sees, is trying not to make a big deal out of it. He's playing around with his pipe, looking inside it – an engine flares up from inside the house, someone's on Colin's scooter in the ballroom – and he says matter-of-factly, staring and poking into his pipe, good show, then. I'll talk to your dad and we'll see about getting that sorted out.

Theo remembers Paz lying under the bushes. The other dogs, bigger and different, live. Some people could live in a house like that. Some couldn't. No more butterflies from Theo's windows: he wonders if they are all gone.

I feel like I'm in the wrong family.

Gus laughed. I've said that for fifty years, but they won't let me leave.

I mean, other families aren't like ours.

Oh, you'd be surprised, son. Families are all basically the same family, if you look at 'em long enough. We all do the best we can, and maybe that's the best we can do. You know, your da and mum are doing the best they can, and they love you. They're artistic types, and that kind of queers things a little. Like living with royalty, except without the manners. Both about equally twittish.

Theo's frowning and squinting, at his dad in the centre of one circle of people and Roger in the centre of another, like two wheels moving something.

Maybe, son, and Gus is reaching a big rough hand out to cup Theo's head, normal isn't normal. Just figure out what your limits are. Don't pay attention to the rest. That's what I do.

Do you.

Aye. I had to do that a long time ago. It's worked out okay. I think it will for you too. It's like staking a claim: here, this, even if it's just this chair, is mine. Let the world rush past and I'll just watch and try to keep me arms and legs out of harm's way.

But why should you have to. It's like running away. Why should you have to.

Here Gus shrugs – it's not running away, it's running toward something, sort of an island, maybe. And you can invite whoever you want onto your island. Might be a tight fit, but it's yours. Gus grins: It's your story.

Theo isn't sure about this, but Gus is looking at him as if he wants Theo to agree, so Theo nods yes. Okay.

In the limo to the airport, Theo asks Adrian: The lady. Does my mother know her.

Yeah.

What's her name.

The lady.

No.

Her name's Marian Pearl. Marian for Maid Marian in Robin Hood.

Adrian pushes open the red-brown wood gate covered with ivy, which bumps on the red gravel walk, and crunches toward the door with his rolling walk. There's glass, and a face in it – Roe, Gus's used-to-be-wife and Adrian's mother. Theo likes her: she is loud and funny and a lot like his dad and she's always mad at Adrian. She's opening the door, and Adrian's calling out, hello missus. She's walking down the steps and putting her hands on her hips, stopped, frowning – you look like death. I shouldn't let you in, it's probably bad luck.

Everybody tells me I'm immortal, Roe. No worries there, darling. I get it from you: Adrian waves his arm around, looking at the house and the garden. Looks more and more like a tour council ad. This blessed plot, this sceptred isle, this England. More waving, then Adrian gives frowning Roe a hug and kisses her cheek and she kisses him, looking put out. Adrian says: here's our boy.

Roe stares at Theo and her face breaks into a huge smile. Oh, aren't you a beautiful sight. How nice to see you, my love. I hope your father hasn't done too much damage that can't be undone.

Hi Roe.

Theo's grinning, and his cheeks are hot. He's buzzing, feeling jumpy, happy. The path is lined with yellow flowers. He puts his arms around her as she hugs him and musses his hair and gives him a powdery kiss and rubs his back.

Come on in, love: she's talking to Theo not Adrian, who's just standing looking into the house, saying, hello, my darling.

A little girl stands there, her hair is huge and crazy, curly, and it has a band or ribbon in it. She's wearing a tiny Arsenal football jersey and a pink skirt and she's barefoot.

Who put those traitorous colours on her.

I've become an Arsenal fan, so you'll have to live with it.

Adrian's bending and grinning, squatting, and the girl is walking out, not shyly, but slowly, picking her way down the steps, old stone, and walking, but she doesn't stop at Adrian: she's coming right at Theo, looking up, squinting in the sun. Adrian and Roe are both watching.

Theo looks down at her and smiles, holds out the book. I brought you a present. I'll read it to you if you want. It's called The Little Cricket.

I can read.

Roe smiles and looks at Theo from behind the girl, smiling and shaking her head 'no' so Theo sees.

Okay. You can read it to me then.

Okay.

She flounces into the house between the two adults. Roe's looking at Theo: We've got an appointment at your school in a little while, so let's get you smartened up and have a bite and we'll be off.

Adrian's already inside, and Roe's going up the steps in her thick shoes. Theo's following and up the steps when he starts to say something but doesn't, just turns to run back down the path. Adrian always leaves doors and gates open, and cabinets. Everything, even the bathroom door.

At the fence Theo stops, and swings it shut, the black limo in the lane gleaming between the slats, a dark animal behind bars. She would need looking after. Theo listens for the click, and rattles the latch on the gate – then he pulls, just to be sure the car's caged and his sister's safe out here, in the world.